Before Now

By Cheryl McIntyre

Cover design by Daryl Cunningham

Cover photo by Vince Trupsin

Cover model Brandyn Farrell

Edited by Dawn McIntyre Decker and Rebecca Friedman

Agent Rebecca Friedman

June 2013

Other books by Cheryl McIntyre:

Sometimes Never

Blackbird (a Sometimes Never novella)

Dark Calling

For you.

Table of Contents

Prologue Park

1 Lucy

2 Park

3 Lucy

4 Park

5 Lucy

6 Park

7 Lucy

8 Park

9 Lucy

10 Park

11 Lucy

12 Park

13 Lucy

14 Park

15 Lucy

16 Park

17 Lucy

18 Park

19 Lucy

20 Park

21 Lucy

22 Park

23 Lucy

24 Park

25 Lucy

26 Park

27 Lucy

28 Park

29 Lucy

30 Park

31 Lucy

32 Park

33 Lucy

34 Park

35 Lucy

36 Park

37 Lucy

38 Park

39 Lucy

40 Park

41 Lucy

42 Park

43 Lucy

44 Park

45 Lucy

Epilogue Park

Prologue

Park

Have you ever looked back and tried to figure out where your life took a wrong turn? The exact moment—that precise action—that turned your whole life to shit? And now you wish like hell that you could go back and change it?

Here's life lesson number 1: You can never fucking go back. What's done is done. Whatever damage you've caused is permanent. Life doesn't have an undo button—no matter how much you *wish* it did.

Which leads me to life lesson number 2: Don't waste your time wishing. It doesn't work and you just wind up looking like a fucking loser. Don't believe me? Let's try a little experiment. Wish in one hand and shit in the other. Now tell me which hand filled up faster.

Life lesson number 3: Life is shitty. Fucking deal with it. You want something? Take it. Take it and fuck everything and everybody else. There is not a line outside your door waiting to hand it to you.

I can pinpoint the exact moment it all goes wrong for me. I do something that I've done probably fifty times before. Jessie has one rule for borrowing his equipment: Return it promptly. He was cool enough to hand it over, the least I can do is honor his simple request.

I leave the party, and my girl, to take Jessie's shit back to him. That's it. This simple fucking act that I've done so many times before. Only, when I come back, I've lost my girl. My best friend has betrayed me, and the new kid has everything that's mine.

I lower myself onto the bed beside Hope and notice the spot's warm, like someone had just been sitting in it. I hope it was Guy, because if it was Mason, I'm going to lose my shit with him. I don't like the way he's been looking at Hope. I don't like the way she looks at him, either.

I've had this feeling lately, like this itch I can't quite reach, and it's been driving me insane. I don't know if I'm being paranoid or not, but I feel like something's shifted between me and Hope and I'm scared we can't get it back. I haven't mentioned it to her. I'm too afraid to find out if I'm right.

I press into my girl and kiss her on the cheek. I want to remind the new dude she's mine. I feel Hope's body stiffen and my gaze automatically flicks to Mason. New or not, he gets what I'm doing and he doesn't like it. His face is expressionless, but his body is coiled tight, his hands fisted at his sides. *What the fuck?* I shoot a questioning look at Guy. My best friend. Hope's foster brother. My. Best. Friend.

My stomach churns from the guilt I read in his eyes as he looks away from me. I turn back to Hope and nuzzle her ear. "You smell good," I say softly as I try to fight against the panic flowing through my veins. I just want to get her away from Mason. I want her to myself, like it used to be. "Let's go somewhere." Mason clenches his jaw and I add, "Alone."

"Yeah, okay," she agrees. "We need to talk." But she isn't even looking at me. Her eyes are glued to Mason and he—*fuck*—he looks relieved, and happy, and fucking hopeful as hell.

My head is getting hot from the blood rushing there. Everything feels like it's going in slow motion. Guy says something and Mason follows him out. I don't know how long we sit in the uncomfortable silence, but I feel like I'm going to puke. So I turn to her, hoping she'll make everything all right.

"What's going on?"

And then she just does it. She rips my fucking heart out of my chest. "We need a break."

We need a break. *We* need a break. *We*. I stare at the door Mason just walked through while her words replay in my head.

And then I fucking laugh. Not because it's funny. It's anything but funny. I laugh because I was right. As much as I tried to ignore it, hoped I was wrong, *wished* for it to not be true, deep down I knew it. "*We* don't need a break. You do." I shake my head hard. "Why? Or should I say who?" I already know why. I know who. I just want to hear her say it.

She glares at me like she has a right to be pissed. "We had a deal," she fires back.

"Mm, yeah. Our non-committal relationship that isn't really a relationship. Except it is. For me. It is." It always was. From the moment I met her, I knew I wanted her for life. *How can she do this to me? I've given her over a year and this is all I get?* "So that's it? We're done? Do I even get to know why? What I did wrong?" Maybe I can fix this. I can change. I'll be whatever she wants. Whatever she needs.

I love her.

I never told her that. I should have told her.

Hope's breathing increases until she's panting, fighting for air. *Fuck.* She's having a panic attack. Because of me.

She pulls her hair, something she does when she's trying to calm herself. I know it's going to get bad any second. "You didn't do anything wrong," she whispers. I swallow roughly. Yeah, it's bad when she starts whispering. "I just need…" she trails off, searching for the right word. Or name.

Hope stands up abruptly and flies toward the door. I shoot up after her as she tears the door open so hard it slams against the wall, shaking the windows. I pull her into me, hugging her to my chest. I wish this was enough. I wish I was enough. But it never is. I never am.

"Calm down," I say quietly. "It's okay." It's not okay, but I lie to her, hoping it will work even though I know it won't. "Just calm down."

She shakes her head, back and forth quickly, her brightly colored hair brushing against my chin. I can smell her fruity shampoo and even with the pain suffocating me, even with her freaking out against my chest, I acknowledge the fact that I love the way she smells. And I realize how much I'm going to miss her scent.

"No...it's...not okay."

Shit. She can barely catch her breath. I can't do this. I don't know how to make her better.

"Get Guy," she pleads. I let her go and move as fast as I can down the stairs and out the back door. As soon as he sees me—he knows. His blue eyes darken until it's hard to distinguish the color. He breaks away from the group he's talking to and Mason follows.

"Where is she?" Guy asks.

"Room," I pant. I watch them run back inside and I take a second to breathe. To orient myself with all the fucked up occurrences of the night. I wonder for a moment if this is really my life. It can't be. It just can't be.

When I get to Hope's room, it all hits me at once. This is really happening. She doesn't want me anymore. She wants *him*. She needs *him*.

Mason is kneeling in front of her and she's clinging to him like he's her savior. As if he's all she'll ever want and need for the rest of her life. And I just…*snap*.

It's one of those moments I have often. I know I should pause. I should stop, take a deep breath, walk away. But I can't. All these emotions attack me at once, overwhelming any good sense I may have had. When I get like this—I can't fucking take it.

"This is why." It's not a question. I don't need to ask anymore. "I knew it." I want to hurt her. I want to fucking crush them all. Mason for stealing the only girl I have ever loved. Guy for betraying me. He knew. I know he knew. There's no way he didn't.

And Hope—I want to hurt her most of all for the knife she lodged in my chest. She twists it now as her eyes confirm what doesn't need confirmed.

My brain understands it. But my heart keeps hoping this is some kind of horrible nightmare. *This is not my life*.

I laugh again and the sound is so dark and broken I cringe. Why does it hurt so badly? I cross my arms over my chest as if it will help the pain there.

I step all the way into her room. And then I smirk at her. I want her to know it's coming. I want her to realize that I have the ability to crush her too.

"Does he know?" I ask, referring to her secret. Her demon. Nobody knows but me. *Me*. I kept her secret all this time. I did that. Not Mason.

"Don't," she begs.

But I just smile bigger. I know I'm hurting her and it fucking feels good. It takes some of my pain away, even if only temporarily. "Hm-mm," I say casually. "He must not." I cock my head to the side in the shittiest, most condescending way possible. "Do you think he'll still want you when he finds out?"

"Dude, what the fuck? Back the fuck off," Mason spits.

His voice grates on my nerves. I want to kill him. Part of me wants to jump on his chest and beat him to death with my bare fucking hands. It takes everything in me to not act on it.

I don't take my eyes off Hope. I want her to witness everything I'm saying and doing. I want her to feel what she's done to me. "NO! You back the fuck off. I'm having a conversation with Hope."

"Park, dude, let's go for a walk," Guy says. He sounds far away even though I can see him in my peripheral vision. I ignore him. Fuck him.

Fuck them all.

"Did you know Hope cuts herself?" I drop the bomb as quickly as she cut my heart out.

She lunges at me, slapping me across the face. "You motherfucker. Get the fuck out." Her voice sounds lifeless and I already feel guilty for what I've done. Panic pulses through my entire body. *It's over. It's really over*. I sealed the deal with that one sentence.

I don't know what happened in the hour I was gone to take Jessie his equipment, but she was mine before I left, and Mason's when I got back. Here's life lesson number 4: Do not—under any circumstances—fall in love.

Lucy's Rules to Live By:

1. Make the conscious decision to look at others with an open mind and an open heart.
2. Everybody needs someone in their life they can rely on. Try to be that person.
3. Take a chance.
4. Love whole-heartedly.
5. Make it your goal to make someone smile daily.
6. Always expect more of yourself today than you did yesterday.
7. No matter how many times you're let down, continue believing in the goodness of others.

1

Lucy

Sweat trickles down my spine as I shift in my hiding place. My hair clings to me in an excruciatingly irritating way. It is entirely too hot out here, even with the thin flowing skirt and tank top I have on. I pull the top up, tucking it into the elastic of my bra, and wait.

This is the ultimate waiting game of who can hold out the longest. I never win. Patience is one of those virtues I never did have. And now I have to pee. Sighing, I turn the squirt gun around and shoot myself in the mouth. It's far from refreshing—warm from my death grip wrapped around the handle.

I hear his shuffling footsteps as he makes his way to the staircase and ready my gun. I'm shocked at Jessie's lack of stealth. I am so going to win this one.

The steps creak under his weight as he approaches the second floor landing. I jump out of the doorway and start firing. It takes four finger pumps before I realize the person I'm shooting in the face with lukewarm water is not, in fact, Jessie.

His hand whips up, trying to block my attack. I shoot once more, soaking his palm. "Oh, shit," I yelp. "I am so sorry. I thought you were someone else."

He wipes at his face and laughs behind his hand. "It's okay," he says, his voice soft, but there's a distinct gruffness to it that makes me really take a look at him. He's holding a box labeled *gamer shit* under a nicely shaped arm. I can make out the edges of a tattoo peeking out from under his sleeve. His dark hair is messy as if he forgot to comb it after he got out of bed. The front is flipped up to the side into a chaotic faux hawk. His eyes are the warmest brown I think I've ever seen, almost like melted butterscotch, but it's the thick, long lashes that have me stifling a sigh. He's adorable in a butterflies-in-the-tummy sort of way. The kind of guy that makes you want to smile just because you're in his presence. "It actually feels good."

Yes. Yes it does. I open my mouth with full intentions of flirting, but I'm cut short by Jessie's victory shout. I look up just in time to see him lean over the railing from the floor above, water cooler in hand. I gasp as ice cold water drenches my body, head to toe, as well as the stranger standing in front of me. He drops the box, and by the sound of it, breaks whatever is inside.

I blow water off my lips and push my hair out of my face, pointing a finger up. "That's who I thought you were," I pant.

Sexy stranger runs a hand down his face and cocks a brow. He lifts the tiny squirt gun from my hand. "You were taking on that," he gestures upward with the gun, "with this?" He waves it in front of me and grins. "Doesn't seem like a fair fight."

I smile back at him, relieved he's being cool about the whole thing. "It really isn't, but what's a girl to do?"

He observes me for several seconds before handing my worthless gun back. "Get him while he's sleeping," he says. "Not with that," he adds quickly, nodding at my hand. "Go big."

I look up at him and smile slowly in an obvious way. "I like big." And then I turn around and run up the steps to my apartment to change.

"He got you again?" Bree, my best friend and roommate, asks, laughing.

"I will seek my revenge," I vow as I continue into my room. Jessie is sprawled out on my bed, the picture of ease with his feet crossed at the ankle. His hands clutch a towel behind his head. I don't miss the smug smile on his face.

"You look damp, Lu," he says casually.

I prop a fist on my hip. "Don't act so proud of yourself, Jess. The only way you can get a girl wet is by dumping a cooler of water on her." I attempt to tug the towel out of his hand, but he doesn't let go. Instead, he pulls on it, dragging me down on top of him. I push myself up so I'm straddling him. Prying the soaking wet tank top out of my bra, I ring it out over his head.

Jessie grabs my wrists and pushes me back until I'm on my back and he's hovering above me. "You got the new neighbor," I say.

"Oh, yeah?"

I nod. "Soaked him."

Jessie hops off the bed. "That's nine—nothing."

"Only because you're a cheater."

"I don't cheat," he huffs, insulted. He rests a hand on the door knob. "You are just terrible at this game."

"That's just what I want you to believe. You better watch your back." I smirk at him and lift my brows. "You never know when I might strike."

"Lulu, I look forward to getting you wet again." He winks at me and breezes out the door. "By the way," he calls over his shoulder, "the new neighbor is my roommate—and trust me when I say he deserves an ice bath."

"Wait," I yell. I peer around the doorway. "You know him?"

"Yeah. Since grade school."

"He's really cute. Does he have a girlfriend?"

Jessie smirks at me and shrugs. "He has a lot of girls. I don't know if any are actually his friends."

My brows pull together. "What does that mean?"

He shrugs and chuckles as he turns on his heel, heading for Bree. He smacks a kiss on her cheek. "Bye baby." She throws her hand up, patting his neck, but doesn't look away from her laptop. Jessie strolls past me, back into my room, and ducks out the window. He pauses on the fire escape, glancing back at me. "It means you need to stay away from him."

Hmm. Interesting.

"At least tell me his name," I say.

He shakes his head and grabs onto the railing. "It never ceases to amaze me," he murmurs. I lean out after him.

"All I want is a name to go along with the memory of his gorgeous face."

"Something to think about at night?"

"Maybe," I sing.

He shakes his head again, but laughs. "His name's Park."

2
Park

I slosh into my new apartment with my wet, mangled box. I should be pissed that Jessie poured gallons of ice water over my head, but I can't muster the appropriate anger. He's nowhere to be found, which doesn't surprise me. The chicken shit knows he deserves an ass beating for that one.

I drop the box on the coffee table and look inside. *Come on.* Son of a…

"Hey, man," Jessie says, coming around the corner. I look to the front door then back to Jessie. Where the hell did he come from? He casually lowers himself into the recliner and throws his feet up next to my box that holds my now broken Nintendo. I know it's old as hell, but I love my old school game systems.

I stare blankly at him. "You owe me a new console."

He chuckles lightly and lifts his head. "I don't think you want us to start cashing in I.O.U.'s." He gives me a sharp look.

Good point. The fact I'm standing here right now speaks volumes as to the uneven scales of our friendship. It still sucks I'm out a vintage Nintendo. "Maybe I can fix it. After it dries out."

He smirks at me, resting his folded hands behind his neck. "Casualty of war, my friend. Right place, wrong time and all that."

I grunt. "Hm. Yeah. Do I want to know what that's about?"

He drops his feet and grins. "If I have to explain why I spent my afternoon chasing the hot neighbor around with a bucket of water, then your issues run deeper than I was aware of."

I nod. No more explanation needed. That hippie chick was hot. Especially wet. "Which apartment's hers?"

He points at the ceiling. "Next floor." Slapping his hands on his knees, he pushes himself up and stretches. "You need help bringing up the rest of your shit?"

I'm pretty sure he just tried to intercept my interest in the neighbor, but I let it go. If he's got dibs, I'm not about to step on his shoes. "If you don't mind."

I open the door to a nice round ass in cut off shorts. Jessie groans as he pushes past me. "Need some help?" he asks, his voice strained.

"Damn shoe just came untied." She flings her long, damp hair behind her shoulder.

That's a lot of hair.

She follows Jessie's gaze, glancing back at me. Her big gray eyes crinkle as a smile spreads across her heart-shaped face. She stands up and I notice she has great legs. They're a little on the short side, but they're lean and toned—a runner's legs. I'm usually more about T and A, which she has plenty of, but I find myself having a hard time taking my eyes off her calves. She offers me her hand and I snap my attention to her face. She has that natural look going for her. No make-up— she doesn't need it. Her skin is tan, her cheeks holding a natural glow. And her lips. Her fucking lips are a work of art. Her upper lip is fuller than the bottom, and the way it curves up… I think it's called a cupid's bow. It's amazingly kissable. I shake her hand and she lets her eyes fall over my wet and clinging clothes.

"I'm Lucy." She points up, her other hand still in mine. "I live in 3B."

"Park."

"Yeah. I know." She pulls her hand away and tucks a strand of golden hair behind a heavily pierced ear. She already knows my name? I eye her up and down as I wonder if she was asking about me or if Jessie was talking shit. "You haven't changed your wet clothes."

"All my stuff is down in the car." I'm still watching her, mostly because she's nice to look at, but partially because I'm trying to figure out if she's got something going on with my new roomie.

Jessie clears his throat obnoxiously, drawing my attention back to him. He really doesn't like me talking to Lucy. It makes me want to do it more if he's going to be a dick about it.

"Let's get your shit. I have to work tonight," Jessie states and turns toward the steps.

Lucy moves out of the way. "It was nice meeting you, Park."

I like the way she uses my name. Setting me apart from Jessie even though the sentence alone did that. "It was really nice meeting you too, Lucy."

"My friends call me Lulu or just Lu." She tucks that hair back again, but it stubbornly falls past her ear.

I cock my head to the side and step closer to her. "Are we friends?"

Her lips part and her eyes grow stormy. And then she laughs, a soft melodic sound that has the singer in me trying to match the key in my head. "Jessie was right—I need to stay far, far away from you." She bounds down the stairs. "See you later, Jess."

I throw a look at him. "What the hell was that? You told her to stay away from me?"

Jessie shrugs unabashed. "She's too good to be one of your girls."

"But *you're* in her league?" I let my eyes rake over his disheveled hair, ripped jeans, and worn Vans. He fucking looks homeless and he's judging me.

"Not even close." He shakes his head slowly. "This is non-negotiable if you want to live here."

I cross my arms over my chest and grin at him. "You're serious."

"Yes. Promise me you won't touch her."

I raise my brows and cough out a laugh. *You have got to be shitting me.* "Do I need to swear on a bible or something?"

Jessie's eyes narrow and he moves closer, his voice dropping. "Look, man. I'm dead fucking serious about this. She's my friend, she lives in the same building, and she's sweet. I won't watch you treat her like shit. I want you to promise me you will not touch her or you can't stay."

I laugh again as I rub my forehead. I should be insulted—fuck that—I am insulted. But I can't deny I'd hit it and quit it. And I need a place to stay—especially for as cheap as he's offering. There is no way I'm going back to the house I was subletting for the summer.

"Calm your ass down. I'm cool. I promise, I won't touch the hot hippie chick in 3B. All right?"

He steps back and noticeably relaxes. "All right. We're good."

I follow him down to my car and look sideways at him. "So, you and her got something going on?"

He grabs a box and barks out a harsh laugh. "No. She's just a friend." He turns to face me and tucks the box under his arm. "Now her roommate, Bree? That's mine. You can't touch her either."

I smirk at him. "Objectifying women? How 1950's scumbag of you. Is there any girls in this building you'll give me your permission to *touch*?"

He looks up like he's thinking. "1A, 2C, 3A, and 3D."

I reach in for my duffle bag. "What's wrong with them?"

He shakes his head and walks back inside, ignoring my question.

***

Turns out 1A is the landlady. She's in her sixties and smells like cat piss due to the at least eight cats residing in her apartment. 2C is a forty year old divorcee with a thirteen year old son who tried to shoot me with a pellet gun. 3A is a lesbian and not interested in a threesome. I checked. 3D has a revolving door and I'm pretty sure those weren't cold sores on her lip.

I slam the door and glare at Jessie. "You suck."

He grins widely at me as he slips on his shoes. "You got a hot date tonight?"

"Herpes never go away," I hiss.

He shivers, but then doubles over with laughter. "I don't know why you want to try to hook up with someone that lives in the same building anyway."

"Convenience. And what are you talking about? You're hooking up with that Bree girl."

"Yeah, but I'm dating her. Not just fucking her."

I cringe. That's a concept long forgotten for me. He might as well be speaking a foreign language. I'd probably understand it better. "To each his own, I guess."

He looks at me for a few seconds and nods. "I guess."

<u>3</u>

<u>Lucy</u>

It's Saturday. That means we have Saturday Breakfast. I stretch and yawn as I try to decide what I want to make. Jessie keeps his fridge fully stocked and his window permanently unlocked for me.

I brush my teeth and braid my hair so it doesn't end up in the food—again—and make my way down the fire escape to Jess' apartment. He's sprawled, face down in his bed, one leg hanging off the side, and snoring loudly. I tip toe past as quietly as possible, heading to the kitchen. I start the coffee immediately. I need a dose of caffeine before cooking.

With the sweet nectar brewing, I peer inside the refrigerator and start plucking items out. I can't decide between omelets or French toast, so I choose to make both. The sink is full of dirty dishes. *Of course.* I'll have to tackle those before I start. And they aren't even rinsed.

"God damn it," I mutter to myself, irritated with Jessie. "I get up early to make you food and you can't make sure there are clean dishes to eat off of."

Movement out of the corner of my eye causes me to jump and drop the onion in my hand. Park's leaning against the door frame, clad in only a pair of plaid pajama pants, and watching me with an amused expression. He rubs his face with both hands. "Oh, my God," I breathe. "You scared the shit out of me."

He grins and pushes off the wall. "Sorry. I heard someone moving around and came to investigate."

I pick up the onion and toss it on the counter. "It's Saturday," I explain as I start water to wash the dishes—purposely turning away from his bare chest. I really want to take a look at his tattoo, but I keep my eyes on the building suds.

"Okay…?"

I flip my braid off my shoulder, glancing back at him quickly. "I make Saturday Breakfast. It's a tradition."

"Tradition? Jessie's only lived here for what? Seven, eight months?"

I shrug. I'm not sure. He was already here when I moved in six months ago. "Every Saturday since we met. That makes it tradition."

"All right." He moves behind me, reaching into the cabinet for a coffee mug. His hips brush mine slowly. I can feel the heat coming off his body and smell his cologne—something crisp and clean, with a hint of smoke underneath. He steps past me, placing his hand on my back as he grabs the coffee pot, slowly filling his cup. I don't breathe until he steps back. Without another word, he walks out as quickly as he appeared.

By the time I have breakfast started, Bree's falling into a kitchen chair. She props her long legs on the table. "New guy's hot," she says in way of greeting. I smirk knowingly at her. *Yeah he is.*

"Jessie still sleeping?"

She beams at me and moves to the sink. "Not for long," she whispers. Filling a cup with cold water, she bounces out of the kitchen. Jessie's shout is followed by Bree's shriek and I shake my head, laughing.

"What are you smiling about?" Jessie asks, stalking toward me. He shakes his wet hair, flinging drops of moisture on my face, and I slap him with the dish towel.

"Quit or I'm not finishing breakfast."

He relents quickly, backing up several feet. "Fuck that. I'm starving. Finish my breakfast, woman."

I raise a brow, readying myself to cuss him out when the buzzer sounds. He looks at me questioningly. I shrug. "Whoever it is isn't here for me. This isn't my apartment," I remind him.

We both hold still, the spatula in my hand raised between us, as we listen to the door opening and closing. Park comes back into the kitchen—now fully dressed—followed by a guy in a black wife-beater that shows off a full sleeve of an intricate tattoo. His hair is the color of the blue raspberry slushies Bree's always drinking. He's pretty, even though I don't think that's the look he's going for.

"Hey, man. What's up?" Jessie says, nodding at the new addition.

"Not much." His hazel eyes rake over me and he smiles at me with a mouth full of perfectly straight, white teeth. "Hey."

"Hi. I'm LuLu," I say, introducing myself because Jessie's too rude to think of it.

"Chase. Nice to meet you." He grins widely at me and I can't help but return it.

I turn back to the stove and gesture at the pan. "I made plenty," I say. "Grab plates."

"You did my dishes?" Jessie asks.

I chuckle, nodding. "Yeah. I had to or we'd be eating off the table."

He puts his hands on my hips and leans over my shoulder. "What'd you make me?"

"French toast and cheese omelets."

"Damn," Chase sighs. "I wish that I had Jessie's girl," he sings loudly.

Shaking my head, I glance back at him and laugh. Jessie releases me and pushes a plate at Chase. "She's not my girl." His eyes flick to Bree standing in the doorway and I press my lips together. That's where all his affection lies, but she hasn't allowed him to claim her as his girl yet.

"Bree, my African princess," Jessie coos. "This is my new roommate, Park. And this is Chase. We all went to school together."

"I already met Park," she informs him.

Jessie frowns and crosses his arms. Park leans into him. "Don't worry man. I just introduced myself after I found her walking around our apartment." He holds his hands up in a defensive gesture. "I swear I didn't touch her."

Bree picks up a plate and holds it out for me to fill. She winks at Jessie. "He did shake my hand."

He growls at her. "The death of me," he murmurs.

I hand her back her plate and she skims her fingers across Jessie's bare stomach. "Your turn." He takes the dish from her and places it on the table, then picks her up, throwing her over his shoulder, carrying her out of the room.

Park raises a brow at me and I shrug as I hand him a full plate. Chase laughs. "So," he says, "you single?"

Before I can respond, Park shakes his head, his eyes locking on mine. "She's hands off. Jessie's house rule."

"Damn," Chase groans. "Always the hot ones."

"What did you just say?" I ask incredulously. One side of Park's mouth lifts in a smirk and he shrugs, his eyebrows lifting with his shoulders.

"Oh, man. This omelet is freaking good." Chase kisses the tips of his fingers. "Screw Jessie. Run away with me right now."

I don't know if he's being funny or trying to change the subject. I flip the switches, turning the burners off and stomp out of the room.

"Oh, shit," I hear Chase trill.

I bang my fist against Jessie's door. "God damn it, Jess. Get your ass out here, now."

Bree opens the door, pulling her shirt down over her flat stomach and smoothes her hair. "What?" Jessie hisses from behind her.

"What does it mean I'm 'hands off'?"

He blinks, rubbing his forehead. He moves past me, heading back to the kitchen. I stay right on his heels.

"Thanks a lot," he whispers loudly. Park smiles behind a forkful of food and Chase chuckles, both amused with Jessie's discomfort.

"What does that mean?" I ask again.

"I think it means he told his friends they aren't allowed to hit on you," Bree offers. She sits down next to Chase and starts eating. They all watch me and Jessie like we're putting on a live show. This isn't dinner theater. Or breakfast—whatever.

I glare at his back as he turns away from me and pours a cup of coffee. He's taking his good old time and it's just pissing me off more.

"What is your problem with your friends talking to me?"

He finally faces me and sighs. "I'm trying to look out for you."

I raise my hands, palms up. "I never asked you to do that. Who I date is my decision. Not yours."

He steps toward me, jabbing a finger toward the table. "He doesn't date, Lu. He fucks and forgets."

Park sits back and sets his fork down, but he doesn't say anything. Bree glances from him, to Jessie, to me, her brown eyes wide.

"You already said something to me. What I choose to do with your warning is my decision. You can't run every guy off."

"The shit I can't."

"You're an ass."

"You're naïve."

I close my eyes and clench my teeth together. "I am not as stupid as you think I am," I grind out.

Park folds his arms over his chest and cocks his head to the side as he watches our back and forth. I avoid eye contact because I don't want him to think this is about him. Because it's not. This is about me. And Jessie thinking I'm an idiot.

"I never said you were stupid."

"No, you just implied that I'm not intelligent enough to make decisions for myself."

"I know these guys. You don't."

"Hey," Chase calls, offended.

Jessie ignores him as he steps closer to me. "Think Jared, but ten times worse."

I grind my teeth to keep from saying something I might regret later.

"Listen to him, Lucy," Park drawls. He pushes his chair back slowly and picks up his plate. He pauses beside me. "Good French toast," he adds before moving through the doorway.

I don't miss the use of my full name. His way of making it clear we aren't going to be friends? I'm not sure.

I skip out on breakfast and go for a run.

<u>4</u>

<u>Park</u>

I open my eyes to a head full of blonde hair hovering above me. *Shit. That feels good.* I glance around quickly, trying to remember where the hell I am. It looks like a bottle of Pepto-Bismol exploded. Everything is pink. Everything. From the walls, to the sheets, to the curtains.

And then I remember the hot-ass, stuck up girl in the pink sweater from last night. After Jessie made me out to be a fucking predator of all things female, I decided to prove him right. As soon as this chick turned her nose up at the sight of me, I knew she was the one. I smile as I tangle my fingers into her hair, urging her on. She picks up the pace and I grit my teeth.

It didn't take long to have her bent over her bed screaming my name. She went from *"fuck you"* to *"fuck me harder"* in less than an hour. That has to be some kind of record. I chuckle. It isn't even a challenge anymore.

What the hell is her name? Something with a P. Parris or Page. Penny?

I tap her shoulder, signaling for her to move her head or get a mouth full. She sits back on her heels and grins at me. She's not nearly as pretty as I thought she was last night. But her hand keeps moving and I decide I don't give a shit what her face looks like because she has a truly amazing talent.

I close my eyes so I don't have to look at her as I come. It's fucked up, I know, but I don't even remember her name. She's just some girl that acted like she was better than me, so I brought her down to my level for a few hours.

I'm not complaining about the wake-up call. I needed to get up anyway. I grab a handful of tissues—fucking pink—from her nightstand and clean myself up. As I shove my legs in my jeans, she wraps her hands around my waist from behind, and I cringe.

"What are you doing?"

"I have to go," I say, detangling her pink polished fingers from my stomach. "Got shit to do. I'm already late."

"Oh." She sighs and I can imagine the disappointed expression on her face. I don't bother to look. Instead, I throw my shirt on and plop down on the edge of the bed to put my boots on. Her hands slide up my back and I have to force myself not to shake her off.

"When do you think you'll be done?"

I laugh and shake my head. "Look…"

"Piper," she provides coolly.

Piper. That's it. "Piper, I had fun, but I'm not looking for a relationship."

Her teeth snap together and she stares at me. "Me either."

I laugh again, this time with bitterness. "Yeah, I've heard that before." I kiss her cheek and push myself up. "Thanks for the wake and take. See ya later."

"Fuck you, Park."

I grin as I snatch up my keys. "You already did. Twice."

I duck out the door just as something shatters against the wall.

***

I avoided the Saturday morning breakfast this past weekend. I also learned to avoid Monday afternoons after walking into the bathroom to find Lucy in her cut-off jean shorts and a tank top, bent over the bathtub scrubbing soap scum away. Apparently Jessie pays her to clean once a week. Now I make a mental note to add the laundry room on Wednesdays to my list of places to steer clear. She's too tempting and I can't afford to be tested.

I almost walk back out when I see her folding towels in front of a dryer. She's in another one of those long skirts, only she has one side pulled up and tucked into the waist. I have a great view of her crazy sexy legs and it physically hurts to look at her. She smiles as she pulls the headphones from her ears. "Hi Park. Haven't seen you around lately."

I place my bag on a washer and scratch my neck. "I've been busy."

"You taking summer classes?"

I turn my back to her and start dumping my clothes. "No."

"Been working?"

"Yeah."

She gets quiet and I glance back at her. Her arms are folded in front of her, emphasizing her chest. When my gaze makes it back to her face, she narrows her gray eyes at me. "Are you going to be weird around me now or are you always like this?"

Her fiery attitude catches me off guard and I grin at her. "Like what?"

She shrugs her slim shoulders. "I don't know...cold?"

I chuckle. "That's me in a nut shell."

"What are you out of the shell?"

"This is it," I say hoarsely. I don't want her to know more. Hell, I honestly don't know if there even is more.

I stare at her, at her big eyes and full lips, contemplating throwing her on top of one of these washing machines. I don't know what she sees when she looks at me, but there's raw heat in her gaze, like she's full of passion. Like she wants to see what I'm full of. Like she already can. And I want to be a part of it. I want to feel it.

She licks those damn lips and I have to discretely adjust my jeans. If she wasn't the forbidden fruit, I wouldn't hide. I'd show her exactly how sexy I find her. I'd let myself feel something good for a little while.

But she is forbidden.

"Okay," she relents. "So, I was thinking about making dinner for everyone—"

"I have a gig tonight—"

"—tomorrow." She tucks her hair behind her ear. "Do you DJ with Jessie?"

"No." I turn back to my washer and pour in some detergent.

"What do you do? You said gig."

"I sing."

She arches her brows. "In a band?"

"No. I'm a wedding singer," I deadpan. "Yes in a band. *A Fool's Paradise.*"

Realization colors her features and she squints at me. "Park…"

"Yeah?"

"No. Nothing." She bites her lip and shakes her head like she knows better than to tell me what she was about to say. Now I really want to know.

"What were you going to say, Lucy?"

"Nothing. I just remembered you."

I cock a brow and move in front of her. "You remember me?"

"Not you, just something…never mind."

"Oh. You've seen us play?" I chuckle. Our shows get pretty intense.

She picks up her basket and backs away from me. "I'll see you later." She pauses, biting at her lip again. If she keeps that up, I'm going to start biting it for her. "You'll come tomorrow? For dinner?"

I hold her gaze. "Probably shouldn't."

"That stuff with Jessie—it wasn't about you. I just hate him acting like that. He thinks he's my big brother. I'd like us to be friends. You should come."

"Friends?" I nearly spit the word. Fuck friends. I don't need another *friend*.

"Yeah." She grins and adjusts the basket in front of her.

I smirk at her and let my eyes graze over her body. "I don't know how to be friends with someone I'm attracted to." If she's not going to listen to Jessie's advice, I can at least be honest with her. And it is the truth. I have no clue how to be friends with a girl anymore.

Her lips part and that stormy look glazes her eyes. "You're attracted to me?"

I nod, dropping the smirk because she looks sexy as hell shifting her feet nervously. "Can't help it. You're hot."

She rolls her eyes. "Well, learn to help it, Park, because I'm not the kind of girl that has one night stands. But I'm nice, and I'm a pretty loyal friend. I think you could use a good friend."

I swallow tightly as she shifts the basket on her hip and starts for the stairs. "Be there at six," she calls.

Fuck that. I'm not going.

***

I roll over, my hand landing on something soft and warm. I squint one eye and try to focus on the girl in my bed.

Motherfuckinggoddamnsonofabitchingshit. They are not allowed in my bed. I never bring them home. I always—*always* go to their place. I must've been beyond wasted last night. I hate this part. I hate trying to get rid of them. And now she knows where I live. Which means she can come back.

I nudge her shoulder. Her short, dark hair spills into her face as she moves with my hand. "Hey. Wake up."

The girl opens her eyes and blinks at me. "What?"

"You need to go," I rasp.

She closes her eyes and I'm afraid she's going to fall back asleep. I poke her in the ribs. "Hey."

"I heard you. Gimme a minute. I'm still drunk."

I rub a hand over my face. *Shit. So am I.* "I'd let you stay, but my roommate will get pissed."

"Well we wouldn't want to anger Jessie," she says sarcastically.

Wait. I'm too out of it to catch up. "You know Jessie?"

She laughs, her eyes still closed. She points a long, slender finger at her chest. "Cousin."

You have got to be fucking shitting me. I let my head drop back on my pillow and stare up at the ceiling. No.

No.

I did not do this.

I'm having some weird-ass dream.

I did not have sex with Jessie's cousin.

I turn my head and she's peering at me out of one eye. I am so screwed. Jessie's going to kick my ass out on the street. Life lesson number 5: Don't mess with your friend's family. Especially the crazy ones.

"I'll be gone before he wakes up. He'll never know. Now chill out and go back to sleep."

"No. You need to go. Now. I'll pay for your cab."

She sighs heavily. "How gentlemanly of you." She sits up, her naked body exposed to me. Yeah. I was wasted beyond belief. She's anorexic skinny. Not something I've ever found attractive. I can see every ridge in her spine as she leans over to grab a cigarette.

"You can't smoke that in here. Jessie makes me smoke on the fire escape."

She rolls her eyes and tucks the cigarette behind her ear. I watch her get dressed, fighting the urge to help her so she can get the hell out of my room. "So..." She clears her throat and screws her lips to the side. "I'll see you around."

I grab my wallet from the jeans on the floor and hand her two twenties, trying really hard not to acknowledge the fact that I'm paying a girl I just slept with. "Yeah. See ya."

She stops in front of the door. "Just so you know, you couldn't...we didn't..."

"We didn't?"

She narrows her eyes at the hopeful connotation in my voice. I can't help myself. I sigh with relief. "No. You were too drunk to get it up." With that, she throws open the door and stomps down the hallway, not bothering to be quiet. When the front door slams, I fall back on my bed and into a sleepy oblivion.

***

I step out of the shower, not bothering to dry off as I wrap a towel around my waist. Picking up my iPod, I open the door, letting the steam out, and pad back to my room.

There's a knock at the door and I cringe. My head is killing me, plus I'm pretty sure I already know who it is. I purposely locked the window after Jessie left for Lucy's dinner. I stalk to the front door and fling it open, not bothering to mask my irritation. How am I supposed to avoid her when she searches me out?

"What?"

Lucy crosses her arms. "Why aren't you in my apartment?" She looks past me, trying to see inside and I feel my lips lift in a crooked smile at her refusal to acknowledge I'm in nothing but a towel.

"I'm not going," I say. Her eyes drift back to mine and I can read the disappointment clearly in her gaze.

"You're being stubborn."

I rest my arm on the door frame above my head and lean toward her. She doesn't react in any way and I grin at her. "I'm following orders." I flick my eyes over her body, from her loose hippie braid, all the way down to her bright orange Converse. I smile at that. When I've made my way back to her face, she's watching me take her in. She sighs and shifts her weight to her other side. I lean out further, deliberately moving closer than is necessary, but she doesn't back up. It's like she doesn't register my bare chest, inches from hers. I'm trying to mess with her, but her indifference to me is making me want to up my game, and turning me on at the same time. *That backfired like a motherfucker.*

"Jessie knows I invited you. He's okay with it."

I drop my hand and step back. "He's okay with it?" I ask, disbelieving.

She nods and her gaze moves over my chest. *About time.* "Well, I told him and there's nothing he can do about it." *To you, maybe.*

"Why are you pushing this? Why's it so important to you?"

"I don't know. I like you, I guess."

I grin at her. "You like me?"

She laughs and bites her lip. "I told you, I think we could be good friends."

"Oh, we could be *great* friends, Lucy," I say, letting my smile turn animalistic. "But then I'd end up homeless."

"I'm serious."

I rest my hands on my hips, right above the towel. "So am I."

She growls at me. The sound sends a shot of need to all the right places and I have to force myself stay where I am. She talks so big about friendship, but I'm sure I could get her in bed if I actually put forth the effort. I bet I could run the tip of my tongue over that mole below her ear and make her whimper. I bet I could brush my fingers along the inside of her thigh and have her begging me to move higher. I bet—

"Park," Lucy breathes.

I clear my throat and focus on her face. Damn she's pretty. She's got beautiful eyes. And that mouth—the things I'd love to do to it.

"Park," she hisses.

"What?" I croak.

"Stop looking at me like that." Her cheeks are pink, her eyes glossy. Her chest is rising a little too quickly. She isn't nearly as unaffected by me as she pretends. The girl's just a damn good actress.

"Looking at you like what?"

"Like you're thinking about me naked," she says, her voice quivering.

I stand up straight and shake my head. "This is why we can't be friends."

She raises her hands and let's them fall, slapping her thighs. "Fine. I don't know why I even bothered."

I shrug. "I don't know why you bothered either," I say flatly and close the door in her face.

5

Lucy

I almost drop my tray of drinks when I see Park sitting in the corner booth of my section. It's been over a week since he slammed the door in my face and my stomach tightens at the sight of him.

I don't know what it is about him that draws me in. He's an ass. He's arrogant. He's a slut. He's also breathtakingly gorgeous and the way he looks at me makes my body react without permission or apology.

With a deep breath, I drop the drinks off and head for his booth. He has his arm draped over some girl's shoulder. She looks up at me with bloodshot eyes and I realize she's drunk. This is why I hate the midnight shift. Every drunk wants greasy diner food after the bars close. I usually get happy or talky drunks, but there's the occasional overly emotional drunk, the handsy drunk, or the mean drunk. She doesn't look happy or talkative.

I clear my throat. "Hey Park." He looks up quickly and I see the surprise on his face.

"You work here?" His voice is full of annoyance and I grind my teeth. The stench of liquor is heavy in the air. I am not in the mood for this.

"Nope. I just decided to steal a uniform and walk around taking people's orders."

He smirks at me, his eyes piercing. I turn to the girl. She's watching me now, a scowl marking her features. I press my lips together and turn to the opposite side to address the others.

Chase smiles. "Hey Lulu. How's it going?"

I grin. "Hey Chase. It's going. Can I get you a drink?"

"Yeah. I'll have a Coke. And I actually know what I want." He hands me his menu and I tuck it against my side. He opens his palms and shakes them a little. "I need a gigantic cheeseburger and crispy fries."

I laugh quietly. "I can do that." I turn my attention to the girl next to him. She pushes her long, blonde hair behind her shoulder and leans closer to her menu.

"I want a Sprite, but...do you have salads?"

Chase groans. "You drive me insane, Annie. Get a freaking burger 'cause you know you want one."

She leans back and looks sideways at him. "Fine," she sighs. "I'll have what he ordered."

I nod and reluctantly face the girl next to Park. "Same," she says curtly.

"Drink?" I keep my eyes on my notepad.

"Do you serve beer?"

"No."

She sighs loudly, as if I'm responsible for what the diner serves. "A Diet Coke then."

I finally raise my head to look at Park. He grins widely and his eyes rake over me from head to toe. It's not like he hasn't done that twenty times already, but accompanied by the shitty grin and leering eyes, it makes me feel dirty. I shift uncomfortably. "What do you want, Park?"

He lifts a brow and somehow manages to smile bigger. "What I want isn't on the menu."

I take a deep breath and meet his gaze with a glare. "So you're not ordering?"

He shakes his head slowly. "What's good here?"

I bite my lip and his eyes focus on my mouth. There's a flutter in my stomach. I feel my cheeks warm and I look away. "The burgers are good. The chicken sandwich is all right. The buffalo strips are amazing. Or—"

"Amazing?"

"Yep."

His voice drops and runs over me like a caress. "Are they hot?"

I close my eyes, but open them quickly and glance at him. "They're spicy."

That smirk is back and he holds out his menu without taking his eyes off me. "I like spicy."

I clear my throat. "Do you want a drink?"

"Milk."

I almost laugh. "Milk?"

"Milk. It does the body good." He winks and the girl next to him paws his bicep.

"Hell yeah it does." She scoots closer to him and I almost throw up in my mouth.

"I'll get your orders in right away," I say and turn to leave. Chase catches my wrist causing me to pause.

"Thanks, Lu," he murmurs. He gives me a small smile.

"Sure. No problem," I chirp.

I don't know why I let Park get to me. I flirt all the time. Guys flirt back. The occasional girl, even. It's all in fun. But he makes it—*not* fun. Either he has me wanting to abandon all my morals, or he has me cringing, feeling filthy and worthless. How he's able to do that is beyond me. I don't even know the man.

The more I think about it, the angrier I get. I wipe the counter a little more forcefully than I need to. He has a girl right beside him, yet he flirts with me. He'll be buried deep inside that walking disease as soon as they leave here, but he still finds the need to mess with my head.

I take a cleansing breath and berate myself for assuming the worst about the girl with Park. She could be nice. I glance over and she glares at me before returning her attention back to whatever Park's talking about.

Okay, maybe she's a bitch.

It doesn't matter what she is. I don't know her and I'm pretty sure I'll never see her again after tonight.

The drunk guys at table 4 wave and call to me. "Hey, goldie." I blow out a breath. Got to love drunken frat boys. "Hey," one calls again. "Come here." He wiggles his finger and I toss the rag and cleanser on the bar.

"What do ya need?" I ask sweetly. College boys tip well if you're sweet.

The two guys break out in obnoxious laughter, throwing each other a look. "Baby girl, I need to take you home."

I smile *sweetly*. "Oh, sorry," I say *sweetly*. "Can't. I have to work." I turn my head and roll my eyes. "Anything else I can help you with?"

They howl with laughter. "You can help me with this," the other one says. He points at his lap and makes his eyebrows jump up and down.

I cock my head to the side and shake my head in apology. "I don't know how to make it bigger." I wish Bree was here. She would have these guys on the floor, licking her shoes.

The guy chuckles. His friend smacks the table top a few times. "What time do you get off? I'll teach you how to make it bigger."

I place my hand on his shoulder and lean into him. "Don't look, but my boyfriend is sitting at that booth over in the corner." I grip his shoulder tighter as he starts to turn his head. "Don't look. He's pretty big and he doesn't like it when guys hit on me, as you can imagine. Don't worry." I let my hand slide down to his back and give him a pat. "He hasn't noticed yet, and I won't tell." I stand back and grin. "Is there anything else I can get you?"

He raises his brows and shakes his head. "No. I'm good."

"Great." I beam at him as I drop the check on the table and bounce off.

I pick up the order for Park's table. He doesn't look at me as I set out everyone's plates. I prop the tray on my hip and look at Chase.

"Can I ask a favor?"

He leans back against the seat, running his long fingers through his blue hair. "Sure."

Hmm. That was easy. "If two guys come over here, pretend to be my boyfriend?" I glance quickly at the girl next to him. "If that's all right."

She chuckles. "Yeah, not a problem."

"Thanks," I sigh.

She sips her drink then adds, "Those dudes are dicks. We could hear them over here."

Chase nods. "No problem, Lu. Do you want me to go talk to them?"

I wave him off. "No. It's all good. They're fine. I don't think they'll say anything else now that I have my big, strong boyfriend with the weird hair." I wink dramatically and he grins.

"You sure? I don't mind." He makes a show of standing up and throwing his napkin on the table, making me laugh.

"Yeah. Thanks again, Chase."

"Is it always like this?" he asks, sitting down and picking up his burger.

I shrug and lower the tray to my side. "This shift brings in all kinds." I can't help it, my eyes flick to Park who is watching me stoically.

"Anyway..." I look around their table. "Everything okay? Anybody need anything else?"

"It's great," the girl next to Chase says. She moans as she takes another bite. "This is so good."

Chase smiles at her then turns to me. "I think we're good."

"I could use more napkins," the girl next to Park barks.

I press my lips together and nod. She's going to run me. I can tell. This is not going to be fun at all.

6

Park

I watch as the douche bags that were messing with Lucy pay their bill. They shove each other out the door and I shoot Chase a look. "I'll be back," I say, pushing my plate back as I stand.

"Where you going?" Taylor whines.

"To take a piss." I brush her off and stalk after the guys. Chase gets up and falls into step beside me. We don't say a word as we head outside. He moves to one side of their car as I go to the other. Both guys pull up short as soon as they see us coming.

I press my hip against the door and cross my arms. Recognition flashes in the guy's eyes and I stare flatly. He adjusts his baseball cap and puts his hands up, palms out. "We were just playing. I didn't know she had a boyfriend."

I try not to recoil at his assumption. "Now you do," I state simply.

Chase moves in on the other dude. "Show women respect."

My lips twitch, fighting off a smirk, and I push off the car. Baseball Cap steps back. "You tip her?" I ask, my voice dropping low.

"Yeah, man."

"How much?" Chase growls.

"Five bucks."

I shake my head and hold my hand out. "You tipped her twenty for having to put up with your shit."

He stares at me blankly and I kick his shoe, causing him to reach out for the side of the car to balance himself. He's a pretty big dude, but I'm bigger. The gym and I have become good friends over the past couple years. He realizes this, too, as he sizes me up.

The other guy reaches into his wallet and shoves a twenty into Chase's hand. "Here. Can we go now?"

Chase looks at me over the roof and I raise my brows. "Get the fuck out of here," he spits. "You come back here, it better be with an apology."

We stand on the curb, waiting for them to back out of the parking space. They flip us off as the car peels out, tires squealing. I chuckle and follow Chase back inside. He tucks the money into his pocket and I glare at him.

"What are you doing?"

He grins stupidly. "What?"

"Put it on the table." He sighs, but places it between the salt and pepper shakers as we pass by.

Chase shakes his head and laughs.

"What?"

"You like her."

"No I don't," I fire back. The denial comes out too quickly. I sound like a third grader. But he doesn't call me on it. He just shrugs.

"I don't know why not. She's pretty cool." He looks past me where Lucy's bent over, clearing a table. "And she's not bad to look at."

I push him toward our booth and slide into my seat. I know she's pretty. She's more than pretty. She's sexy as hell. But I'm not allowed to have her. If Jessie kicks me out, I have no place else to go. I can't go back to the sublet I abandoned. Chase still lives in the dorms, so he's not even an option. Hell, back home with my mom isn't even doable—not with my poor-ass excuse of a father hanging around. And no matter how much I'd like to have Lucy, I'd like a roof over my head more.

The farther Lucy stays away from the better. For both of us.

I'm losing my buzz and that pisses me off. Taylor presses her leg against mine and leans into me. I can't even lift my arm to eat. She's getting on my nerves and I'm not sure if it's her or if it has more to do with my waitress.

She raises her hand and snaps her fingers. "Excuse me. Server?"

Lucy scowls in my direction as if I'm the one snapping at her like an ass. "Are you actually doing that?" Annie laughs and looks at me incredulously. "Where did you find this girl?"

I rub my forehead and shake my head.

Taylor rolls her eyes. "What? It's her job."

"Did you need something?" Lucy asks, her voice sugary. It doesn't match the barely contained anger in her eyes.

"A box."

"Please," Chase adds.

"No problem." Lucy looks down at my full plate and frowns. "I guess you need two? Something wrong with your buffalo strips?"

"Guess I'm just not in the mood for spicy tonight," I clip out. I don't know why I'm being a dick to her. She really seems like a nice person. And Chase was right when he said I liked her. But therein lies the problem.

Her lips pout out for a second before she turns that fake smile on me that she used on the douche bags earlier. "Not everybody can handle the heat."

I watch her strut her tight, round ass away with a huge grin on my face.

***

I wake up. In my own bed. Alone. Not hung over.
I feel pretty good.
This is weird.

I hear the banging of pans in the kitchen and remember it's Saturday. I grab my cigarettes and make my way to Jessie's room so I can grab a quick smoke on the fire escape. If I bend out over the side a little, I have a perfect view of Lucy and Bree in the kitchen.

Bree turns on music and they start dancing as they move around making breakfast. When Lucy starts swaying her hips in front of the stove I turn away. I don't need that image in my head. I lean over the railing and blow out a puff of smoke.

I have a jolting realization. *This is it. This is my life.*

What the fuck?

"Here." I glance over my shoulder as Lucy leans out the window with a cup of coffee. "Black, right?"

"Yeah." I take it and my fingers brush over hers. Her eyes flick to mine. She ducks back in and it occurs to me belatedly to say thank you. I push my cigarette butt into the old beer bottle on the ledge and sip my coffee.

What the fuck am I doing? Who the fuck am I?

I flex my fingers. I haven't thought about this shit in a long time. I close my eyes. A shot of panic flows through my veins as the image of a girl with multi-colored hair and a bad attitude seers itself behind my eyelids. My fingers twitch with the desire to pick up my phone and call Hope. I make a fist.

Damn it.

Why am I thinking about this? About her.

Laughter drifts out the open window and I bend until I can peer inside. Lucy's head is tipped back and she's cracking up over something. The muscles in my stomach go taught. Her beauty hits me like a punch in the face and pulls me inside.

I stand in the doorway to the kitchen, watching her as I sip my coffee. Bree realizes I'm here, throwing me a quick smile. I nod at her before turning all my attention to Lucy as she moves from one foot to the other, bobbing her head to Guns N' Roses. Her braid flies from side to side as she rocks out on the air guitar.

Jessie slides past me and jumps up on a chair to serenade us. "Take me down to the paradise city," he sings loudly. And extremely badly.

Lucy spins around and Bree bends over, laughing until tears are pouring down her face. Jessie keeps singing obnoxiously off key.

Large gray eyes meet mine and I smirk before backtracking to my room where I stay until I'm sure she's left.

<u>7</u>

<u>Lucy</u>

"How did you talk me into this?" I ask Bree, tugging on her hand. I love live bands, but I hate crowds.

Bree laughs, tucking a strand of thick, black hair behind her ear. "I didn't have to try too hard, Lu. You wanted to come. Admit it."

I shrug. I did. A lot. I've never seen Park perform. I caught him singing once on the walkway before he went into his apartment. He has an incredible voice. I can only imagine how he'd sound with a band behind him.

"They're really good," she says. She's been to two of their shows with Jessie. I passed, but when she asked me tonight, I couldn't resist anymore.

Bree puckers her lips and nods her head to the band playing a cover of a Steve Miller Band song. This reminds me of how we met. We bonded over our unique tastes in music, back in the eighth grade, when I saw the Billy Idol patch on her messenger bag. Most people assumed because her mom's white and her dad's black that she must like rap and R&B. They looked at me with my free love, give peace a chance, flower power, hippie parents and assumed I must like music right out of the sixties. And although all that's true, what they didn't realize was that we knew and loved a hell of a lot more music than that.

Bree has a passion for old southern rock, musicals, and anything from the eighties. I get giddy over old school rap, folk, and any and all rock. So when she tells me *A Fool's Paradise* is good, I take her word for it.

"When do they come on?"

"Ten, I think." She looks at Jessie for verification and he nods.

He puts his arms around our shoulders and pulls us into his chest. "I'm getting drinks. What do you want?"

"Rum and Coke if you can get it," I answer.

"Me too," Bree agrees.

"Psh. I can get it, woman. Do not doubt my awesomeness." He saunters off, running his hands through his dirty blonde hair.

"Mm. I do not know what I'm going to do with that boy," Bree sighs.

I laugh. "Please. We both know what you're going to do with that boy as soon as we get home."

She smiles at me, flashing a mouth full of white teeth. "I think I love him."

I gape at her. And then I squeal and jump up and down as tears come to my eyes. Jessie's been in love with her pretty much from the moment I introduced them. But she's played it so cool with him, treating their relationship more like a friends with benefits deal than actually dating. He's never pushed her and it looks like it finally paid off.

Her hands shoot out and stop my flailing. "Shh. Stop. Don't make a big deal out of it."

"But it is a big deal," I gush. "Are you going to tell him?"

Her brows crease. "He hasn't told me yet."

"So?"

"So I don't want to be the one to say it first." She skims her fingers over her red sundress and looks away.

"Oh, my God. You're being stupid."

Her head snaps back to me. She raises her brows. "You're stupid."

"You're lame," I say flatly.

"You're mom's lame."

My retort is cut off by a hand on my elbow. I look back and Chase leans in. "I wasn't sure it was you," he says. "I've never seen you at a show before."

Bree drapes her arm over my shoulder. "I hogtied her and threw her in the trunk."

"Ah, they aren't that bad." And then he moves to the side and I catch sight of the blonde haired boy behind him.

"Guy," I trill.

He leans in and hugs me. "Lucy Lu. How the hell you been?"

"Good. Not the same without your daily stick figure Kama Sutra sketches, but still good." He laughs and I receive a cocked brow from Bree.

"You know each other?" Chase asks, his brows lifting in surprise.

"She was in my Human Sexuality class last semester," Guy explains.

I pull Bree closer, sliding my hand around her waist. "This is my best friend, Bree, I always talked about. This is Guy." I gesture back and forth between them and they shake hands.

Guy turns back to me and tips his head forward. "So you're the girls from Park and Jessie's building."

I don't have a chance to ask him what he means because Jess hands me my drink and draws Chase and Guy into a conversation about a trip they took in high school.

The band shouts out a thank you and clears the stage. I check the time on my phone in anticipation.

"Twenty more minutes," Bree says.

I sip my drink, looking around at all the people here to see a college band, until Jessie shoves a shot in my face. "Cheers, ladies." He, Bree, and I clink glasses and I swallow down the burning liquid. I chase it quickly with my rum and Coke.

"What the hell was that?" I ask, blowing out a breath.

"Wild Turkey," he says, hissing through his teeth.

"It's nasty," Bree coughs. "Don't do that to me again." She takes my hand. "Come to the bathroom with me."

I trail behind her, allowing her to tow me through the close bodies. She shoves me through the door and turns me toward the sink. I look at her in the mirror, a question in my gaze.

She ignores me and pulls out my rubber band, working her fingers through my hair, and untangling the braid. When it falls loosely around my waist, she grabs my shoulders and shifts me to face her. I dodge the mascara brush as she brings it to my eye.

"What are you doing?"

"Your make-up."

"What? No. I hate make-up."

"Lucy, I'm trying to help you," she huffs as she places a hand on her hip and taps her foot.

"Well don't," I say firmly.

"He was watching you." She moves around me and coats her own lashes, her mouth rounding into an O.

"Who?"

She looks at me in the mirror. "Who do you think?" Twisting the brush in for more, she starts on the other eye. Girls flow in and out and I have to keep moving out of the way.

"I have no idea." But my heart starts racing in my chest and my tummy pulls tight with excitement.

"Park's been in the back corner, surrounded by scantily clad girls, but he's had his eyes on you since we got here. I can't believe you haven't noticed. I even felt the heat and smelled the passion and he wasn't eye fucking *me*." The girl washing her hands glances over with a knowing smile.

"I don't know if he wants me or hates me."

Bree raises one shoulder as she glosses her lips. "There's a fine line between love and hate."

"I said want or hate."

"Okay. There's a fine line between lust and loathing." She pauses. "That's pretty good. I'm going to have to patent that." She holds her hand out, offering me the tinted lip gloss.

I take the gloss, sliding it over my lips, before rubbing them together. "Happy?"

"Yes." Bree shoulders her purse. "So do you want or hate him?"

I shake my head. "Well I don't hate him."

"So you want him?"

"Don't we all?" A girl sighs as she tosses a paper towel in the trash.

"He's a slut," I say matter-of-factly.

The girl shrugs. "A sexy slut." She walks out and I look at Bree. She laughs and nudges me to the door.

"Just see where it goes," she suggests. "By the way," she adds, "he's right over there." She points and when I follow her finger, he's looking at us. Bree wiggles her fingers and he salutes her with his glass. His eyes rest on me and I know what she means about feeling it. His gaze rakes over my body slowly. I can nearly sense my clothes pressing into me like I'm being touched by his hands as opposed to his eyes.

Turning on my heel, I follow after Bree, back to the boys.

Jessie hands us new shots—tequila this time—followed by fresh rum and Cokes. He's straight up trying to get us drunk.

It's a good thing too, because *A Fool's Paradise* hits the stage and I have an eargasm I feel all the way to my panties.

Park has a stage presence that is ten times hotter than the sexy asshole that lives in the apartment below me. There's no coldness to him. Only raw passion. His voice is husky, sultry, as he rasps out the song. The way he holds the microphone, it's like he's making love to it. The way he looks at the audience, it's like we're making love to *him*. Like he can't get enough of *us*. It's sensual and exciting.

When he captures my gaze and holds it, I know I'm in trouble.

8

Park

We always play a mix of our own songs as well as covers. The band gets pissed at me because I have a hard time following a set list, but I have to sing what I'm feeling. I've always been that way. When I was in the band with Guy, Hope, and Chase, they never questioned it. They knew me and always just went along with it.

Sometimes I really miss those days.

I don't know for sure what I'm feeling right now. The only thing I'm sure of is I haven't been able to take my eyes off Lucy since she walked through the door. I don't know if it's her—her innocent charm, her rocking body, her lack of interest in the other guys having the same issue as me... Or maybe it's because she's forbidden. Whatever it is about her, it's been painful to look and know I'm unable to touch.

I drop the mic to my side and look at the guys. "*Hurts So Good*," I say.

They nod and the drums start the bom bom tsk, bom bom tsk, bom bom tsk. I follow the guitar in and skim the audience for her face again. My eyes burn into her as I belt the lyrics.

I have no idea what I'm trying to tell her. I don't know where I got the balls to do this in front of Jessie. But I realize I don't give a shit. I watch Lucy's lips part in appreciation when I tell her to sink her teeth right through my bones and decide it's worth Jessie's wrath.

She knows as well as I do it's not just a song as she moves her body to the beat of the music. *Fuck.* It's like having sex without ever touching. Lucy sways her hips as I caress her with my voice. Our eyes lock and I can see that passion glowing inside her. I drop my voice low, never breaking our gaze, and plunge to my knees. The girls in the crowd scream as I lean back until my shoulders graze the stage. "Come on baby," I growl into the mic before springing back up. She's stopped moving now, watching me with an intensity that makes me want to cut the set short and take her home right now. She definitely knows I'm not just performing.

And so does the rest of the audience. Heads start turning to see who I'm singing so intently to. Her cheeks blaze with embarrassment, so I turn to a girl closer to the stage and serenade her for awhile, but I make sure Lucy gets the last line.

I try to be careful after that. I stick to the playlist and make minimal eye contact with her. I catch Jessie's scowl a few times, but I ignore him. There are fifty people between us. I think it's safe to say I've kept a no-touching distance.

I end the last song and thank the audience. Usually I jump off the front of the stage, choose a girl to get drunk with, and have her take me home.

Not tonight.

I step backstage and slip out the side door for fresh air. I lower myself to a crate and rest my back against the cool brick wall.

The door swings open a moment later, but I don't look to see who's joining me. "Hiding?" Guy's voice asks from the darkness.

I smirk as I stare up at the stars. "Nah. I'm not scared of you. Just needed some air." And then I pry a cigarette from my pack with a chuckle. I shield the flame from the wind and light up.

"Your voice won't last if you keep that up." He sinks down beside me. He was always saying shit like that back in the day. The band was huge to him. He pushed us to be great. He was always on my ass, encouraging me to quit smoking. Quit drinking.

He hasn't tried to encourage me in a long time. Probably since about the time I quit our band and formed a new one.

"It's all right. I'm sure I'll die before my voice gives out." I wince as soon as the words leave my mouth. I can feel his eyes on me, but I refuse to look at him.

We're both quiet for awhile. I wait for him to call me on that one or say what he came here to say. He seems to be waiting for me to talk. I don't give in.

"She's home."

Two words make me flinch. "How long?" I croak as I look sideways at him.

"A month. She wants to see you."

I expel my hit and laugh. She wants to see me. Life lesson number 6: You don't always get what you want. In fact, it's pretty fucking rare.

"Is he with her?"

"Yes."

Of course he is.

I flick my cigarette into the darkness and stand up. "I'll think about it."

I'm lying and he knows it. I have no intentions of seeing her. If I never see her face again it'll still be too soon. Besides, I'm sure I'll spend eternity in Hell beside Hope Love.

I go back inside, grab hold of the first girl that says my name, and a bottle of Jack. I plop down and pull the girl into my lap. "What's your name?" I ask her.

I don't know why I ask. I won't remember in an hour.

***

I wake up wet. I shake my head and instantly begin puking. Soft hands turn my head then proceed to push me onto my side.

"You have to roll over, Park," Lucy groans. "Come...on..." She's panting and I want to see what she looks like right now, but I can't keep my eyes open. I also can't seem to stop vomiting.

I try to help. At least I think I do. My limbs are numb. I think I feel her shirt under my palms.

"Park. Can you hear me?"

I nod and that forces more vomit up. I hear footsteps moving away from me. I guess she got tired of my shit already. That's quicker than most. Guess I set another record.

Ugh. I can't stop spinning. Life lesson number 7: Something about drinking less. I'll figure it out later.

"Bree, come help me get him inside before Jessie sees him."

"Holy shit," Bree whispers. "Is he alive?"

I moan as another wave of nausea hits me. Nothing comes up this time, but that doesn't stop my stomach from convulsing. I cough and open my eyes. I don't feel like I should be alive.

Lucy's bent over me, her hand resting on my arm. "You need to come inside. Can you walk?" If I could laugh, I would.

I close my eyes. I can't even focus. I guess I could crawl. Using my legs, I push myself to the side and flip over. My face rests in my puke and I realize how fucked up this situation is.

"Ew," Bree mutters. "Gross, Park."

"Just help me carry him," Lucy hisses.

"I'm not touching him. He has puke all over him—is that a French fry? Uh, God." She makes a strangled noise. "Nu-huh, Lu. He's disgusting. Plus, there's no way we can pick him up."

"Ugh." I open my eyes again as Lucy's hands wrap around my waist. I lift my head and feel the warm moisture run down my face. It fucking reeks. I reek. And it is a French fry. *That is disgusting*. Real life people—it isn't pretty. That's life lesson...? Fuck, I can't remember. Just add it to the list.

"Almost up," Lucy grinds out. I can tell her voice is strained so I double my efforts and somehow make it to my feet. I sway and she squeezes me to her side. I shouldn't like it.

But I do.

I think I black out because the next thing I know, I'm in the bathtub, Lucy's kneeling between my legs, and cold water is pelting my face.

"Oh, my God. Don't do that to me again."

I look up at her. She's pale, but her cheeks are red from exertion. She's drenched, her hair's plastered to her, and her eyes shine with tears. Her shirt is covered with my puke. I lift my hand, cupping her cheek in my palm. I want to tell her I'm sorry. That this is part of the reason she needs to stay away from me. That I'm no good.

But nothing comes out.

She turns her head away, making my hand fall to my lap. "You fell over and wouldn't wake up. You hit your head. There's blood." She's talking too quickly. I'm having a hard time keeping up. "I think I should call an ambulance."

"No," I croak. "Be fine."

She shakes her head and grabs the hem of my shirt. She fights it until it's over my head and she throws it behind her. When her hands go to work on my jeans, a shot of adrenaline gets my heart pumping. "This isn't how I pictured this," she murmurs.

"You pitcher...?"

That didn't come out right, but she understands what I'm asking. "Yes. No. Just shut up, Park." My jeans finally slip past my hips, taking my boxers along. She stops and forces my underwear to where it should be and I try to help because I know she shouldn't be responsible for me. Nobody should have to deal with this.

Smacking my hands away, she hisses, "Just stop. You're making it harder."

I blackout again.

The scent of honey suckle and mint brings me to. *Fuck*. Lucy's washing me. She's fucking *washing* me.

"I'm sorry," I say. Her hands pause in my hair and she meets my gaze. "I'm sorry I'm such a loser."

"You're not a loser, Park. You're just reckless."

I laugh. It hurts my throat. She has no idea how reckless I am. Her hands massage the shampoo into my scalp and it feels so good. I sigh.

"And you have bad breath," she adds, titling her chin up so her nose isn't so close to my mouth.

"Sorry."

"Stop apologizing or I will definitely take you to the hospital."

I laugh again. Wow. My head is really pounding. "You're kind of funny, Lucy." She fills a cup with water and tips my head back. She's careful to keep the soapy water out of my eyes. "You're nice, too."

That makes her laugh. "I tried to tell you."

"Yeah." I close my eyes. When I open them again, she's pulling her shirt off. She tosses it on top of mine. I watch as she lathers up all that hair. As she tilts her head to rinse, I run my eyes over her neck, her chest, her stomach. My eyes pause on the belly button piercing. How did I miss that? She sheds her jeans next and she's in front of me in her bra and panties. After everything she's done for me, I shouldn't be such an asshole, sleaze ball, but I'm getting turned on witnessing her half naked, dripping wet, and soaping up her body.

She's oblivious to my perusal and that just makes me feel shittier. I'm a fucking creep. Worse yet, I have to fight my hands from reaching for her. I want to pull her against me and help her wash her body. I want to trace my fingers over her curves and feel her pulse under my mouth, hammering in her throat. I doubt she wants my vomit mouth anywhere near her.

She shuts the water off and looks down at me. Our eyes lock. "Fucking gorgeous," I whisper. She feels around blindly for a towel, as if refusing to look away. Maybe she's as unable to tear her eyes off me as I am her. When she finds it, she sinks to her knees, patting me dry.

Fuck. I want to touch her so bad.

"Can you make it to my bed?"

I swallow loudly. "Your bed?"

"I want to keep an eye on you. My bed's big enough for both of us." She holds out her hand and I take it, letting her pull me up and guide me to her room. I can't remember the last time someone took care of me.

"You should probably take those off," she states flatly, gesturing to my boxers. "They're all wet." She turns around and I can't help but chuckle. I'm not shy, but she obviously is. I shove them down and kick them off. I lose my balance and fall onto her bed.

She takes clothes out of her dresser as I cover myself up and I watch her disappear out the door.

***

I wake up pressed against a warm body, smooth legs tangled with mine. I blink a few times, trying to remember who the hell I went home with last night. I glance around the room, not recognizing my surroundings. The Grandmaster Flash poster next to the Credence Clearwater fabric scroll throws me off. There are different sized, silk butterflies hanging from the ceiling at varying heights and it makes me dizzy.

Mother of God, my head hurts like a bitch and my mouth tastes like shit. The girl shifts, a soft sigh leaving her lips, and I try to get a look at her. Long, golden hair lies across the pillow and I freeze.

I know that hair. I've spent many nights imagining what it would feel like to run my fingers through it.

Lucy rolls, burying her face in my chest. The scent of her shampoo hits me and images flash through my mind.

Oh, my God.

I was coming after her last night. I ditched the girl that was ready and willing. I couldn't get Lucy's face out of my head, no matter how much I drank. I wanted her and was done letting Jessie control me. I was drunk enough to not care about being fucking homeless. I had full intentions of telling her this. *Hell.* I wanted inside her so fucking bad I had full intentions of telling her all sorts of shit.

And then…Lucy took care of my drunk ass. She cleaned up my puke and watched over me. She told me I wasn't a loser.

I let my hand skim over her hair. It's softer than I envisioned and I like it way more than I ever should. I think I kind of like everything about this hippie chick.

This can't be good for either of us.

9

<u>Lucy</u>

I shift my leg, snuggling closer to the solid warmth beneath me. My inner thigh rests on something that feels suspiciously like a... *Oh, my... Holy shit.* I slowly open my eyes. Yes, that's Park's naked chest under my face, so that means my leg is definitely on an ever hardening penis. *Park's* ever hardening penis.

How did we end up under the same blanket? I was so careful to use my own separate cover since he was drunk and naked.

Park Reed is naked, in my bed, with my thigh on top of his goods. I feel his chest vibrate under my heated cheek and I know he's awake—and he's laughing at me. Probably because my body went completely rigid with the realization that I'm touching him intimately.

"That had better be nothing more than morning wood you're sporting there, buddy," I say. I mean to say it bravely, as if I am completely unaffected by his—him, but my voice is thick from sleep and it sounds kind of sultry and sexy. I feel him go fully erect under me and I turn to stone. Okay, *that* has nothing to do with a morning reflex.

"I need you to move away from me right now, Lucy," he breathes and I'm not sure if I can. My body is screaming at me, begging me to move closer. This is not me. This is not who I am. I do not just hook up with guys. Even if they are undeniably gorgeous.

"Lucy," he pleads, and I roll away, tucking the comforter in between us.

"Sorry. We had our own blankets last night. I didn't mean to lay on you." I close my eyes and fight to even out my breathing.

The definition of lust is: an intense sexual desire or illicit appetite.

I know. I looked it up.

My appetite is intensely, and illicitly, desiring sex with Park right now.

Lust is a bitch.

I wish I didn't like him. I wish I could think of him as the dog Jessie insists he is. That would probably—though admittedly, not entirely—help this attraction. I take a long, even breath. I will not be another notch on his bedpost.

The bed moves and I tip toward him. I open my eyes and he's propped on his elbow looking down at me. Maybe it's because he just woke up, or the massive hangover I'm sure he has, but his eyes are that warm brown from the first time we met. Not the cold, shadowy eyes I've gotten used to lately. All his features are soft, open, and it makes me want to crawl back on top of him.

"Thank you," he murmurs. "For helping me last night. You didn't have to do that." He shakes his head. "Most people wouldn't have. So, thanks."

I nod my head. "You were really drunk. How's your head?"

He shrugs. "I'll live."

I bite my lip and sit up. "You hit it when you fell. It wouldn't stop bleeding." I take another deep breath. "You scared the shit out of me."

He prods his head with the tips of his fingers, searching for the wound. I place my hand over his and guide his fingers to the large bump on the back of his skull. He hisses when he makes contact. "Ah. Okay." I drop my hand and he offers a half smile. "Sorry for scaring you."

"Did you drive like that?"

Park winces. "No," he states adamantly. "I don't drive when I drink." The way he says it makes me wonder if there might be a story there, but I don't ask.

"I know it's not my place to tell you what to do, but you…might want to think about cutting down. You were passed out on your back. You could've choked and died if I hadn't found you out there." I cringe with the memory, but he seems unattached, as if I'm talking about someone he doesn't know.

"I'll die when I die, Lucy. We all have an expiration date."

I throw the blanket off my legs and get up. I don't know why his blasé attitude irks me so much, but it does. Maybe he doesn't comprehend how bad it was, but I was there. I remember.

"Okay, well, I have to get ready for work, so…" I cross my arms and wait for him to get the hint. I actually have awhile before my shift, but he's irritating me. He cocks his head to the side and stares at me.

"You're pissed." It's a statement, not a question, and absolutely no inflection whatsoever.

I breathe out a surprised laugh. "Go home, Park, and do whatever it is that you do while waiting for your time to *expire*."

He sits up, careful to keep his lower half covered. "It's been awhile since someone was pissed at me about what I did to myself instead of what I did to them."

His honesty catches me off guard. And then his words slam into me. Everybody should have someone that cares. Someone that doesn't give up on them. Someone to always care what they're doing. Right at this moment, I make it my goal to be that someone for Park.

"I'll go get you some clothes. You go take a shower. There's Ibuprofen in the medicine cabinet. And when you're done, I'm going to check your head, and make you breakfast."

His eyes widen in surprise. "You've done enough. I should just go."

I head to the door without looking back. "Go take a shower, Park. You still smell like alcohol. I think it's coming out of your pores. And there should be an extra toothbrush in the top drawer. Please use it."

I hear him chuckle as I shut the door behind me.

***

It's been almost a week since I had breakfast with Park. In that time, he's made a point of trying to repay me. On Sunday, he was on the fire escape smoking a cigarette when I came home from grocery shopping. He scaled the railing and bounced down the steps in his hurry to help me carry the bags up to my apartment. On Monday, he helped me clean his bathroom, singing to me the entire time. It was fun until we got into a Comet fight and he used the back of his hand to wipe the green powder from my nose. He paused, his eyes meeting mine, his Adam's apple bulging in his throat as he swallowed tightly. I started breathing heavily and he closed his eyes, backing away from me. The sexual tension wound around us, growing hot and unmanageable.

On Wednesday, I found him in the laundry room. He kept me company while our clothes washed and we talked about music. It should have been a safe subject, but he got really excited and passionate about it, which just made me that much more attracted to him. Especially when I realized he has great taste. I got uncomfortable due to my rising desire and made an excuse to get away, even though my clothes were still drying. I don't think he bought my generic explanation, but he made no mention of it. Instead, he insisted on bringing my basket up to my apartment for me—*with everything folded.*

Now it's Friday. I'm working the midnight shift. And guess who comes sauntering in with all his gloriousness. Yep. Park plops down, alone, in the back booth that I've come to think of as his, and pulls out a book. He's fresh from a show and his hair glistens with the sweat he worked up performing for all the screaming college girls.

I sigh. I can't believe he has a book. I didn't take him as a reader and now my attraction hitches up about ten more notches. Pretty soon it's going to be too high to ignore. I don't know if that scares me or excites me.

"Hi," I say as I stop next to his booth.

He sets the book aside and turns his heart fluttering grin on me. "Hey, Lucy."

"What are you doing here all by yourself?"

He trails a finger over his bottom lip as his gaze scales over me, and my breath catches. Does he do that on purpose? Does he even realize he does it? It's like he swallows me whole every time he looks at me.

"I thought I'd come check out those buffalo strips since I never got to."

I arch a brow. "I don't know," I tease. "You couldn't seem to handle the spiciness. Are you sure you're ready for the heat?"

He drops his hand and now his tongue moves over his lip. He meets my gaze. "I'm ready," he says, his voice gravelly.

I clear my throat. "Milk?"

Smirking smugly, he leans back and picks up his book. He opens it and starts reading. "It does have its health benefits," he murmurs.

"Yes it does," I agree, eyeing his sculpted arms. He glances up at me, turning his head to see me better. He arches his brows.

"What's that?"

"Nothing. I'll put your order in," I add before backing away from his table.

Park sits there all night until my shift is over. After I'm safely in my car, he hops into his own and leaves. He doesn't go home, however, because when I get there, his parking spot is empty. But when I cook Saturday Breakfast, he shows for the first time in a month.

I feel the shift happening. I just don't know where it's taking us.

10
Park

Guy shows up as I'm leaving for the diner for Lucy's midnight shift. He brushes his blonde bangs out of his eyes and hops in my car without question as to where we're going or why. This is the kind of friendship we have. He's been my best friend for most of my life. First day of kindergarten, I was scared shitless. I used to be a mama's boy, and I wanted no part of being somewhere she wasn't. I watched my dad come and go too many times. I didn't trust that my mom would still be there when I got home. Guy could sense my fear and instead of using it against me, he looked out for me. Every day for the first two weeks of school, he was glued to my side, acting as a shield. And when I finally adjusted, he and I became inseparable because I wanted him there, not just because I needed him there.

In high school, shit turned around. He came out and a lot of people didn't accept he was openly gay. They gave him shit on a daily basis and I tried to be *his* shield. But I'm just not as good as he is. I slacked on my job a lot and he never complained about me being a horrible friend. He never complains about anything. He's that kind of person. Calm. Easy going. The super glue of our group.

In all the years I've known him, we've been in three fights. One over which Transformer was better, Optimus Prime or Bumble Bee. We were kids and that was serious shit. But obviously I was right—Prime all the way.

Our second fight was over a girl. Something I didn't think would ever happen, not just because he's gay, but because we're that close. I never thought a girl could come between us. That time he was right. I was so wrong and deserved his wrath. Hope—she was my…well, I'll never know what she was to me, but she was the one and only girl I have ever loved. And she was—*is*—his best friend. I never minded sharing him with her or her with him. Together, we were the perfect trio. Until we weren't.

Shit was fucked up in high school. We had the normal teenage bullshit. But then we had the band. Guy,

Hope, Chase, and I. We formed the band and it helped fill some hole for each of us. But it also added a lot of stress and responsibility that we weren't ready for. And Hope… God, Hope had issues. *Has*. She *has* issues. I was a coward. I didn't know how to help her, and I felt special that I knew something nobody else knew about her. It was *our* secret. So I did nothing to help her, and that was where I fucked up. One of my many fuck-ups along the way.

I thought Guy would never forgive me when he found out I kept her secret. And in a way, he never really has. Not fully, anyway. But I haven't forgiven *him,* either, for keeping her other secret. He's my best friend too, but he didn't tell me about Mason. Sometimes I wonder whose betrayal hurt me more.

This brings me to our third fight. Five weeks ago, I came back to the apartment we were subletting for the summer. Classes had ended and I did so damn good on all my exams I had decided to celebrate. As usual, I went too far. I was shitfaced beyond belief when I came home. I wanted to call Hope. I missed her. I fucking missed her so bad and I wanted to tell her what she did to my life when she walked away. How I used to light up when I thought of her, but now all I associate her with is loss and failure. My loss. My failure. I wanted her to understand that I didn't love her anymore. Not like I did. But I missed her and what we used to have.

I just wanted to feel again.

Guy doesn't do confrontation, and he doesn't get physical, but that night, he had my drunk ass flat on the ground. After he pried my phone out of my hand, he laid into me. Everything that he'd held in all the years we'd been friends, he let it all out.

I listened to him tell me what a shit friend I was. What a shit boyfriend I'd been to Hope. What a loser I was. And then he really went for my jugular. He brought up the biggest fuck up of my life. He looked me in the eyes and reminded me of the night I almost killed him.

He left pissed off and I started packing my shit. The next day, I moved in with Jessie.

I blink, coming out of my bad memories. When I pull into the diner's lot, Guy looks over at me and smirks.

"Shut the fuck up," I grind out.

"I didn't say a word."

"You were going to."

He opens the door and starts for the restaurant. I sigh and follow. If he starts his match making bullshit, I'm out. I'm not even playing around. The dude lives for this. That and my embarrassment.

He knows something that most people don't.

I was a virgin until I came to college.

That girl, Hope, she was my world. My everything. She wasn't ready and I never pushed her. I was content to wait until she was ready. She never was. Not with me. She met someone that made her—makes her—happier than I ever could. Someone that took—takes care of her better than I did.

I thought if I waited, she would come back. She didn't. It wasn't until almost a year later when she went off to college in another state—with the guy she left me for—and I came here, that I finally realized it was definitely over. I went a little nuts. I started drinking worse than I ever did in high school and I started fucking my way through the female population.

The past year is a blur of physical release and emotional torture. I've lost myself somewhere along the way, little pieces of who I used to be are spread like breadcrumbs, but I don't think I'll ever find my way back.

Guy attempted to set me up several times, but after Hope, I haven't ever wanted a serious relationship again. That's laughable, because we were never serious. She didn't want to label us, which meant I thought she was mine, but she didn't want to be tied to me. Now the word *relationship* makes me physically ill. I gave my heart to a girl just for her to rip it out of my chest and stomp it into the dirt. I am never doing that again. Fool me once—fuck you. Fool me twice—I'm a fucking idiot who deserves what I get.

"Guy!" Lucy calls excitedly. She rushes over to give him a hug. I don't receive the same greeting. She tucks a loose strand of hair behind the ear with all the piercings and smiles. "Hey Park."

I nod and walk past her to my booth. I forgot my book in the car because Guy threw me off. I guess it'd be rude to sit here with him and read anyway.

I wait for him to join me, but he has his head bent toward Lucy in private conversation. She's nodding and he's smiling. I don't know why it irritates me. I shake it off and start looking at the card advertising some new pie. It doesn't even look very good, but I read it four times before Guy slides in across from me.

"She is so sweet," he states matter-of-factly. "She said she'd bring you a milk."

I look at the window, but all I see is my reflection. It's the last thing I want to look at right now—then I see her gliding toward me. I turn to face her just as she sets my glass in front of me. "I wanted Coke," I say curtly.

"Oh," she says, her brows drawing together. "Okay. Sorry. I'll take this back." She gives Guy his ice tea and he shrugs. That fucking pisses me off.

"Don't do that," I spit.

He narrows his eyes at me. "What?"

"Don't apologize for me."

"I didn't."

"You shrugged. You might as well have said: 'Sorry, Lucy, I don't have a clue why he's such a dick.'"

He sighs. "Well, someone has to do it." And then, as if just realizing what I said, he adds, "Why *are* you such a dick?"

I grin tightly. "Guess I'm just special that way."

"If you're mad at me that's fine, 'cause I'm not real happy with you, either, but don't take it out on Lulu. She doesn't deserve your shit."

My head gets light as all the blood rushes there. "She doesn't deserve my shit, or I don't deserve her? Come on, Guy, say what you really mean."

He takes a drink and sets his glass down so calmly that I want to reach out and tip it over. "You deserve a good woman," he says quietly. "Because I know you're a good person. You've just buried him so deep I'm having a hard time finding him anymore. You need to get yourself straightened out before you get involved with any girl. If you don't, you'll wind up taking her down with you. Do you want to do that to Lucy?"

This is usually where I walk away, but I'm tired. I'm just so fucking tired. "This is it," I say firmly. I jab the table with my index finger. "I've changed. This is who I am now."

He nods, taking another drink. "You've changed, but this isn't who you are."

Lucy stops hesitantly next to me and places my Coke down. She puts her hand on my shoulder and squeezes. I flinch at the intimate way she touches me. Like she sees I'm pissed off and wants to calm me down. It's fucked up that it works. "Do you need me to come back?"

"I think I'm going to take off," Guy says, his eyes on me. He throws a five on the table and stands. "Lu, take care of my boy."

She looks at him and nods. "I'm trying," she says softly.

I flinch again.

Guy leaves and Lulu takes his seat. She reaches for my hand and I draw it back. "Are you all right?" she asks.

I stare at her, trying to understand what her motive is. Why does she continue to be nice to me? "I'm fine."

"Are you sure?"

"Why wouldn't I be?" I snap.

"I don't know," she says quietly. "You look upset."

Upset. Not pissed off. She wasn't calming me, she was offering me support. I sit back because I can't decide if I want to yell at her to go away or pull her into my lap. "Why do you care?"

Now she flinches. "I thought we were friends." She searches my face for something. "It's like we take a step forward and then you shove me five steps back. Why do you do that? Why do you push me away?"

"I don't know," I say truthfully. *Maybe because I want you close and it fucks with my head.*

Her lips part and her gaze flicks over me again. "Well stop it." She stands and picks up Guy's abandoned glass. "I'm stubborn as hell, Park. You might as well make it easy on yourself and just give in to me."

11

Lucy

Every time Park steps outside to smoke a cigarette, I think he's going to leave and not come back. I have to keep answering questions from my co-workers about his newly constant presence. Who is he? Does he have a girlfriend? Am I his girlfriend?

Kimmie slides up next to me as I'm pretending to wipe down the counter. Really I'm watching Park watch the stars while he smokes.

"Whatchya doing?" she asks with a huge grin. She knows exactly what I'm doing.

"Math," I deadpan.

She bobs her red ponytail. "Adding up all the things you'd like to do to him?"

I huff a breathy laugh. "More like subtracting clothing."

"Oh, I hear ya. He's going on my list." She wiggles her eyebrows and smiles wickedly.

I turn my whole body toward her, gripping the counter behind me. "You're list?"

She nods, picking up the washcloth so she can actually wipe the counters down. "Greg and I have a list of people that we can sleep with and it's not cheating."

I press my lips together to keep from laughing because knowing Kimmie, she's dead serious. "I thought those lists were supposed to be famous people?"

"Yeah, but I don't know any famous people."

"I think that's the point. Isn't it cheating if you have sex with somebody that isn't your boyfriend?"

"No." She shakes her head. "Not if they're on the list."

"But couldn't you just sleep with someone and then add them to the list?"

She cocks her head to the side. "I hadn't thought of that. I'll have to keep that in mind." She winks and saunters over to one of her tables.

Three guys come staggering in and I seat them in Kimmie's section. Mine is pretty full and I know she needs the money. She gives me a grateful smile as I walk back to my station.

Park plops down in his seat and I bring him another Coke. He grins at me. "Thanks."

"We don't want a ginger," one of the drunks bark. "Where's that other waitress?" I look over my shoulder at the guys I just sat. The one with the goatee waves his hand at me. "There she is. Come here."

I start over and Park grabs my arm. I look down at his hand wrapped around my wrist and then at his face. He's staring at the guys. "If you need me, I'm right here."

I feel my eyes widen. Park can make out with a girl he just met in a bar full of people, groping her for all to see. He can drink his weight in liquor and pass out in front of my door. He can leer at me and make his sexual innuendoes. None of it fazes me. But this—Park offering to have my back…this shocks me.

"Thanks," I say quietly. He drops his hand and I go on over to their table. "Hey guys. Is there a problem?"

"Not now." They break out in laughter.

"You can have them," Kimmie tells me. "They're drunk as hell." She pats my shoulder and leaves me to deal with these idiots by myself.

I pull out my pad and pen and cock my hip against the table. "All right, boys. Listen up. I know you've been having some fun tonight—"

"Hell yeah," goatee slurs. His eyes are red and glossy as he looks me up and down.

"And you can keep having fun as long as you're respectful. If you're nice to me, I'll be nice to you."

He licks his lips suggestively. "Baby I'll be so nice to you."

I raise a brow and frown at him. "See, that right there. You can't do that or I'll have to ask you to leave. But if you can behave yourselves, we'll get along fine." I glance around and the others nod. Goatee just grins stupidly.

"What can I get you to drink?"

The less wasted ones order and when I turn to goatee, he leans toward me, his chiseled arms resting on the table top. "Pretty girl, I'd drink your bath water," he says. His finger slides toward me slowly and he reaches out, skimming it down my thigh. Then he hooks it under the hem of my shorts. I try to back up, but he slips his other fingers under, tightening his grip. "But the only thing that's going to quench my thirst is a sip of your sweet, wet—"

I don't get to hear the end of that sentence—thank God—because Park's there, shoving the guy's face into the table. One of his friend's stands up.

Park points to him. "Sit the fuck down." The friend listens and Park's grip tightens around Goatee's neck. "Let her go before I fucking break your hand." I feel him release me, and I take a quick step back, but I can't pry my eyes off Park. He takes a deep breath to calm himself. "I'm going to let go, and you are going to apologize, then you are going to get up and leave without making any more of a scene."

I look around quickly and he's right. It's a scene. My manager has his hand on the phone, ready to call the police. The other waitresses are huddled together, watching the events unfold, and every customer in the diner is craning their neck to get a look.

"Fuck you," Goatee spits. His cheek is smashed against the table, his face red with rage. I can tell he's struggling, but Park looks calm and composed. The bulging of the fine veins in his forearm and the whitening of his fingers are the only tell. He shakes the guy, slapping his cheek into the laminate top.

"I'm not letting go until you agree," Park growls.

"We'll go," one of the others says.

The third one glances over at me. "He's just drunk. We'll get him out of here."

I nod, but Park still doesn't let him up. I touch his shoulder and the hard muscle beneath my fingertips makes me draw back. "Park."

He turns his head slowly to look at me. "Step back, Lucy. Now."

I do and Park shoves away from the guy who comes up swinging. He catches Park in the jaw and I release a shocked scream. His friends dive for his arms, but he's bigger than them, and he's furious. He shakes them off and goes after Park again. But Park's recovered from the first hit and sidesteps the next wild throw. Then he lays Goatee out with an uppercut to the chin. As the big guy falls back into the table, I move forward, grabbing Park's arm.

It takes him a moment to turn to me, and when he does, he captures my face between his hands, looking me over. "Are you okay?"

"*Am I okay?* Are *you* okay?" I trail my fingertips over his reddened jaw line. It's hot to the touch and I'm pretty sure it'll bruise. He closes his eyes and steps back, dropping his hands as he curls them into fists. I notice his knuckle is split and bleeding. I take a napkin off the next table and press it carefully to the wound.

"I'm fine." I peer up at him and he sighs. "I'm fine," he repeats.

***

I wake up to Park crawling through my bedroom window. He pauses when he sees I'm awake, one leg in, and one leg out. He holds up a paper bag. "I brought breakfast. Coffee and bagels."

I sit up, smiling like an idiot. I can't help but look at him like my own personal hero. The feminist in me recognizes what he did as being alpha male bullshit, but the woman in me thinks it's hot. I actually think he handled it pretty well. He didn't hit that guy until he had to. I only wish he had given me the chance to try and resolve the issue on my own before he jumped in.

"You brought me breakfast?"

He closes the window with one hand while juggling everything in the other. "Peace offering," he says, shrugging. "Just in case you were pissed about last night."

I pat the bed in front of me. Park's eyes flick from my hand to my face, back and forth several times before he lowers himself and offers me a Styrofoam cup. He pops the lid off while I hold it and adds two sugars and a creamer. When he looks inside the bag for something to stir it with I close my gaping mouth. How the hell he knew how I like my coffee is a mystery to me. The fact that he cared to know makes my stomach twist.

He gives me butterflies.

"I thought they put something in here…" he trails off and I pull myself out of my thoughts. I follow his gaze to my leg, folded beneath me. The sheet's only covering half my body and I adjust it. And then I realize why he's staring. I usually sleep in shorts, but it got too stuffy last night. I ended up just wearing my tank top and panties.

"I'll go get a spoon," he says, lifting his eyes to meet mine. But he doesn't get up. My heart starts racing and my body is screaming at him to kiss me—my brain is worried about morning breath.

He closes his eyes. His long lashes rest on his high cheek bones. My gaze trails over his perfect face, resting on the purple bruise. I suck air through my teeth and his eyes flick open.

"Does it hurt?"

His brows draw together and his mouth opens in surprise. "Unbelievably," he murmurs.

I release the sheet from my death grip and he watches my movement as I hesitantly bring my hand up to his jaw. I trace the tips of my fingers over the swollen skin. It's rough from not shaving and it's the most amazing thing I've ever felt.

Park's breath shudders out, blowing against my neck and goose bumps explode across every inch of my skin. I shiver. And then, as he witnesses my reaction, he shivers.

Oh, my God.

My fingers pause on his warm skin. I bring my palm up, cupping the side of his face and without consciously making the decision, my thumb caresses his lips. His eyes capture mine as he trails his tongue over the length of my finger and closes his mouth around it.

I gasp. My whole body goes hot and need rages through my core, shooting out to all the essential places. For a moment, I think, *screw it. He can add me to his bed post, his belt, his little black book, and any other place he wants me.*

I tug slightly, putting pressure down on his teeth, and wrapping my other fingers around his chin. I guide him toward me, pulling until the back of my thumb is touching my own lips, and then I slide it out of his mouth. I feel the wetness from his tongue as my thumb skims across my lips and I lick at it automatically.

His hands are on the mattress, one on each side of my thighs, holding him from falling into me. He bunches them into the sheet. Our faces are less than half an inch apart.

Neither one of us moves. He's staring at me with so much longing that it's making it hard to breathe. He shakes his head, slowly at first, then with more resolution.

"I can't," he says gruffly. He's backing away before I can make sense of his words. He clears his throat and opens the window. "Enjoy your breakfast, Lucy."

I watch him leave, my full name playing on a loop in my head.

<u>12</u>
<u>Park</u>

I'm on my way out when I bump into Lucy. She's not paying attention as she works her fingers through her hair, taking the ever present braid out. She looks tired.

"Oh," she gasps. "Sorry."

I grin. "It's okay." It's been two days since I nearly kissed her and I realize how much I missed this face, this voice, and this set of perfect lips.

"Hey, are you leaving?"

"Uh, yeah. I was going to head out for awhile."

She bites her lip as she regards me. "Can you wait? Just like, five minutes? I have something for you, but I need to change real quick." She spreads her arms out and I look at her uniform. The bottom half of her shirt is wet with a dark stain.

"Fountain machine went crazy today. I smell like root beer."

I lean toward her and sniff, wrinkling my nose.
"That's not all you smell like," I tease her. She actually
smells good. She always does. "Take a shower. I can
wait." In the month and a half I've known her, Lucy has
always showered after work "to get the grease smell out
of her hair."

"Really? You don't mind?"

"Nah. I was just going to grab a beer." I see the
flash in her eyes. Disapproval or disappointment.
Definitely one of the dis words. We both know what I
really mean. I was going to go get drunk and find a girl
to stay with tonight. "No hurry," I continue. "Just come
find me when you're done."

She nods and I watch her bounce up the steps
before going back inside. Jessie and Bree are watching a
movie. By watching a movie, I mean there's a movie
playing while they make out on the couch. They don't
even notice me pass by.

I go to my room, turn on some music, and lie
back on my bed. Three songs later there's a soft tapping
at my door.

"It's open."

Lucy steps in and kicks the door closed behind her. Her hair is still down, but now it's wet. It curls at her hips in a way that makes me want to wrap it around my fingers. Her cheeks are pink, her lips glossy. Fucking kissable. And she has on the tiniest God forsaken sleep shorts I've ever seen, showing off her incredible legs. I'm in my own personal Hell.

Stepping in front of me, she pulls one hand from behind her back. I take the book she extends to me. "It's the second in the series you were reading the other night."

"Umm, thanks, Lucy. That's really nice of you." I say it casually, but really, it means a lot to me. Not only did she pay attention to what book I was reading, but she took the time to go buy the next in the series for me. I don't like the way it makes me feel. I'm not comfortable with a girl causing any emotion in me, especially when it stirs the ones I've kept buried.

"Well, it's a backhanded gift. I've been wanting to read these books, and since you had the first, I thought if I got you the second you'd let me borrow them when you're done."

"Oh, I see. You're one of those. You give the gifts *you* want."

She grins and brings the other hand from behind her back. "Guilty," she says holding out a six pack.

I chuckle, taking it from her. I gesture for her to take a seat on the opposite end of my bed then I pop the cap off a bottle and hand it to her. I retrieve the book from my nightstand and toss it in front of her before leaning back against the wall with my own beer and book.

"You keep bringing me gifts I might start thinking you actually like me."

She blinks slowly and looks at the wall behind me. "I do like you, Park."

My eyes roam over her face. *Yeah. I know. Just haven't figured out why, yet.* "You're growing on me, too."

She smiles widely at me and takes a drink. "I needed this after the day I had."

"What happened?"

"Besides the exploding fountain machine, two tables stiffed me after running me like an Alaskan sled dog, a girl didn't show for her shift and we, of course, got slammed. I dumped a tray of drinks—on a table of customers, and my manager bitched me out after the customers were through yelling at me. That was on top of the normal shit that comes along with waitressing. For some reason, everything that goes wrong in a restaurant is the waitress' fault. Did you know that?"

I nod. "Everyone knows that. It's the waitress's job to buy, prepare, and serve the food, right?" I wink at her and she laughs, shaking her head.

"We also apparently choose the menu, wash the dishes, set the thermostat, and pick the music. People can be so rude. It gets stressful sometimes." She leans back on her elbow and I pull one of her legs up, taking her shoe off and resting her foot in my lap. She watches me, but doesn't question my actions. I press my thumb into her arch and her head falls back as she moans.

I readjust her leg and shift my body. I'm afraid of how things would progress if she realized that noise made me go instantly hard. She'd probably jump out of my bed and make another excuse to get away from me. I'm not ready for her to go. I can't take my eyes off her face, at the pleasure so evident in her features. It makes me want to please her so much more and I know we're getting close to crossing a line.

I clear my throat and take another sip of beer. "What's your major?"

Lucy raises a brow at me. I know it sounds like a lame-ass pick-up line, but I'm trying really hard to gain some control of myself here.

"General education so far. I'm still undecided." She tips her bottle up and I watch her throat work as she swallows and my hand starts moving quicker on her foot. She sighs. "What about you?"

"What?"

"What's your major?"

"Computer science," I answer.

Lucy sits up and her gaze moves over me. "Computer science? Not something with music?" she asks not hiding her surprise.

I pull her other leg up and go to work on that foot. "Nope," I say.

"Why not?"

I clench her heel in between both hands and she releases a breathy whimper. "Oh, my God. You're really good at that."

I grin at her. "That's not all I'm good at."

Her lips part as she stares at me. "Nice try," she finally says. "Answer the question."

I look away. "What question?"

She leans over the bed, setting her beer on the floor and picks up the book as she lies flat on her back. "The one you're avoiding." She peers at me as she flips a page. "If you don't want to talk about it, just say so. You don't need to deflect with sexual overtones."

Damn. Just straight up calls me out on my shit. That's sexy as hell.

"I don't want to talk about it."

She presses her lips together and nods. "All right." She returns her attention to the book and I watch her read for a while before I settle back and start on mine.

***

I snap the book closed with a yawn. Sitting up and stretching my arms above my head, I look down at Lucy's sleeping form. Her long hair hangs off the end of the bed, her breathing is steady, relaxed. I watch her chest rise and fall. And then I hurry to cover her up because even unconscious, she still turns me on.

I want to crawl over her, burry my hands in that hair, and let my mouth learn the shape of her body.

Fuck.

I rub my face, refusing to look at her again. I flip the lamp off and lie down, facing away from temptation.

I know for a fact that all I would have to do is run my hands up her legs with the right amount of pressure. She would probably turn into my touch. One caress over the right body part would have her begging for me in her sleepy state.

I am a fucking creep. I should wake her up and tell her to run.

Jessie fucked with my head the moment he said I couldn't have her. All I can think about is getting balls deep inside the girl. I want her taste in my mouth, her sweat on my chest, her scent on my sheets, her moans echoing off my walls. I want to look into her eyes as I make her come.

Lucy rolls, hooking her leg over mine and I go still. My entire body is begging for me to stroke my fingers over her smooth skin.

Fuck. Mother fucker. Mother fucking shit.

I hate Jessie. I loathe him with everything I am right now. I can't take this torture anymore.

I think I need to look into finding a new place to live. Soon. Very fucking soon.

13

Lucy

"Hey," Park says when I sit up. I blink against the sunlight a few times, groan, then flop back, pulling the cover over my head.

I hear his low, sexy chuckle and try not to shiver. He pulls the blanket out of my hand, allowing it to slide down my body slowly, almost teasingly. It's like a soft caress that has me instantly turned on. "Lucy," he says huskily. I peer at him out of one eye. But he's not looking at my face. His gaze is glued to my body as he continues to drag the blanket further off me. He licks his lips and I can't help my reaction to him. A chill runs over me. Goose bumps burst across my arms and legs, and my nipples tighten visibly. I'm thoroughly awake now.

Park makes a noise in his throat and finally meets my eyes. "Lucy," he nearly chokes my name. "Please get out of my bed before I do something very fucking stupid."

My breathing is erratic. My heart hammering in my chest. "How stupid?" I say thickly.

He moans and closes his eyes. "I don't know," he says softly. I can feel the desire in his stare when he finally looks at me. It's pure hunger. "It's starting to feel like the smartest move I could ever make."

"Why," I whisper.

He growls. Oh, my God, he growls and I lose all ability to breathe, or think, or...breathe. The blanket is swept away and Park lowers himself until he's hovering just above me. His arms lock on either side of my head. "I can't control myself when I'm near you," he mutters.

"Why do you try?"

His breathing races until it matches mine. He transfers his weight to one arm and traces his fingers over my face, from temple to chin. "Because you don't do one night stands and I need a place to live." And with that he pushes himself up, rolling away from me.

Right. Just a one night stand. That's it. Nothing more. I'm so close to shouting that I've changed my mind. Hell, I'm close to begging him to demoralize and corrupt me all day long.

But that's not who I am.

I stare at the ceiling for several heart beats, trying to regain some sense of control over my raging libido. "I have to pick my brothers up today," I say, turning my head to look at him. He raises a brow, but doesn't respond. "Do you want to come with me?"

Now his brows pull together and he shakes his head. "Why?"

I sit up and hug my legs to my chest. Park eyes my legs before sitting up beside me. "I like hanging out with you, Park," I say honestly. "I know it's dumb to you, and I'll probably wind up being sorry, but I just..." I shake my head and bite my lip. "I want to be with you."

His eyes narrow before he looks away. He glares at the floor for an awkward amount of time. The room is so full of his silence, thick with indecision, I nearly suffocate on it. I stand up, feeling stupid for opening my mouth. His fingers wrap around my wrist and he sighs loudly.

"What time are you leaving? I need a cold shower before I can go anywhere."

I grin at him. "I need to leave by eleven," I say as I head for the door.

"I'll be ready," he calls. I shudder, because the way he says it—it feels like he means so much more than the car ride.

***

"And where have you been, my slutty friend?" Bree sings as soon as I close the door. She crosses her arms, smirking at me. "I know you didn't sleep in your bed last night. I know this because when I snuck in your window first thing this morning, your room was empty."

"You stayed all night with Jessie?" I ask, my voice filled with the surprise and excitement I'm currently feeling.

Bree grins and shakes her head. "Don't change the subject on me. You did the deed with Park Reed." She smiles at her little rhyme before forging on. "First, I want to say: It is about damn time you got laid.

Secondly, I want every single detail." She perches on the end of the couch and clasps her hands in her lap expectantly. "Is he as good as they say? What does he look like naked? Is it big? I bet it's big."

I toss my shoes in the pile by the door and pad to the other side of the couch. "Sorry to disappoint, but we didn't have sex. We slept together—literally—and that is all."

She eyes me skeptically. "I call bullshit. You might not have had sex, but there was more going on than sleeping. Spill." She makes herself comfortable as if expecting some long, entertaining story and I sigh.

"He almost kissed me again."

She grins knowingly. "And...?"

I take a deep breath and let it out in a rush. "And he didn't."

Her brows scrunch. "Okay, but there was touching and panting, right?"

"No. Well, he kind of touched my face for like a second, but that's it. There may have been some heavy breathing, but mostly from me. For such a slut, he is irritatingly prude when it comes to me."

"Why? You're hot?"

I laugh at her dumbfounded expression. "Dare I say Park is kind of a good guy? He said I don't do one night stands. And I think Jessie may have threatened to kick him out, too. I need to have a talk with him about that. He thinks this is Jared all over again."

"Jared was a creep," Bree says quickly.

"Yeah, I know," I agree, remembering Jessie's old roommate. He and I seemed to hit it off right away. We started dating and it was great until he realized it was going to take more than a few dates to get me to spread my legs. We had all gone to a party that Jessie was working—Bree, Jared, and I. I was having fun, drinking and dancing. When Jared led me into a room, I didn't think much of it. It wasn't the first time we had snuck off to talk. But he didn't feel like talking anymore. This was our fourth date, and in his mind, I owed him. He was clumsy from the alcohol we'd consumed, pawing at me like a dog in heat. I had to shove him off me before he understood the word 'NO.' And then he had no issue hitting on my best friend. We were interchangeable in his mind and his bed. Sad thing is I was falling for his game. We had fun together and I seriously believed it could turn into something special. When Bree shot him down with direct threats of castration, he hooked up with some other girl that night.

I cried like it was my first broken heart and, God, it felt like it was. Jess kicked him out the next day. I think that was more because of Bree than me, but ever since, he feels some weird responsibility for me. Thus, Park. I have to admit, the similarities are eerily present, but I'm not the same girl I was then. Hell, I'm not the same girl I was a month ago. And…

"Park isn't Jared," I say.

"No. He's not." Bree picks at the polish on her nails, holding back what she really wants to say.

"What?"

"It's just…Park doesn't hide who he is. Jared was a dick in sheep's clothing." She pauses to make sure I appreciate her misquoting of a timeless phrase. I roll my eyes and she continues. "You know Park's a pig when it comes to women. I think, as long as you remember that, you'll be fine."

I shake my head. "That's the thing, he is constantly contradicting his asshole persona. He does these really sweet things all the time. He defended me at the diner. And he won't sleep with me because I told him I want to be friends—because I don't have one night stands." I groan. "Why did I tell him that?"

Bree laughs. "Uh, because you *don't* have one night stands? You've been with exactly two dudes. You aren't a hoochie." She grins mischievously. "But it's never too late to join the club. I think you'd make an excellent tramp."

"Awe, thanks, B."

"Anytime, Lu."

"I need to get ready. Park's going with me to pick up the monsters."

Both brows lift in surprise. "Really? Meeting the family?"

"Yep. Do you see how all those lines blur for me?"

"Yeah, but those lines aren't blurring for Park. You need to remember that. If you guys end up sleeping together—where you aren't really *sleeping*—you need to know that's all it is. Jess said Park has never been in a real relationship. Ever."

"It's cool, Bree. Right now, it's just a lot of attraction. Lust isn't love. We're friends and I'm okay with that."

"Fine line, Lu. Fine line."

"Got it," I say thickly.

Truth is I *really* like Park. I think there's more to him than he lets people see. A lot more. I care about him and I don't know how long I'll be able to keep everything separate.

14
Park

I didn't know what to expect when I followed Lucy to her car, but the ride has been surprisingly easy so far. When she starts talking about her parents, we fall into easy conversation, and I can't recall ever enjoying spending this much time with a girl outside of her bed.

"They are seriously crazy," she laughs. "My dad will offer you a beer just to test you. Don't take it. Also, you'll probably 'catch' him smoking a joint, which he'll offer you a hit of. Don't hit it."

"Why? What is it?"

"It's pot."

"Then why—"

"It's a test."

"But if he's smoking it then why does he care if I do?" I ask, confused.

"They're crazy," she says, her voice rising to a higher pitch. I love the sound and it makes me smile instantly. "You don't even get it."

"I get crazy parents. Trust me."

She shakes her head. "No. You think you get it, but you really don't. My parents tripped too much acid when they were younger. They're seriously twisted." She bites her lip, fighting a smile. "And they're going to tell you stories about me as a kid. Do not believe anything they say."

I chuckle. "Skeletons, Lucy? I didn't picture you as the type. Now I'm thoroughly intrigued."

"No. I'm serious, Park. Don't believe anything they say. It's a game with them." She shakes her head, laughing quietly. "They try to one up the other with the most outrageous and embarrassing stories. Every time I bring somebody new to the house, they freaking do it. It only ends when you call bullshit. This one time, they had my friend Mandy believing I drank toilet water until I was seven."

I grin at her. "*Did* you drink toilet water until you were seven?"

She bites down on her lip and shakes her head, her hair swaying around her thighs. "Oh, they're going to have so much fun with you."

I gaze out the window, watching the sun reflect off the other cars for a moment. "They sound pretty cool."

"They are," she agrees. "So, I should probably warn you about my youngest brother, too," she says slowly. I look at her sideways and she shrugs. "I just want you to know all this ahead of time. When my parents adopted him—"

"Your brother's adopted?"

She glances at me quickly. "Yeah. We all are."

"You all are," I say slowly.

"Mm-hm…"

Who the hell is fucking with me? I want out of the car. I need to get away before I freak out.

"You're adopted?" I verify one more time, my voice barely audible.

She nods, her brows merging in confusion over my reaction.

I push down the rising panic and try to ignore the feelings I shouldn't be having for this girl. This is a sick reminder. It's too similar. I rub my hands over my face.

"I knew a girl… Guy's family fostered a girl. She was…" *Shut up. Just shut the fuck up.*

"Hope," she provides.

I freeze. My blood is ice. "You know Hope?" My knees start bouncing and my hands are shaking. *How does she know Hope?*

"Guy told me about her." She bites her lip again, shooting a quick look at me. *Guy. Of fucking course. What the hell did he tell her?* "Your band name—*A Fool's Paradise*—it's named for her. Right?"

I feel the bile rise to the back of my throat. My heart is racing too fast, too hard. I think I'm having a fucking heart attack. I'm only nineteen. *Can nineteen year olds have heart attacks?*

"What did you just say?" The words barely come out, but she hears me. Her cheeks redden and she shakes her head.

"Nothing. Never mind." She releases her grip on the steering wheel and waves her hand in between us as if that will dismiss the tension in the car.

"What the fuck did you just say, Lucy?" Her body tenses at my tone, but she still doesn't answer me. "Answer the fucking question," I say tightly.

"A fool's paradise—the illusion of happiness, false hope. I just thought...after Guy told me—I shouldn't have jumped to conclusions. I'm sorry."

"Pull over."

"What?"

"Pull the fuck over," I demand. "Now."

She glances at me, but complies. As soon as the car stops, I throw the door open and start walking back the way we came. I can't be around her right now. I don't know if I want to yell at her to shut her mouth or if I want to cover her mouth with mine. Either way, I need her to stop talking. I feel translucent and I want to crawl out of my own skin. Her talking to me at this moment just grates against all the wrong nerves.

I need a drink. I need a whole lot of drinks.

I just want her out of my head.

"Park?"

"I'm going home, Lucy."

"Let me take you back at least."

I stop walking, resting my hands on my hips. I kick the dirt with my scuffed up boots and stare up at the sky. "I don't want you to take me back. I don't want to be anywhere near you."

"Why?" I barely catch it over the noise of the other cars. I turn around and lower my gaze to meet hers. "I don't understand…"

"You are fucking with my head and it's already been fucked with enough. Just stay away from me, Lucy. I'm begging you."

"I'm so sorry, Park. I didn't mean to…" She shakes her head, biting down so hard on her lip the plump skin whitens. "I won't say anything else to upset you."

Her eyes get glossy. I spin away and continue walking. I can't deal with that shit too.

***

"So you seriously just got out on the middle of the freeway and walked away?" Chase asks as soon as I heave myself into the front seat.

I shoot him a look and lean my head against the window. "I don't want to talk about it."

"I didn't want to get out of bed on my only day to sleep in this week and come pick your dumbass up off the side of the damn road, yet here I am."

I sigh. I knew that answer wouldn't fly with him. "She brought Hope up." I shake my head and rub my forehead. "Or I did, I guess. But she said something about being adopted and *A Fool's Paradise*. I fucking freaked."

He glances at me, brows raised.

"Yeah, I overreacted a little." *Fuck. I'm such a dick.*

"Really? I couldn't tell," he says, heavy on the sarcasm. "You are an idiot."

"Fuck you. I know. I don't need you to always tell me what's wrong with me."

"That's why you're an idiot. You know what you're doing is fucked up, but you just keep doing it anyway."

"Got it," I hiss. "Can you not talk and just drive?"

Chase huffs a dry laugh. "My car, man. You want a ride then deal with it. If not, I'm more than willing to pull over and watch you walk your ass home."

I don't respond. He drums his fingers on the steering wheel and I know he's thinking. Probably deciding which of my flaws he wants to point out next. This could take a while. I have a lot.

"What I don't get," he starts, and I groan. "Lulu's freaking sexy and she's sweet. She likes you for some ungodly reason, and instead of jumping on the opportunity to get to know a girl like that, you treat her like shit."

He didn't ask a question, so I don't give an answer. Fuck that. I don't need his Dr. Phil bullshit right now. Yes, Lucy is nice. And yeah, she's fucking gorgeous. She's also perceptive. She wiggled her way under my skin and saw shit she wasn't supposed to see. I don't know how to deal with that right now.

I should just fuck her and get her out of my system. Fuck it and forget it. Life lesson number 8: Fuck. And fuck a lot. Don't make love. Don't even have sex. No feelings. Just feed your basic animalistic needs. Never the same girl twice—unless it falls within the same night or following morning—and never get attached. Don't take their number. Why? Because after you fuck them—forget about them.

Life lesson number 9: Always bag it. Seriously. Always. And if the girl's shady—double bag it.

Wow. I really am a worthless piece of shit.

"You know," Chase says suddenly, "if you don't want her, I think I'll ask her out."

I turn my head slowly and glare at him. *She's mine.* I don't know where it comes from, but it keeps running through my head until I want to shout it like a fucking psycho.

"What?" he asks with mock surprise. "If you aren't going to do it, I might as well. And I don't think Jessie really cares if *I* take her out. And if he does, oh well. He'll get over it." He strums his fingers again, looking all too pleased with himself. I want to bash his face against the steering wheel.

"I bet she's crazy in bed, too," he goes on. "Ya know? 'Cause she's so nice. *Giving*. They say it's the quiet ones."

He's goading me. I know it. But I feel the tension building in my head as the image of Lulu straddling him plays over and over in my mind.

"And all that hair...? Something to grab hold of—"

"OKAY," I roar. "Shut the *fuck up*, man. I get it. All right? I *fucking* get it."

He chuckles quietly, pulling into the complex's lot and I jump out of the car as quickly as I baled from Lucy's.

"What? You're not going to ask me up?" Chase calls after me.

"Fuck off," I throw over my shoulder and stalk through the door.

15

Lucy

I'm in the middle of making dinner when there's a loud knock on the door. Ozzy runs to answer it and I start to follow behind him, a saucy wooden spoon still in my hand. Bree shoos me back into the kitchen.

"I got it," she says, running after my little brother.

I go back to stirring noodles and spaghetti sauce. And then I hear his voice.

"Can I talk to Lucy?"

I can picture Bree crossing her arms and puckering her lips. "Why? So you can act like a—" She sighs. "Ozzy, go watch the movie."

Ozzy's bright orange head runs past the kitchen and I hear Bree finish her sentence as if she had never paused. "Dick? Because she already has a full understanding of that."

Park clears his throat and he sounds uncomfortable. "I want to apologize."

I lean around the wall and his gaze flicks to meet mine. He has a large box in his hand and he shifts it, trying to slide past Bree. She cuts him off with her arm on the door frame.

"It's all right, B," I say. "Let him in."

Bree looks back at me, her lips twisting disapprovingly, but she backs up and gestures dramatically for him to enter.

"What is that?" I ask when he stops in front of me.

Park sets the box on the table and offers a half smile. "Peace offering."

"Huh. Another one. How about just saying you're sorry? Or can you only do that when you're drunk?"

He takes a step forward leaving him too close to me. I look up at him and he inhales a long breath. It comes out in a rush of words. "I'm sorry I acted like an ass. I'm an idiot. I know it. You didn't do anything wrong. It's my bullshit and I shouldn't have taken it out on you. And I lied when I said I want you stay away from me. I just needed to clear my head. I probably should have explained that instead of freaking out." He pauses for another breath before forging on.

"But you need to know this is who I am. This is what it's like to be my friend. And this is why I don't have a lot of them. So if you can accept my apology, knowing that I'll probably do something similar again—and very soon—then we can try to be friends. If not, then that sucks, but I get it."

I press my lips together to keep from smiling. He sounded so sincere and awkward through that whole speech. I'd already forgiven him the moment he showed up at my door.

"You want to be friends?"

He nods slowly, his brows crinkling in confusion.

I shake my head and throw his words back at him. "I don't know, Park. I don't think I can be friends with someone I'm attracted to."

His brows smooth out and his posture relaxes as he grins at me. "I knew it," he says, his voice taking on this hypnotically sexy tone. "So we won't be friends."

"Then what will we be?"

He nibbles on his lip as he regards me. "You still opposed to one night stands?"

"Absolutely."

"Hm." He crosses his arms and lets his brown eyes travel the length of my body. "That is a damn shame." He shakes his head and smirks at me. "Well, we sure aren't enemies."

I lick my lips and nod in agreement. "No. We're not."

"So if we're not friends, and we're not enemies, and we can't...have sex, then what's left?"

I know what's left, but I also know Park doesn't date. I'm pretty sure he's allergic. I wouldn't want to see him all rashy. I shrug. "I guess we'll have to come up with our own name."

Bree peeks her head through the doorway. "How about Lurk?" She beams at me. "Oh, or Parcy!"

Park stares at her blankly. "What the hell is she saying?"

"I have no idea," I say quickly, shooting her the "go-away-now-or-I'll-murder-you-in your-sleep" look. She laughs and bounces away.

"On second thought," I decide, "how about we don't give it a label."

Park flinches and narrows his eyes on me. He looks away quickly. "Fine," he says roughly. "Yeah. We don't need to name this. We are what we are." He shrugs stiffly. "Maybe we'll be friends. Maybe we won't." He picks up the box from the table and I'm replaying the whole conversation, trying to figure out what I said to piss him off now.

"Where can I hook this up? I thought your brothers might want to play some Playstation with me."

Oh, my God. That's so sweet. I smile, but he doesn't return it. "Um, in the living room," I say quietly.

He nods and ducks out of the kitchen without another word.

***

After Bree and I get the dinner mess cleaned up, she goes downstairs to "watch a movie" with Jessie. I go to the living room and try to play a video game.

I do not play video games. I never have. I'm not even positive exactly how I should hold the controller as I perch on the front of the couch. Ozzy and Jeremy have no issues and laugh hysterically at me every time my guy dies—which is constantly.

Park is even chuckling at me as I fling my arms, trying to make the stupid little man on the TV jump. Finally he slides in behind me, his legs on either side of mine and his chest pressed against my back.

His rough cheek brushes mine as he wraps his hands around the controller, his fingers over mine. He smells good, that crisp, clean scent with the familiar lingering of his cigarettes. His breath is minty from the tic tacs Jeremy handed out after we all ate garlic bread. And he's warm. Very, very warm.

"This is the button to jump." He presses his thumb down on mine and the guy on the screen jumps.

"Uh-huh," I whisper, but I have no idea which button I just pressed.

"No matter how much you swing your arms, he'll only jump if you press this button." He presses down again, but now my head is turned and I'm looking at his profile. I note he has a scar on his earlobe that I never saw before. I shiver as I think about pulling it into my mouth and sucking on it.

Whoa. Where did that come from?

Park's arms tighten around my waist and he twists his head to look at me. Our noses brush and I shiver again, my arms breaking out in goose bumps. He releases my hands and runs his fingers over my forearms like he's mesmerized by how they feel.

"This is going to be a problem for me," he says into my ear. His breath grazes my skin and damn if I don't shudder again. His body jerks and he grips my arms.

"What?" I breathe.

"There is no way I can get up. Not for a while at least."

My brows draw together. "What do—" And then it occurs to me as he chuckles into my hair.

He clears his throat and places his fingers back on mine. "You guys ready to play another round?"

My brothers agree enthusiastically. Ozzy pushes his glasses up his little nose and talks smack to Park.

Park plays along, teasing him like he's known him longer than a couple hours. He starts clicking at buttons quickly and I just end up settling back against him. I let him play, guiding my fingers wherever they're supposed to go. I try to figure out what I'm going to do about these feelings I shouldn't be having for him.

16
Park

I put my index finger to my lips and wink at Lucy. She smiles and nods. I tip my head to the left and raise my Super Soaker. She slides along the wall—secret agent style. I hold back a chuckle. She takes this game so seriously.

Halfway through breakfast, Jessie leaned into Lucy and very calmly said two words that had everyone jumping up and forming teams. "Water War."

I claimed Lucy as my teammate immediately. Bree took Ozzy and Jessie joined Jeremy. Leaving our pancakes, we all took off to find a form of water weapon.

As great as Lucy is, she sucks at Water War. When she grabbed that little squirt gun she shot me with the first time I met her, I plucked it from her hand and threw it over my shoulder. She was mad until I produced Super Soakers. Chase and I had filled them with cheap tequila and took them to a party. We shot girls in the mouth all night. Good times.

Lucy made me wash them out before she agreed to use them. It set us back. That's why we're sneaking around by the staircase.

The floor creaks above us as we approach the landing. I spin around and grip Lucy's waist. I roll us along the wall, pressing my body into hers, and then pulling hers into mine as we turn. I'm being dramatic, but it gives me the excuse to feel her against me.

Her shirt comes up slightly and I trail my fingers across her bare back. I feel the muscles pull tight, twitching against my hand, and I apply more pressure. Lucy's head drops forward, resting on my shoulder.

I walk my fingers up her skin and slip them under the clasp of her bra. She tilts her head so she can look at me. I can feel her breathe against my chin, soft and warm. I want to inhale it. Taste it. Drink every ounce of her breath.

The quick padding of little feet gives away Ozzy's approach. Lucy jumps back, falling back into game mode. She holds out three fingers, folding them in as she counts down.

Three.

Two.

One.

I grin at her as we spring around the corner and fire. They double-crossed us. Jeremy and Jessie joined Bree and Ozzy's team. Before I can fully comprehend what's happening, I'm being hit by four different streams of water. Jessie and that damn water cooler being the most efficient. I'm soaked.

Lucy's fairly dry, and laughing. I turn my gun on her. She tilts her head to the side to keep her face out of the attack, and I lunge at her. Wrapping my hands around hers, I angle her gun up and spray until I've drenched every inch of her head.

She squirms in my arms, her back pressing into my front, and she squeals loudly.

And then I feel a sharp pain in my leg. I jerk back and try to shake my calf, but there's a kid attached.

"Son of a—" It takes everything in me not to kick Ozzy off. His teeth are embedded deep into my flesh and it hurts like hell.

"Oswald," Lucy cries. "No. Get off him." She drops down to her knees and squeezes the kid's cheeks in between her fingers, trying to pry his mouth from my leg. When he releases me, I jump back out of biting range.

Lucy hugs him to her tightly, rubbing his back. I kind of want to hit him.

"It's okay, Oz. I'm fine. We were just playing. I'm all right. I promise."

Jeremy laughs and shakes his head. "He got you good. You're bleeding."

Lucy gasps and pulls back from her little brother. She grabs his face and looks at his mouth. "Gross Oz. You got his blood in your mouth." She glances at my leg and then up at me. "I'm sorry. Are you okay?"

"He bit me." I know I'm stating the obvious, but that little shit *bit me*.

Jessie chuckles and covers his mouth quickly. I glare at him and he holds his hands up, shaking his head, but the smile's still there.

Lucy stands up, pulling her brother to her side. "I tried to warn you—"

"I don't recall you saying shit about your brother being a zombie wannabe." As soon as I say it, though, I realize that's what she was trying to tell me when I freaked out yesterday.

It must show on my face because her only response is the arching of her brows. "We should get you guys cleaned up." She turns to Ozzy and narrows her gray eyes. "You know you're in trouble, right?" He nods slowly, dropping his gaze.

"So who won?" Jeremy asks as we head back to the apartment. I limp behind everyone, blood soaking into my sock.

"We won," Bree says, placing her hand on his shoulder.

Lucy has this little smirk on her face that I'll make her pay for later. I'm not seeing the humor in this situation. It hurts like hell. I shoot a look at Ozzy when he peers over his shoulder at me.

"I'm buying you a muzzle," I hiss. And even though his eyes hold some semblance of remorse, he laughs at me.

Fucking kids.

Life lesson number 10: Do not have children. They're short, evil demons with homicidal tendencies. In fact, I should go get my balls clipped just to be safe.

I adjust my jeans and sigh. On second thought—fuck that. I'm in enough pain as it is.

Bree says something about helping the flesh eater rinse his mouth. They head up stairs and I turn into my apartment. I rip a paper towel off the roll and start cleaning my leg. There are over six hundred different species of bacteria in the human mouth. I bet kids have even more germs than that. When I was a kid, I would consistently just wet my toothbrush instead of brushing my teeth. I didn't care about hygiene until I hit puberty and realized girls didn't want to kiss a dude with bad breath and B.O.

I cringe. Who knows how long it's been since Ozzy's brushed his teeth. I probably have thousands of critters slithering into my blood stream.

"You need some help?" Lucy asks. She leans her hip against the counter and crosses her arms.

"I need rubbing alcohol."

She wrinkles her nose. "You should use peroxide. Alcohol will burn."

"I know what it will do." *Burn the fucking creepy crawlers right off.*

She bites her lip like she's fighting a smile. "You're kind of a crybaby," she says quietly.

"It hurts."

"Yeah. I know."

"Then why you calling me a baby?" I sound like a baby.

She gazes at me. "You're pouting."

"I am not." Okay, *seriously*. What the fuck is wrong with me? I am straight up being a sulky little bitch.

"Will you feel better if I kiss it?"

I raise a brow and nod. "Definitely."

Lucy bends down, resting on her knees. She leans forward and suddenly I'm not in pain anymore. Her hair is wet and it sticks to me, tickling the hairs on my legs. She glides a soft kiss to the skin above the bite wound. When she sits back on her feet and looks up at me, I want to grip the back of her neck and crush my mouth to hers. I want her so fucking badly.

Clearing her throat, Lucy drops her gaze. "Let's see if we can find you a band aid and a lollipop."

She pushes herself up and takes my hand. I purposely step into her, our chests making contact. My fingers bunch the hair at the back of her neck and I pull her closer. Her gray eyes get that stormy look that I can't get enough of. I love knowing I cause that. It makes me go hard and I want her to know. I want her to understand the way she affects me, too.

I trail my hand down to the small of her back, resting it at the sexy curve above her ass. I push until her hips press into me. She gasps and it's like a punch to the gut.

What the fuck am I doing?

I drop my hands and step back. *Damn it. I'm sorry*. But I don't tell her. I just stare at her, watching the different emotions passing over her face. Each one is more beautiful than the last. Fear. Confusion. Passion. Anger.

"I know I said we don't have to label this, but I can't live in limbo. I can't keep waiting for you to decide what you want. Either I'm worth it to you or I'm not. If you don't want a relationship that's fine, but don't lead me on. All these *almost* kisses are driving me insane. Kiss me or don't. Quit acting like you want me…just to push me away."

"You don't want a relationship either." I don't know why that's what I choose to say when really I want to apologize—to explain I wasn't trying to lead her on. I want her so much. It's getting harder to control, but I'm not ready for more. More is fucking scary as hell.

She laughs harshly. "I want a relationship, Park. *You* don't."

"You don't want one with me," I say and it's apparent I'm asking a question. A really big question.

Her eyes narrow as she flicks them over my face. "I don't want what you can't give." She turns around and pauses halfway through the doorway shaking her head. She whirls back on me. "No. You know what? I do want it. I want to be with you more than I've ever wanted anything else in my life. What I don't want is to be hurt and I think you'd be really good at hurting me. So just...don't."

I wonder how big of a prick I am because I want to lie and promise her I'd never hurt her. I want to say whatever I need to to make her stay.

"I don't want to hurt you, Lucy, but I will."

She blinks quickly and I know she's holding back tears. "I don't even know what to say to that. Congratulations, you're a bastard?"

I shake my head slowly. "This is who I am."

She closes her eyes. "And this is who I am. I don't sleep around. I don't know how to turn off my emotions and just have a one night stand. I need more than that." When she looks at me again, her expression is unreadable. "I don't want to keep doing this. I don't want to wait to be enough for you. If we can't be more than friends, then you can't try to kiss me anymore. It means two very different things to us."

No it doesn't.

"Okay."

"Okay?" She pushes her fingers through her hair. I fist mine to keep from reaching for her.

"Okay," I repeat.

"Yeah. *Okay*. Great. I've got to take my brothers home. I'll see you later."

I watch her as she leaves me standing in the kitchen. As soon as the front door closes, I sink into the chair. My head drops to my hands. My leg fucking hurts again.

Lucy's Rules:

1. Make the conscious decision to look at others with an open mind ~~and an open heart~~.
2. Everybody needs someone in their life they can rely on. Try to be that person.
3. Take a chance.
4. Love whole-heartedly. (<u>Unless in the presence of Park Reed—in which case, guard your heart at all cost</u>.)
5. Make it your goal to make someone smile daily.
6. Always expect more of yourself today than you did yesterday.
7. No matter how many times you're let down, continue believing in the goodness of others. (?)

17

Lucy

Regret: A sense of loss or disappointment; a feeling of sorrow or remorse over an act or decision.

I regret every single word I said to Park in his kitchen three days ago. I miss him. He asked me to accept him for who he is and I shot him down. I can't believe I did that. I told myself I'd be patient with him. That I wouldn't give up on him. I don't know how to make this better.

When Chase and Guy sit in his booth, I almost start crying. It just seems so wrong. *That's Park's spot.*

I put my hand on my hip as I look at Guy. He pushes his blonde bangs out of his eyes and smiles, but I don't feel like smiling right now. "He send you to keep an eye on me?" I demand.

"Actually, he kindly suggested a nice place for me to go grab a bite to eat when I said I was hungry."

"Which was Hell," Chase interjects, "if I remember correctly?"

"Yes," Guy agrees. "But I like the pie here better. Not as sulfery."

"Mm." I nod. "A little better atmosphere as well."

"Less screaming with despair," Chase concurs.

"Similar décor, though, I'm guessing," Guy states glancing around the small diner.

I laugh for the first time in three days. And then my vision blurs as my eyes fill with tears. I blink them back quickly. "How is he?"

"He's Park," Chase says flatly. "He's indecisive and moody."

"But *how is he?*"

"What do you mean?"

I feel my eyebrows crinkle. "He's always moody and indecisive. I want to know... Is he drinking? Is he...?" *Sleeping with every girl he meets?*

Guy sits back and stares at me for a long moment before he slides over and pats the seat beside him. "Come sit for a minute."

I look over my shoulder at my manager. He's busy flirting with Kimmie, much to her dismay, so I take advantage of his distraction. I scoot my bottom onto the cool vinyl and Guy wraps his arm around my waist.

"Talk to me Lucy Lu."

"Okay... About what?"

Guy smiles and stares at me again. "How long?"

I look down at the table. "How long what?"

"Should I...?" Chase stands up. "I forgot—something...in the car." I watch him as he walks away and my stomach starts churning with nerves.

"Exactly how long have you been in love with Park?"

"I'm not in love." *I'm not.* I don't love him. I care about him. And yeah, I think about him a lot. But love?

"You love him," Guy says, his voice taking this surprised tone that irritates me. I mean, is it that hard to believe someone could love Park? He's gorgeous and sweet. He's smarter than he lets on and the man is filled with so much *hunger*. It's beautiful. He's beautiful. I could drown in his heartache. I could suffocate on his anger. I would happily bleed his passion. He is completely lovable.

"I don't love him. I like him. I lust him. I do not love him."

"He doesn't love you, too." Guy watches my reaction closely, but I don't give him one. "I'm not sure how much, but I see this change in him." He sighs, his hand squeezing my hip at the same time. "You just have to be careful. He's self-destructive. When things start going good, his timer starts ticking. Counting down until..." He flicks one hand in the air, opening his fingers wide. "Boom."

"He blows up?"

Guy smiles, but it doesn't reach his eyes. "Pretty much. And if you aren't really careful, you'll get hit with the shrapnel."

"You say that like you know firsthand."

Guy looks at the salt shaker as if it holds the right answer. He pulls his lip into his mouth, chewing on it as he thinks. "I've seen it happen." He turns to me. "I told you a little about Hope. My sister that he used to date."

I flinch at the name, remembering how Park lost it the last time she was brought up. "Yeah."

"Right. Well, she was the same way."

"Was?"

He nods his head and narrows his eyes, studying me again. "She's different now. Happy."

"What changed for her?" I want to know how to help Park be happy.

Guy laughs and shakes his head. "Love, Lucy." He rubs his face. When he drops his hands, they smack the table hard and I startle.

"I think you should go for it," he says suddenly. "Just jump in with both feet."

"Uh..." I slip out of the seat. That would be great if he didn't just warn me I'd have my heart ripped to shreds. "I have to get back to work."

Guy claps his fingers around mine. "Just think about it."

***

I do everything in my power to *not* think about what Guy said. In fact, when Bree says she wants to set me up with one of Jessie's friends, I don't fight her on it.

I let her pick my outfit and do my hair. I even give in and let her weigh my eyelashes down with mascara. Jessie seems all right with the whole thing, so I know whoever I'm going out with must be a decent guy. He must be everything Park isn't.

I don't even know his name.

Not-Park shows up fifteen minutes early. This annoys me, but if I'm being honest with myself, it has nothing to do with his timekeeping. It's more the fact that he has very blonde hair. It's almost white—and it's 100% natural. I know, because he made a point to tell me. He also has bright blue eyes and a dimple in his chin.

He reminds me of a Ken doll.

When Not-Park smiles, I notice he has perfect teeth. They're whiter than his hair and I can see the pink of his gums.

"Kyle is majoring in business," Bree says. "He only has one more semester before he graduates. His family owns their own business. A restaurant. He wants to expand and open another location around here." She continues to list his qualifications. I zone out, imagining Bree standing behind a podium as Kyle struts up and down a walkway, trying to sell him to the highest bidder.

"Lulu loves Mexican food," Bree says loudly and I know I missed something.

"Mexican's great," I agree.

Kyle smiles and I return it. He seems really nice. I bet he's the relationship type. He probably doesn't screw everything with two legs and a vagina. I mean, he knows what he wants in life apparently. He wants to finish school and open a restaurant. He seems reliable. Promising.

"Ah, good," he says. "You had me nervous there for a second." He offers me his hand. "You ready?"

"Sure." I let him hold my hand and ignore that his is a little sweaty.

"You look really nice. Bree said you were pretty, but I wasn't sure if she was biased." He grins. "She isn't, obviously. You're stunning."

Stunning. I'm not sure I've ever been called stunning. And then I wonder what Kyle would think if I'd worn my cut-off shorts and tank top like I would prefer. How would he feel if my hair wasn't curled and my face was free of make-up?

I feel like an imposter. Little Lucy playing dress-up in Mommy's clothes, on a date with a perfectly nice boy I have absolutely no interest in.

Because Kyle's hair isn't black and messy. Because his eyes are blue and kind instead of brown and warm with hidden pain. He's too tall and too husky. I prefer the tight swimmer's build and six foot, tattooed frame of—

I am so mad at Park.

He has ruined men for me.

I realize as Kyle opens the car door for me that he doesn't smell right. He's all musky woods scented. I miss that light undertone of smoke and ash.

Ugh. I just miss Park. Damn him.

Before I step into the car, my eyes flick up to the second floor fire escape. I shouldn't have looked. My chest tightens and my face grows hot as I meet his dark gaze.

Park's bent over, forearms resting on the railing, cigarette between his lips. He's too far away and covered in shadow. I can't make out the expression on his face, but his body looks rigid. Frozen. He doesn't appear happy to see me.

Kyle touches my elbow, pulling my attention back to him. I blink slowly and allow him to help me in. He closes the door and as he runs around the back of the car, a half smoked cigarette hits the windshield. The burning cherry explodes across the glass as the filter rolls down the hood. I look back up to the fire escape, but Park's gone.

18
Park

I close the window and stalk out to the living room. *Where the fuck is he?* I might kill him. I want to.

I go to the fridge for a beer. I chug it down and go for another when I hear Jessie and Bree. They sound happy and it pisses me off more. Why do they get to be happy? Why does everyone else get to be fucking blissful when I don't even get a taste?

"Hey man," Jessie says as he reaches past me, grabbing out two beers. "Bree wants to watch a movie. You want to hang with us?"

I clench my jaw and pop the top on my bottle. I glare at him as I take a long drink. He raises his brows and starts to turn away. "Did you do that?" I ask.

He sighs heavily. "Did I do what, Park?"

I push out of my slouch and step close to him. "Did you hook Lucy up with that douche bag?"

"Kyle? He's cool, man."

"Kyle," I repeat. Even his name is douchey. "Who the fuck is Kyle? Do you know anything about him?"

Jessie barks out a harsh laugh and rubs his chin. "I'm not in the mood for your shit today." He turns around and walks away from me like he's ending the conversation, but I'm not done. I follow him to the living room.

Bree's curled up on the couch and he settles in next to her. Something rolls inside of me. I can't explain it. There's no *name* for it. The closest that comes to mind is rage.

"Is it a date? Are they dating?" I need to know.

"Jesus, Park," Bree huffs. "They aren't getting married. He's taking her to dinner."

I narrow my gaze on her. "Did you set this up?"

"Yes. I did. I'm sick of seeing her turn down guy after guy because she's waiting on you to notice her."

I notice her. "What guys? What are you talking about?"

Bree rolls her eyes. "Dudes hit on her all the time. She can't work a single shift without somebody asking her out. But she says no to all of them. Why? Because she thinks there's more to you than your drunken, whoring ways." She shakes her head, glowering at me. "It's time for her to get out and have some fun. It's not the end of the world. It's *just dinner.*"

I set my empty bottle down on the table and cross my arms. "Lucy isn't like you," I state slowly.

Bree sits up, dropping her feet to the floor. "What do you mean by that?" Jessie shifts next to her like he's getting ready to hold her back and it makes me smile. *Bring it the fuck on.*

"She doesn't want to just have fun with guys. She's not about stringing them along. She wants one guy. You and me, Bree, we're the same. We're cool with cheap fun and meaningless sex. But Lucy is better than us. She wants a relationship."

"Are you calling me a whore?"

"Are you a whore?"

"Park, you need to shut up," Jessie says firmly. "Don't talk shit to Bree or I'm going to get pissed."

"You should be pissed. You're in love with this chick and she just keeps yanking your fucking leash.

Don't you wonder who she's fucking when she isn't with you? Doesn't it eat you up inside? Don't tell me you don't think about it."

Jessie doesn't say anything. He can't. He's pissed off—because he knows I'm right.

"Shut your mouth," Bree hisses. "I'm nothing like you, Park."

I laugh. I laugh loud and long as she fumes, watching me. "You are exactly like me. That's why you don't like me. It's like looking into a mirror, reminding you every day how screwed up you are."

"I don't like you because you're hurting my friend."

"Ditto," I say, locking my eyes on hers.

"What happens between me and Bree is our business," Jessie utters. "I know you're mad, but you're overstepping by miles right now. Lulu wanted to go out with Kyle. That's it. You can't blame anybody for it."

I look at him hoping my disgust shows on my face. "I can blame you. You and your stupid-ass rules."

He closes his eyes and drags his fingers through his hair. "Just go pick up another girl and get this out of your system."

I flinch away from his words. I feel sick from the thought. "I don't want another fucking girl," I murmur. Bree turns her head quickly to look at me. I shake my head and walk away.

Fuck this. I'm done.

***

I must have fallen asleep on the landing waiting for Lucy to get home because I open my eyes to her kneeling over me. "You drunk?"

I rub my face and yawn. "No."

"You all right?"

I almost laugh. "No."

She stands up and offers me her hand. "Come on. I need someone to keep me company." I let her help me up so I can absorb the sensation of her skin against mine.

I follow her inside thinking how great she looks in that dress and then I remember she was wearing it for another guy. All the earlier jealousy roars to the surface and I try to reel it in, but it's stirred up too many old feelings. I'm losing the battle quickly.

"How was your *date*?" I don't even bother to hide the disdain in my voice.

Lucy drops her purse on the coffee table and plops her ass down on the couch. She slips her heels off and sighs. "It was…" She trails off and bites her lip.

"What?"

"Boring."

I laugh, mostly with relief, and lower myself beside her. "Boring, huh?"

"It was the most mind-numbingly boring dinner I have ever attended." She leans back and I do the same. When she turns her head to look at me, I realize she's wearing make-up. She looks pretty, but it just isn't her. I like her natural better.

"You want to know something?" she whispers.

"What?"

"From the moment he showed up at my door, I compared him to you. I hated every minute because I just kept reminding myself that he wasn't who I wanted to be with."

My heart skitters around in my chest before beating frantically. "You shouldn't say things like that to me, Lucy," I murmur hoarsely.

She licks her lips and I stifle a moan. "Why not?"

"Fuck, Lucy." I sit forward and grab my head. "You're all puppy paws and kitten whiskers. You're too damn good and I don't know what to do with that."

"I am so sick of everyone acting like being nice is a bad thing. It doesn't make me stupid or weak. I'm not some naïve, vanilla, little girl."

I turn my head slowly and let my gaze fall over her. "Oh, you're vanilla, Lucy. Trust me. But that just makes me want to drizzle hot fudge all over your body, and take my damn good time licking it off."

"Then why don't you?"

Really good question. "*I can't.* I promised Jessie I wouldn't touch you." I don't know if I'm explaining it to her or myself. Both. Definitely both.

She sits up and twists her body to face me. "Is that the only reason?"

All I can do is nod because I'm just not sure anymore.

"Then don't touch me," she breathes. Her lips press into the hot flesh of my neck and I shudder. She skims her tongue up to my ear. "But I never promised I wouldn't touch you." Her mouth covers my earlobe, sucking gently, and my hands twitch at my sides.

When she knows I have no intention of stopping her, Lucy slides her leg over my thighs until she's straddling my lap. I pull my hands back, forcing myself not to touch her—even though I want nothing more than to grab her and trace every inch of her body. She works her way over my jaw and stops at my mouth. Her lips hover so close to mine I can nearly feel them.

I lock my gaze on hers and the storm is back in her eyes, darkening the gray. She lets her nose caress mine, but she doesn't kiss me. Instead, she rocks her hips against mine and my hands curl into fists. I don't know how much more I can take.

"I want you, Park," she says softly. Her lips brush mine with every word. "All of you."

I pull back just enough so I can look at her, read her expression. *Fucking beautiful.* "Tell me you're mine," I demand. "Tell me you belong to me."

Her eyes dart over my face. She doesn't move in any other way, frozen in my lap. "I'm yours, Park—only yours—if you want me."

I grab her face and crush my mouth to hers. She gasps, but recovers quickly, opening her mouth, welcoming me. Her fingers lock into my hair, pulling me closer as she glides her hips back and forth. I go instantly hard and it encourages her to keep going. Her tongue explores my mouth and I groan. I need her. Now.

Running my hands down her back, I grasp her ass and grind into her. She breaks away from the kiss and lets her head fall back with a moan. I take advantage and drag my mouth down her throat. I cup her breast and kiss the golden cleavage peeking out of her dress. And then I decide it's not enough. I hear the fabric rip as I force it out of the way.

Lucy doesn't seem to mind that I ruined her dress. In fact, it seems to give her ideas. She takes hold of my shirt and pushes it up quickly. I lift my arms for her and she flings it over her shoulder. Her hot tongue slides down my chest and she bites at my nipple.

"My turn," I say, my voice husky. I slip my hands under her dress and work it off her body. She goes to unhook her bra and I grasp her hands, pulling them up above her head. My fingers smooth the skin down her arms, over her ribs, and then up her back. I unclasp the hooks and she drops her arms, letting me slide the straps off.

Sitting in my lap, her breasts exposed to me, Lucy shivers as I take a moment to appreciate her. *Absolutely gorgeous.* I trace her nipple with my thumb before taking it into my mouth. I suck hard, letting my tongue knead her flesh. She digs her fingers into the hair at the nape of my neck and rocks against me again.

I release her with a pop. "Right now," I say roughly. "I need you right now."

"My room," she utters.

I stand up, bringing her with me. She locks her legs around my hips and kisses my neck. I feel like I can't get there fast enough as I move toward her open door.

I lower her to the bed. Her long hair fans out around her. She is so sexy. I slide her panties down her legs. *Ah, God.* She's flawless.

"You sure about this?" I ask quietly. *Please say yes.*

Not taking her eyes off me, Lucy nods once. "Positive."

19

Lucy

I watch Park unbutton his jeans and wonder how I got here. When I woke up this morning, I was miserable, afraid he would never talk to me again. And now I'm in heaven. I wonder if he realizes how big this is for me. There's nobody else I would take this risk for. I have no idea what this means for us, but I won't think about that now. I can't.

He drops his pants and it doesn't surprise me that he's bare beneath. My eyes soak up the sight before me. Every hard plain of his sculpted body. As he lowers himself over me, I realize this is truly happening. Every fantasy I've had since I met him is dull and diluted compared to the real thing.

The warm wetness of his tongue is the most incredible feeling in the world. He takes his time, kissing and sucking at my skin as he travels my body. When he gets to my thighs I tense with anticipation. He circles his hands around my hips and brings me down to meet his mouth. I release his name in a strangled cry.

Park's tongue delves deep inside of me before sliding up and flicking across my center. He nibbles and sucks, gentle and rough. The sensations he's pulling from my body are almost too much to handle. Delicious heat coils low in my stomach, searing a path straight to my core. I rise up, gliding into the rhythmic caress of his mouth. He makes a noise, his lips vibrating against me and that's it for me. I knot my fingers into his hair as I shake with ecstasy.

He places one last kiss there and sits back. "This is mine." His eyes meet mine to verify I understand before his teeth nip at my breast. "This is mine." He moves to my other breast and flicks his tongue over the nipple. "This is mine." Next he skims his lips over my mouth. "Mine." A kiss to my forehead. "Mine."

Park lies beside me and pulls me onto him. He grips my ass. "And this is mine." I rub against him and he sucks in a breath. His hands get lost in my hair as he guides me toward him. "All of you. Mine."

He rolls us and leans over the bed. Taking a condom out of his wallet, he tosses it on the bed beside me, and I smooth my hand over the silky smoothness of his erection. He closes his eyes, enjoying my touch. I love touching him, but I can't take it anymore. I need to know how it feels to have him inside me.

"Park." My voice comes out thick, pleading. His eyes meet mine and he holds my gaze in understanding.

"I got you."

Most people say I love you in this situation, whether they mean it or not. Park's three words mean so much more to me. They're a promise for right now. No bullshit about the past or the future. Just this moment in time, he's taking care of me.

He kisses me softly before positioning the condom. When he moves into me I wrap my legs around him and nearly scream. He starts a slow, smooth motion that has my body begging for more. His hands alternate gripping my hips, caressing my sides, brushing through my hair. His mouth moves from my lips, to my neck, to my breasts. He has this great rhythm that is completely chaotic. An ever changing pattern. It's such a contradiction and I realize somewhere in the back of my mind—this is Park. A chaotic contradiction.

He draws his lips over my ear as he says my full name. I feel something building inside, growing, rising higher.

"Harder," I plead breathlessly. He complies immediately. I drag my nails across his back and he growls as he nips my neck. I gasp and drop my legs so I can thrust my hips up to meet his.

Park moans and pushes my hands up beside my head. He interlocks our fingers as he watches me. "Not yet," he rasps. He frees my hands and pulls my leg over his hip. "I want you to come with me."

Oh, shit. If he keeps talking like that I'm not going to make it. I whimper as he slips his arm behind my back, causing me to arch into his waiting lips. He brushes them over my chest and then my neck.

"Oh, my God. Park. Please." I don't know what I'm begging for. All I know is I can't take a second more. It's not possible to feel this good. This euphoric.

"I got you," he says again as he works his hand between us and his thumb presses down, moving quickly over my sensitive spot. My entire body clenches as I spiral out of control. I cry out his name loudly and he covers my mouth with his. He thrusts into me twice more and shudders with his release.

We're both panting as he rolls to the side. He pulls me against him and rubs gentle circles into my back. "I just want you to know, if I end up homeless tomorrow—totally worth it."

***

I don't know what I was expecting the morning to bring. I guess not much because when I open my eyes and find Park's large sleeping form beside me, I'm a mix of shocked, excited, nervous, and extremely scared of the happiness overshadowing it all.

He stayed.

I take a shaky breath as I look at his face, peaceful and relaxed in sleep. His lips are parted, his sooty lashes lie on top of sculpted cheek bones, and his dark hair lies untamed from the usual messily styled faux hawk. I want to run my fingers over the tattoo on his arm like I've imagined doing since the night I saw it up close in his drunken state. What does it mean to him? I want to trace every black inked line of the words scripted around the dark roses and figure out the significance behind it.

But I don't.

I'm afraid if I wake him he'll leave.

There was a lot of big talk in the heat of the moment about belonging to him, but I don't know how much of that was true.

Every word of it was real for me.

But I can't be sure about him—no matter how much I want it to be.

I slip out of my bed slowly, careful not to jostle him, and pad softly to the bathroom. I start the shower while I brush my teeth. My whole body blushes pink as I recall the details of the night before. The way Park's hands felt when he touched me. His lips. His tongue.

I sigh, throwing my toothbrush in the holder before I step into the shower. I pull the curtain and let the spray beat down on my head. Standing here alone under the hot water, I come to terms with the fact that it may crush me if Park takes back what he said.

I want more. A lot more.

I hear the door open and close softly. The shift in the air chills my skin and goose bumps burst across my arms.

My stomach tightens as I peek around the shower curtain. Park's standing in front of the sink in all his naked gloriousness. He cocks his head to the side and grins at me as my eyes soak up every inch of his body.

"My toothbrush still here?"

I nod, feeling ridiculously shy, which is ludicrous. It's a little late for that. "In the medicine cabinet."

He finds it quickly and I can't help staring at him as he does something as normal as brushing away his morning breath—while he's naked. His eyes drift over to me and he smirks around the plastic in his mouth. With a shake of his head, he spits into the sink and straightens up.

"Lucy, I'm two seconds away from jumping in there to give you a closer look."

Before I can respond, there's a knock at the door and my eyes go wide. Park's head swings from me to the door and back. Without a word, he pries the shower curtain out of my hand and steps right in front of me.

"Um…" I clear my throat and try again. "Yeah?" I call.

"I need my brush," Bree yells. "I'm coming in."

I shake my head at Park, not knowing how to stop her, and then it's too late.

"Jessie went to pick up donuts," she says. Park's looking at me with a devious smile and it takes me a second to respond.

"Oh. Okay," I say, my voice quivering slightly.

Park takes a small step, pushing his body into mine and I have to cover my gasp with a cough. One dark eyebrow rises and he trails his hands down my sides.

"I told him to get coffee too, so don't make any."

"Uh-huh," I breathe as Park's hand dips between my legs and his lips brush across my collar bone.

"You all right?" Bree asks, sounding amused.

Park presses me against the cold wall. One of his talented hands grips my breast while the other rubs me before he slips a finger inside. His hot mouth works at my neck and I almost moan my reply.

"Yep," I squeak. "I'm good."

Releasing me just long enough to pull my leg up, Park rests my foot on the side of the bathtub. He moves to my lips, sealing his mouth over mine, allowing his tongue to explore.

"Okay," Bree chuckles. "Just come on down when you're done in there."

"Mm-hm," I mumble into Park's mouth.

"By the way," Bree continues, "you left your dress in the living room—along with Park's shirt."

Park freezes and I turn my head, my lips skimming his cheek. "Bree," I begin, but then I stop, not knowing what to say.

She laughs softly. "Don't worry. My lips are sealed." The door opens, but before she leaves, she clears her throat. "Treat her right," she says firmly and we all know she's talking to Park.

He looks me in the eyes as he answers her. "I'm going to do my best."

Bree laughs again as her suspicions are confirmed and the door clicks shut. I still don't move as Park's words sink in.

20
Park

The expression on Lucy's face does me in. It's the combination of her gray eyes, bright with excitement, her delicate brows pulled together in confusion, and her perfect lips parted in appreciation of my vow.

I can see she wants to believe what I say—part of her does—but there's another piece of her that's reluctant to trust me.

"I wouldn't be here right now if I had no intention of trying," I murmur. "I will strive to do right by you. Don't doubt me."

I mean it. Right now, at this moment, I mean every single word.

Her eyes flick over my face before she smiles. My heart kicks up, beating quickly in my chest. She doesn't say a word. Instead, she pushes her mouth against mine and kisses me hungrily.

I growl, my hands grasping her thighs, and spreading her legs wide. I move into the space I've created, letting her feel how much I want her. *"Park."* She moans loudly and I can't wait any longer. I push inside her and she pinches her eyes shut as she clings to me.

"Park," she sighs and I move quicker, on a mission to keep my name on her lips. Lucy pushes up on her toes, trying to get closer to me. I grip her ass and lift her. As her legs wrap around my hips, I bury myself as deep as I can. She gasps and a small smile forms on her lips. I kiss it because it's the most perfect thing I've ever seen. I want to feel it. Taste it.

Lucy's fingers are digging into my shoulders and this little pinch of pain turns me on even more. I hammer into her as she pants against my mouth.

"Open your eyes, Lucy. I need you to look at me." It takes her a moment to comply, but when she does, I'm rewarded with that stormy passion I am all too fond of. "Fucking beautiful."

She bites down on her lip and I shake my head. "Don't hold it back." Her eyes close again as she fights to keep quiet.

"Lucy," I groan. "Look at me." As her eyes pop open I feel her clench around me. "Does it feel good?"

She nods quickly, her nails cutting into me.

"Tell me," I demand.

Shaking her head, her muscles squeeze, tightening around me until I'm ready to explode.

"Tell me, Lucy." *Ah. Fuck.* I slam into her hard and her gaze locks onto mine.

"Harder," she grunts. *Jesus.* I do what she wants and in return, she gives me exactly what I want. Her head lolls back against the tiled wall and she moans my name loudly as her body quivers around me. I follow her right over the edge, kissing her roughly.

Lucy touches her fingers to her lips and grins at me. "That was…"

"Fucking perfect," I finish for her.

She nods in agreement. "Fucking perfect."

I don't think I've ever heard her drop the F-bomb and for some reason, I find it incredibly hot. I press a kiss to her mouth as she slides her legs down to stand.

"I'll see you downstairs," I say, my lips still on hers.

She nods, smiling. "Save me a donut." And then she slaps my ass.

As I wrap a towel around my waist and go to find my clothes, I can't help the grin that forms. I pause and huff out a surprised laugh.

I'm fucking happy.

***

I walk into the apartment and straight into my room to change. When I'm done, I make my way out to the kitchen, and drop myself into a chair for a donut. I notice Jessie watching me. My gaze flicks to Bree as she dunks a cream stick in her Styrofoam cup of coffee.

"We cool?" Jessie leans forward, resting his arms on the table.

I look at him for a few seconds. It's not really a question. It's more of a request. He's trying to make peace with me. Hell, I've been over it since the moment Lucy's lips touched my neck. "Yeah. We're cool."

I pull the two remaining cups out of the holder and add cream and sugar to Lucy's, setting it to the side. "What does Lucy like?" I ask as I flip the lid on the pastel colored box. When I'm met with silence, I look up. Bree's grinning at me and Jessie's brows are furrowed in thought.

"What?"

"Jelly," Bree tells me. "The red kind."

I pick one out and set it on a napkin next to her coffee before I pluck up a chocolate glaze for myself. Jessie's still watching me as I take a big bite and knock the lid closed.

"What?" I ask again, my mouth full. I'm fucking hungry and I'm in a good mood. We're over the bullshit from last night. I don't want him to start something new with me now.

"Nothing," he says slowly. "You're just acting weird."

I stop mid-chew and cock a brow. "Weird how?" I glance at Bree and her eyes are wide as she looks at Jessie, waiting for his answer.

He shrugs. "I don't know. You're being...*nice*."

I chuckle as I shove another bite in my mouth and try not to take offense to that. "Maybe I'm not as big an asshole as you think I am."

"Maybe." He shakes his head and sips from his cup. "Or maybe you took my advice and got laid."

I swallow, nearly choking on the chunk of donut as it catches in my throat. If he only knew what I did with his *advice*. I smirk at him as I lean back in my seat. "Maybe," I throw his word back at him because it's a good non-committal remark.

Jessie stands and smacks my shoulder. "Well, whatever you're doing, keep it up. You're not nearly as pissy as usual."

I laugh. "I have full fucking intentions of keeping it up."

Bree spits coffee across the table and starts coughing. With a worried expression, Jessie pats her back. "You all right, baby?"

She nods and then laughs nervously. "Wrong pipe."

I hand her a napkin and wink at her. She rolls her eyes.

This is kind of fun. Too bad Lucy isn't here so I can mess with her too.

Right on cue, she comes bouncing into the kitchen and plops down beside me. Her hair is loose and wet. The scent of her shampoo hits me, stirring something inside. She reaches for the cream and I place my hand on top of hers.

"I already did it."

Gray eyes skip over to me. It might not be obvious to anyone else, but I notice the slight flush to her cheeks. I keep my hand in place, circling my fingers over her wrist. Under the table, her foot comes to rest on my leg. My lips twitch as I hold back a grin.

"Thanks," she finally says, pulling her hand back.

"You're welcome." With my eyes still on hers, I lick glaze from my finger. I watch her mouth open as she observes my movements. I'm laughing internally as that infamous storm takes root in her gaze.

Without missing a beat, Lucy sticks her finger deep inside her pastry. Slowly, she brings it up to her mouth, gliding her pink tongue along the side before wrapping her lips completely around her finger. With a little groan, she licks every bit of jelly off. "Mm. That's so good."

"Jesus, Lulu," Jessie chokes. "Don't do that kind of shit."

She flinches like she forgot he was in the room. Hell, I forgot about him for a second too.

Bree bursts out laughing, and as her amused gaze rakes over both me and Lucy, I know it's at both our expense. In a quick motion, she glides her chair back, and takes Jessie's hand. "Take me to your room. Lucy just gave me all sorts of ideas."

With a deep growl, Jessie throws Bree over his shoulder, and rubs his hand over her thigh. "I take it back, Lu. Do that shit anytime you want."

I watch them leave the kitchen and then I turn slowly to face Lucy. "You are in so much trouble," I state darkly.

"Oh, I hope so," she breathes, making me go instantly hard for her.

I swear the room grows hotter as we stare each other down. Several heartbeats pass before I launch myself at her. I pull her out of the chair and grip her ass with both hands before I kiss her. We stumble back into the wall and her fingers twist into my hair, holding me firmly in place. I don't know where the hell she thinks I'm going. There is nowhere else I'd rather be at the moment.

"Just so you know," she pants in between kisses, "I'm not usually like this."

I pull back enough to look at her and I smirk. "Like what?"

"This..." She shakes her head, searching for the right word, so I decide to help her out.

I suck her earlobe into my mouth as I push my hips into her. "Horny?"

"*God. Yes.*"

I chuckle. "Lucy, I'm not judging you, but if I were, I wouldn't be thinking anything bad."

Working her fingers under my shirt, she grazes her teeth along my throat, nipping me gently. *Holy shit. That feels so good.*

"I blame you," she mumbles, he nails skimming across my stomach.

"Fuck," I hiss. I pull her head back and crash my mouth down on hers. I don't know if I've ever kissed a girl like this. I literally cannot get enough. My tongue moves frantically, drinking from her. I want her taste in my mouth permanently. By the time I pull back to catch my breath, we're both at that point where it's nearly impossible to turn back.

"I don't think I can take the blame all myself," I say, my voice thick, husky. "You affect me just as much, if not more."

Lucy opens her mouth to respond and the buzzer sounds. We both jump at the shrill noise and I glare at the wall. Whoever the hell just interrupted us is going to pay dearly.

21

Lucy

"Shit," Park grunts. "Hold that thought." He moves around me, heading for the living room. I pick up my donut and peek around the corner. I watch as he swings the door open.

Two things happen simultaneously.

Park's entire body noticeably tenses and he says a name that makes my heart clench in my chest.

"Hope."

I can't see her because Park's body is blocking the doorway. My stomach churns. He isn't moving. I'm not even sure he's breathing. I need to see her. I need to know what she looks like. This girl that affects him in so many ways.

Dropping my donut in the trash, I push myself forward. I can't make sense of all the questions swimming through my head. Why is she here? Why won't he move? Why does she have this effect on him?

Is he in love with her? Does she want him back? Does he want her? What does this mean for us?

It must only take me seconds to get to him, but it feels like forever. I pause just behind him and reach out, touching the tips of my fingers to his taut shoulder. He jumps and almost steps into me. He's purposely blocking me and I don't understand why.

"Can we come in?" Guy asks.

I lean around Park's arm and wave them in. As Hope steps inside, my eyes trail over her, and my confidence takes a major hit. She's pretty. Really pretty. If I was a lesbian, she'd be my type, pretty. It's her uniqueness I think—the dark hair, streaked with a deep blue, the gauges in her earlobes, the old band tee shirt that hugs her torso perfectly. She's small and feminine, but has this badass vibe going on.

"What are you doing here?" Park asks quietly. His body is still wound tight. I'd know that even if I wasn't touching him. His whole demeanor says: Get the fuck out.

"We were in the neighborhood?" Guy says, but it sounds like a question. He smiles as he shrugs. "Hey Lucy-Lu."

"Hi," I rasp.

Park glances down at me before shifting his gaze to Hope. She sighs and does this little half wave thing. "Hi. I'm Hope."

I swallow, stepping away from Park, and extend my hand. "Lucy," I say as we shake. "My friends call me Lulu or—"

"You can call her Lucy," Park states.

My head whips back to look at him. His eyes are hard and focused on Hope—who by the way, does not seem like a threat in the least. She actually seems pretty nice. All the questions come storming back in.

"Not that you don't have a spectacular...foyer," Guy says flatly, "but can we maybe move into the living room and sit down or something?"

"No," Park spits. I would be squirming under his glare, but Hope ignores him completely. I don't know what to say. He's being really rude, but I don't know the details of their history. Maybe he has a right to be. But I can't imagine Guy bringing her here to upset Park, either. This isn't my apartment, but my manners take over.

"Come on into the kitchen. There're donuts."

Park shoots me an unhappy look and I bite my lip. He shakes his head and looks away. "You can't stay here," he murmurs.

"You've been avoiding me," Hope says.

He's good at avoiding people. He's done it to me.

"A normal person would assume I wouldn't want to see them," he fires back.

Hope shrugs one shoulder. "I'm not normal."

"I don't want you here." He says it so harshly that *I* flinch.

"Too bad," Hope grinds out. "I'm only home for a little bit longer and I missed you. Quit being a dickhead."

Park pats his jean pockets and sighs in frustration. "You don't get to tell me what to do." With that, he pivots on his heel, and stalks off to his room.

"Well that went better than I expected," Guy breathes.

Hope grins at him. "Progress." She turns back to me. "You said there were donuts?"

"Uh…yeah. Um, in the…the kitchen." I point a thumb over my shoulder. I'm at a complete loss for words.

"Chocolate?" she asks.

I shake my head. "I don't know."

Guy tugs on my hand, pulling me after him. "Where's Jessie?"

"He's with Bree. In his room."

He chuckles. "Ah. He's busy then." I watch as he and Hope each take a seat before I follow. I'm more than a little confused as to what exactly is happening, and I'm majorly uncomfortable.

"So you're Lucy," Hope states. She sits back with a chocolate cream stick, watching me closely.

"So you're Hope," I say.

She smirks at me before taking a bite. "So I am."

"Lulu and Park do not have feelings for each other," Guy explains. "Isn't that right, Lu?"

I just stare at him. I have no clue how to answer that. How do I feel about Park? I have no idea.

Especially now. His whole reaction to Hope screams unresolved feelings. All I do know is my heart feels broken. My stomach feels sick. And I am seriously lost right now.

"I should go check on Park," I finally reply.

"He's smoking," Hope tells me as she finishes off her last bite.

How does she know that?

Picking up a napkin, she takes her time cleaning her fingers, and then looks at me. Like really looks at me. I fidget under her piercing scrutiny. "I can see it."

"See what?" I ask.

"Why he likes you."

"Who?"

She grins. "Whatever he told you about me, it's all true. It's just not as bad as he makes it sound. Different points of view, ya know?"

I shake my head slowly. "He hasn't told me anything really."

Hope lifts a brow. "What do you want to know?"

I blink. "Everything." Then I shake my head yet again. "No. Nothing. Not about you and him. He should tell me that."

Guy makes a noise and my eyes flick to him. He smiles weakly at me. "He's not going to tell you."

"Why?"

"Because," Park says from the doorway, "it's ancient history." He folds his arms in front of his chest and glares at the floor. "Go home, Lucy."

"Stop being an ass," Hope whispers.

Park smiles at her, but it's cold, unfriendly, and it sends a chill down my back. "You can go home, too, Hope."

"Fine," she says. "I'll go to Lucy's. We can get to know each other."

Park is across the room so quickly I don't even register his movement until he's between me and Hope. "Stay the fuck away from her," he seethes.

"I'm not going to contaminate her," Hope throws back.

"*You contaminate everything you touch*," he shouts. Hope rears back at that as if he hit her.

"Park," Guy warns with just one word.

Without taking his eyes off of Hope, Park steps back. "Fuck it. I'll leave. You all have a nice *visit*."

I sit dumbfounded, unable to do anything but watch as he walks away.

What the hell just happened? I close my eyes for a moment and take a shaky breath. I feel like I just lost Park before I ever really had him.

<u>22</u>

<u>Park</u>

I drive for hours. By the time I roll through the drive thru for a burger, it's early evening and I have a massive headache from the chain of cigarettes I've smoked. The music doesn't help either, but the louder I keep it, the more it drowns my thoughts. And the deeper I can sink them the better. I'll take the physical pain in my head over the pain my mind can cause any day.

Pulling behind the back of the building, I shift into park and lean my seat back. I close my eyes in an attempt to relieve some of the throbbing in my skull. But all I see is Lucy, sitting at the table with Hope.

Fuck.

I unwrap my sandwich and shove half the thing in my mouth. It's greasy and tastes like shit, but I choke it down anyway. I need something in my stomach because my next stop is for alcohol. Lots of it. I have no idea how long Hope's planning on sticking around, but I'm going to need to be drunk to deal with it. I crinkle the oily paper in my fist and toss it on the passenger side floor.

When I'm back on the road, I light my last cigarette and add the now empty pack to the trash lining the floor. I skip to a more mellow song, trying to relax. I hate that I allow Hope to get to me. It's not even her, really. It's what she represents. I know that, but I have this gut reaction at the sight of her. No matter how many times I tell myself to get past this shit—I can't. I hold onto it like a life force, as if letting it go will cause it all to happen again.

Her timing couldn't have been more perfect. I needed the reminder because I nearly let myself get close to Lucy. I'm pissed at myself for the slip and I feel like shit for what I know I'm going to have to do, but I can't let it go on. It's already gone too far.

I pull up in front of the small house that is home to my three band mates. I don't come here often, but they're always good for a party. And that's exactly what I need right now. The door's hanging wide open and I can hear the rumbling bass of the TV induced gunfire before I even shut the car off.

Two girls are sitting on the porch smoking a joint like it's legal. I almost don't recognize Remy—also known as Yoko by everybody in the band except the drummer. And that's only because he's her boyfriend. She cut her hair up to her chin and dyed it a deep black. She looks good, but I know how crazy this chick can get, so I usually avoid her. I pluck the joint from between her fingers as I pass by, making eye contact with her friend. She's cute and might just be what I need tonight.

"Puff, puff, pass," Remy says, holding out give-me hands. I raise a brow and take a long hit. "Come on, Park. I need to get my buzz on before the house fills up."

I take another drag and start to hand it back, but shift at the last second, holding it out to the friend. She smiles as she takes it and I know I'll be getting acquainted with some part of her body before the night's over.

"The guys are inside," Remy announces.

I don't acknowledge her as I lean closer to the friend. "What's your name?"

"Erika." Her eyes tumble down the length of my chest and I grin.

"Well, Erika, I think I'm going to be here awhile. Come find me later."

"She has a boyfriend," Remy spits. "God, can't you ever put your dick away?"

"I don't care," I retort. And then I glance over at her. "Why are you so worried about my dick, Rem?"

She lifts her lip in a disgusted snarl. "Kiss my ass, Park."

"You've smoked way too much if you think my lips are getting anywhere near your ass." She opens her mouth to reply, but I throw my hand up in front of her face, cutting her off. "Where's this boyfriend?" I ask Erika.

"He's supposed to come by later."

I narrow my gaze on her mouth. "Come find me later," I say again. "Before he gets here."

"Get out of my face," Remy seethes. I step backwards and she glares at me.

"Remy, it's always a pleasure."

"Fuck you."

I chuckle as I pass through the door. "In your dreams."

"I hate you," she yells after me.

Not more than I hate myself.

I find the guys in the back room, sprawled out on the couches, playing video games. I settle in next to Lewis and he hands me a beer. "Your girl was hitting on me again," I say, twisting the cap and sucking down half the bottle.

He shrugs. "Well can you blame her? You are awfully pretty." Aaron, the bassist, glances over at us, huffing out an amused snort, but he doesn't comment.

I laugh and take another drink. "This face is a curse."

Seth sits forward so he can see around Lewis. "Man, I don't know what the hell you guys are saying. You got a mean mug. I can't even look at your ugly ass." He scratches at his buzzed head and tosses his controller on the table. "You didn't even bring me any presents."

I shake my head. "No, but I found a nice little gift on the porch."

He nods. "Erika." Seth says her name like he plays the guitar—smooth and entrancing. "She's got a boyfriend."

I smirk at him. "I could give a shit." Before he can reply, Erika glides into the room and settles her ass onto my lap.

"Guess she doesn't give a shit either," Lewis murmurs and I chuckle.

"Give me another beer," I say. "My hands are full."

"I fucking can't stand this guy," Seth breathes. "Been here five minutes and he's already corrupted Erika."

"This isn't corruption," I counter. "I'm not making her do anything." I slide a hand up her thigh, resting it in her lap, and trail my thumb back and forth. She leans in as I take the beer from Lewis, and I can feel her breath against my throat.

An image of Lucy flashes through my mind and I swallow with difficulty. I need something stronger than piss warm, generic beer. I tap Erika's leg. "Hey, watch out a second. I need a shot." She gives me a confused look, but slides off my legs and I shoot out of the chair, stalking to the kitchen. I don't bother with a glass.

Instead I drink straight from the bottle until my throat rejects anymore.

As I set the bottle down, I notice movement out of the corner of my eye. Erika. I wipe my mouth with the back of my hand, watching her move toward me slowly.

"I've been to almost all of your shows."

I cock a brow as I study her. I don't recall ever seeing her before. She flips her chestnut hair off one shoulder and wets her lips. They're nice lips, but she has nothing on Lucy's gorgeous mouth.

Wait. No. Fuck.

Get out of my head.

I clear my throat and try to focus on the girl that's actually in the room. "Oh yeah? You a fan?"

She stops in front of me, her fingers slipping into the waist of my jeans. "I'm a huge fan of yours," she says, her voice dropping. "I love watching you perform." She blinks, looking up at me through dark lashes.

"You want to get out of here?" I ask.

She nods and I'm following her out the door, the bottle of Jack in my hand.

***

I zip my pants and kick the trash around on the floor, searching for the cigarette I dropped. Everything is spinning, so I give up, pulling another one from my new pack—courtesy of Erika.

"We can't go back to my place," she says. "My boyfriend is probably looking for me."

I glance at her and smirk. Yeah, that's probably not a good idea. I'm way too drunk to defend myself against some jealous boyfriend. Especially if he finds out I just had my dick in his girl's mouth.

"We can go back to my place." I flick my fingers out, motioning for her to drive.

I know I'm giving shitty directions because my brain is refusing to remember street names, but she manages to get us to the apartment. Somewhere in the back of my mind, I know this is a bad idea. I just don't care. In fact, I welcome it. I'm on a spiral and I just can't stop.

This is why I love liquor. It instantly numbs. Fuck lucidity.

I stumble up the stairs and try to get my key in the door. I miss twice before it opens on its own. I lift my head to find Guy staring at me. If disapproval had a face—it'd look like Guy.

"What the hell are you doing?"

I grin at him. "Hey man."

"What are you doing?" he repeats, his voice coming out in a shrill hiss that makes me cringe. He'd be the voice, too.

"I'm trying to get into my apartment," I sigh. "Can you back up?"

Guy looks past me and points one finger. "You need to go."

"You need to go. I fucking live here."

He rolls his eyes. "Not you. Her." I glance back and Erika shifts her feet uncomfortably.

"Erika," I sing. I forgot about her already. "Hey, come here. This is my best friend. You have to come meet him."

She steps forward and Guy gives a half smile. "Hi. Thanks for getting his drunk ass home, but you can't stay."

I feel my eyebrows crinkle in confusion. "Why can't she can stay? I have plans for her."

Closing his eyes and taking a noticeable breath, Guy shakes his head. "Park, dude, you're drunk and not thinking clearly."

I chuckle, leaning against the doorframe for support. "That's the point," I tell him. I tap my temple. "I don't want to think clearly."

"Lulu's here."

That name stops my heart for a split second before it pounds erratically in my chest. I push off the door and shove past Guy. "Don't care," I mutter as I reach back and grab Erika's hand. I lead her into the living room and take in the sight.

Guess we're having a party. My eyes trail over the many faces—most I recognize, some I don't. I stop on that dude Bree hooked Lucy up with. What's his fucking name?

He nods at me. And I narrow my eyes. "Hi," he says, standing up. He extends his hand toward me. "I'm Kyle."

Kyle. That's right. Douche bag Kyle.

My eyes flick down to his hand then back to his face. I don't move.

His brows raise and he drops his hand. I sit in the empty chair across from him and finish my perusal of the room. Jessie's crazy cousin's here. Awesome. She rolls her eyes as my gaze slides over her. I'm so glad I didn't hit that.

Lucy's tucked into the far corner of the couch and doing a great job of keeping her eyes away from me. Beside her, Hope is perched between Mason's legs.

I glower in their direction. Mason fucking Patel has the balls to come up in my apartment. I laugh. I can't help it. There's nothing funny about this situation, but I can't stop fucking laughing. It's so ludicrous and I'm drunk as shit. It feels like I'm dreaming.

I pull Erika into my lap, wearing her like a shield. I don't even know what I'm doing right now. The fact that Lucy still hasn't looked my way speaks volumes as to the shit this sandwich is made from. But I can't stop eating it no matter how much I might want to. I'm not in control anymore. Right now I'm ruled by this storm of jealousy and some other emotions I can't identify. And they're all amplified by alcohol.

So I'm not to blame when the words come out of my mouth.

"Well, isn't this a cozy, fucked up party." I look around the room again ignoring the couple of guys I don't know, and stopping on Bree and Jessie. Guy moves to my side and I breathe out silent laughter. "You know, Bree, I think you're the only girl in this room who hasn't seen my dick."

23

Lucy

I whip my head in Park's direction. My face ignites and my mouth drops open. *Did he seriously say what I think he said?* His gaze locks on me and he smirks. I feel tears burn my eyes. How could he announce that to the whole room? Especially when he has a girl on his lap. And then I realize what he said. I look at her. At the girl he just admitted to having sex with in not so many words.

I feel someone touch my arm and I tear my eyes away. Hope shakes her head once.

Bree laughs uncomfortably. "Well, I don't think I'm the only one, but I'm sure nobody really wants to get into that." She shoots him a murderous look and he leans his head against the back of the chair as if it's too difficult to hold up any longer.

"Did you fucking get with my cousin?" Jess hisses. "What the fuck?"

Park shrugs carelessly and I clench my jaw as Bree leans into Jessie, whispering in his ear.

"Has anybody been able to get a hold of Chase?" Guy asks. His voice is louder than it needs to be since the room's fallen silent. He's clearly trying to change the subject.

"Yeah," Hope chimes in. "He's picking up Annie and they'll be over."

"Oh, yay," Park barks. "The whole gang back together." He lifts his head and grins at Hope's boyfriend, Mason. "Except you. You aren't part of the old gang."

Mason's brow arches and a dimple shows in his cheek. "No, I'm part of the upgraded version."

"Upgraded," Park muses. "Buyer beware."

"I haven't heard any complaints," Mason retorts, his arms tightening around Hope's waist.

"Is hippie spelled with a y or an ie?" Hope asks suddenly. I wonder how many times these people will attempt to steer the conversation away from Park's drunken remarks.

Guy settles on the floor beside Park's chair, crossing his legs at the ankle, and leaning back on his elbows. "Why?"

"I'm putting Lucy in my phone as Hippie Chick," she says, tapping on her cell.

Park mumbles a comment too low for any of us to hear and I clear my throat. "I think either spelling is acceptable."

She smiles at me before typing it in. "I'm making your ringtone *Lucy in the Sky with Diamonds*," she says, her head tipped down at her phone, but her eyes cast sideways toward Park. He makes a strangled sound deep within his throat. Everyone is staring and I get the impression that Hope's messing with him.

When the song plays from her phone, Park shoves the girl off his lap, and jumps out of the chair. He rips Hope's cell phone out of her hands, pressing a button to silence the music. "No Beatles songs," he rasps.

"She's not me," Hope whispers.

Park's face contorts into something in between rage and agonizing pain. His eyes flick to me and then away quickly before he storms across the room. He stops in front of the girl he brought home. "You need to go. Call your boyfriend." And then he leaves, slamming the door behind him.

***

I wake up to the sound of shouting. A girl screams and I scramble out of bed, stumbling to the window. Three guys are in the parking lot, a girl standing off to the side. She keeps screaming, shaking her head back and forth. I look back to the guys and notice a fourth person on the ground in front of them.

It takes my groggy brain a couple of seconds to make sense of what I'm seeing and then I'm climbing onto the firs escape, yelling for Bree to get Jessie. I have no idea if she hears me or not, I don't even know if she's home, but I keep going. The guys look up at me and take off. One of them pulls the girl into a car and they peel out, tires squealing.

My legs are shaking by the time I drop to my knees next to Park. He's lying limply on his side and I'm afraid to move him.

"Park." My hand hovers over his shoulder. Fear grips my insides, squeezing them until I feel like I can't breathe. "Park," I say again, panic sounding in my voice.

He groans and it sounds wet, like his mouth is full of water. I roll him toward me and gasp. His face is a multitude of colors, the deep red of blood standing out above all others. "Oh, my God," I murmur. My hands flutter around his head. I don't know what to do. I look around quickly for something. Someone. Anyone.

"I'll be back," I pant. "I need to get help."

Park coughs, rolling to his side again. He makes a gurgling sound and I run. I push myself up the fire escape and pound on Jessie's window before pushing it open. The room's empty, so I crawl inside.

"Jessie," I scream.

As I make it to the door, I'm met by Jessie and Guy. "What's wrong?"

"Park." It's all I can get out before I'm turning and rushing back to the window.

"What happened?" Guy asks behind me.

"Three guys. They beat the shit out of him."

"Shit," he breathes. "Get Chase and Mason," he instructs Jessie. I don't hear if he acknowledges him because I'm barreling down the metal stairs. My feet clank along the steps covering all other sound.

Guy skids to a stop and kneels next to Park. His fingers go to his neck, checking for a pulse and I feel like I might throw up. He lets out a visible sigh. Jessie, Chase, and Mason jog over to us. I stoop to the other side of Park and look at Guy. "We should take him to the hospital."

"No," Park grunts. He goes into another coughing fit and I take his hand.

"You have to," I protest. "You could have internal injuries. You're coughing up blood."

"Call," Guy says. I don't know who he's talking to, but I hear Mason requesting an ambulance seconds later.

Park's head lolls to the side and I start to have a meltdown. I think he's lost consciousness, but I'm not sure and it scares me. "Check his pulse again," I yell at Guy.

"Lulu," Bree says from behind me. I don't respond. I can't look away from Guy's fingers as he touches them to Park's throat again.

"He just passed out," he says, his eyes closing in relief.

"Did you see it happen?" Chase asks. It takes a moment for me to realize he's talking to me.

I shake my head. "I just heard yelling. Didn't you guys hear it?"

"We had music on," Jessie says, his voice cracking with remorse. "We were talking. Laughing." He runs his fingers through his hair. "We didn't hear anything except you screaming."

"There were three of them," I explain. "I didn't see what they did to him. I just saw…him on the ground. And that girl, the one he came home with earlier, she was there. She was screaming at them."

We can hear the sirens coming down the street and Bree takes my hand. "Come on, Lu. You need to get out of their way so they can help him." I reluctantly release Park's fingers and let Bree pull me back. My legs won't stop shaking.

"He'll be okay," she says firmly. The flashing lights cast odd shadows across her face. I nod as I watch two paramedics approach.

Guy starts answering their questions immediately. All I can do is stand there and watch as they secure his head and get him on the gurney.

"Only one can ride with him," the younger paramedic says.

"I'll go," Guy says.

"What hospital?" Chase asks? "We'll be right behind you."

I realize I'm in sleep shorts. I'm shoeless and I'm not even wearing a bra. "Don't leave without me," I tell Bree before I run back to the apartment to change. I don't care what happened tonight. I care about Park. I need to be there. I need to know he's going to be okay.

24

Park

I'm heavy, but I'm floating. Maybe I'm weightless. Maybe I'm sinking.

My eyes won't open. They're pinned with the weight of my confusion. Maybe I'm just tired. Maybe I'm sleeping.

"...don't know what to think."

I try to open my eyes. All I see is darkness. My ears are buzzing. There's a continuous beeping that's driving me insane.

"He can be an idiot, but he's a good person."

Is that Hope?

I must be dreaming.

"Is he?" That's Lucy. I try to open my eyelids again. I put everything I have into it, but they weigh a thousand pounds and I'm so exhausted. Maybe I'll just sleep.

"I haven't been around in a while," Hope says. She sounds weird. Stressed. "I wasn't here to see him change. I've just heard the stories and I don't put much stock in other people's accounts. I mean, he's always been an asshole, that's just who he is. But he had this sweet side that he didn't show a lot of people. If he's changed…that's my fault."

"Why?" Lucy asks. I know it's her voice, but it's off. I want to wake up now. I don't like where this conversation is going. I don't like how Lucy said that one word. She sounds upset and it makes me feel strange.

It's quiet while I struggle to move. I just want to open my fucking eyes.

"I loved him," Hope finally says. "I'll always love him. But sometimes I wonder if I used Park."

Lucy makes a noise that sounds like disapproval.

"I know. It's messed up, but it's not like I meant to do it. He was just there. Always there. He knew things about me that I couldn't talk to anybody else about. Even Guy. And I counted on him for that. He was my friend that shared my secret."

"You hurt him," Lucy says. Her voice is soft. It's not a question. It's not an accusation. It just is.

"I never meant to. He was a crutch that I didn't know I was leaning on. I put so much on him and I never meant to. But I tried to tell him. I started to realize that maybe he felt stronger than I did. I tried to make it clear that we weren't—that he wasn't my boyfriend. That I didn't want a boyfriend. I said it all the time. Maybe too much. And then I met Mason and the connection was so...*different*."

"So you dropped him for Mason."

I can't breathe. I can't fucking breathe. I'm definitely sinking. I think I'm dying. I want to die. I want it to stop.

I just want to fucking wake up.

"When other people say it, it sounds bad," Hope whispers.

"It's not bad. You can't help who you love..." Lucy trails off and there's another stretch of silence.

The beeping sounds louder. Faster. I can't take it. Somebody please make this all stop. I can't do this. I need to leave. I need to move. I need—

"I hate the thought of him being in pain," Lucy murmurs.

"I never meant to hurt him." Hope sighs loudly. "I regret that part every day. It's just… I spent my whole life drowning, and then Mason came along, and I could breathe. For the first time in my life, I was happy. I needed that. Park was great and I'll always be grateful to him. He was there when I needed him, but Mason made me not need. That didn't come out right. I still need things. A lot of things. Mason just makes me need different things."

I can't remember the last time I cried, but right now my eyes are stinging like they want to tear up. My head is pounding.

Wake up.

Wake up.

Wake up.

"He…we…" Lucy sounds like she's choking on her words. My chest aches.

"You love him," Hope finishes for her.

My heart is racing. I can barely hear her reply over the rushing echo in my ears. Don't answer that. Please don't answer that. Don't—

"I don't know. I didn't mean to. I don't want to."

"You can't help who you love," Hope says quietly, throwing Lucy's words back at her.

She doesn't love me. I shouldn't be letting myself feel this. It's not real. This is just a dream and when I wake up I'll feel like I lost something.

Maybe I won't wake up.

Maybe I'll sleep forever.

My head hurts so badly. There's so much pressure. I feel like an overinflated balloon.

I wish I would burst.

"He slept with that girl. In the same day as sleeping with me. And then he announced it to a room full of people. I can't..."

"He's an ass," Hope barks. "Dear Buddha, he's a dickhead. But seriously, Lucy, take it from someone that's made an art form of pushing people away—he's trying to make you leave. If he *makes* you go away then it won't hurt as bad."

"That's stupid," Lucy mutters, the resentment thick in her voice.

Hope's right and I hate her a little bit for it. I'm not an idiot. I know I do that. But she's wrong about why

I do it. It's not about making it hurt less. It's about finding out who will actually stay.

"Look, Park isn't some unfeeling bastard. And he isn't dumb—generally. I think his problem is that he feels everything. And the dude's a closet genius. Did you know he's on a full academic scholarship?"

"No, I didn't, but that doesn't surprise me."

She's lying. It surprises everyone that finds out. That's why I never tell people. Of course, this is dream Lucy. She has faith in me and loves me because that's what my subconscious wants from her. How fucking pathetic is that? I have to dream this shit up because in reality I could never have it.

Fuck. I don't want to dream anymore.

The beeping is really loud now. Really fast.

"What's going on?" Lucy asks. She sounds scared. "Is he all right?"

"You need to step out. Both of you." Who the hell is that? I don't know that voice.

"I'm not going anywhere." Lucy's tone is firm, but there's an undercurrent of fear. What's wrong? What's happening?

"Miss, you need to let us do our job."

My head is going to explode. I can't take it. My chest—

"Lucy, we need to get out of their way," Hope says. She's scared too. "Come on. We'll just go into the hall."

That fucking beeping. Why won't it stop? It just needs to stop. It needs to stop. I can't breathe. I can't think. My head hurts. Why does it hurt so badly? Please just make it all stop.

Make it stop.

Make it stop.

Make it—

I relish in the peaceful silence as the pain slowly subsides. I'm weightless again. Floating up. Up. Up.

25

Lucy

    I'm sitting on the floor in the hospital hallway, staring at the door to Park's room. He's not in there—hasn't been for almost an hour. They took him for another head scan. Hope's shoulder presses into mine. Our sides meshed snugly together. Her thigh resting against mine. I barely know her, but I'm so grateful she's here. I couldn't do this alone.

    Though Bree and Jessie are huddled together in the corner, not far from where I sit, they feel miles away. Like they're bubbled in their own little world.

    Guy is squished to Hope's other side. Chase is standing on the opposite wall, his arms and legs crossed in front of him. The girl from the diner, Annie—she's pacing in between us. Park's mom, a pretty, middle aged woman with dark hair streaked with gray, is downstairs with Park. She was the only one allowed to go with him.

Mason went to get coffee a few minutes ago. I don't need it. My body is wired without caffeine. Fear keeps the adrenaline pumping steadily through my veins.

He has to be okay.

He *has* to be.

I was so mad at him. And now I don't know if I'll ever get another moment with him.

I need him to be okay.

I need him…

"Can you stop?" Chase hisses. "Annie. Stop. Sit down."

"I can't sit down," she replies quietly.

"Then stand. I don't give a shit. But stop pacing. It's driving me crazy."

Annie pauses, her eyes raking over Chase slowly. "I'm not good at this."

"Come here," he demands. She moves in front of him and he holds his fist out.

"What?"

"Rock, paper, scissors," he states as if she should've already known this. I can't help but watch them. It's so much better than staring at a door, counting every imperfection.

"Why?" Annie asks, confused.

"Because I said. Come on." He starts pumping his fist into his palm.

"But…what are we playing for?"

"For fun."

She shakes her head, but puts her fist out, matching his. "Rock, paper, scissors, shoot."

"Rock beats scissors," Chase calls triumphantly. "Okay, again."

She smiles and shakes her head again. I rest my head against the wall as I take in their game. Annie likes it, but she doesn't want him to know she likes it. She rolls her eyes a lot, but that smile—even as small as it is—hasn't left her lips.

"Why does paper beat rock?" Hope asks suddenly, pulling me out of my thoughts.

"I know, right?" Guy says. "If anything, rock should beat paper because it's like a natural paperweight."

"But scissors cut paper," Chase disagrees. "Rock can't defeat two things. That's not fair."

"Yeah, but a rock isn't going to smash scissors," Guy throws back.

"Unless they're a pair of those plastic little kid scissors you have to use in grade school," Annie adds.

Chase scoffs. "What drugs are you on? Of course a rock is going to smash scissors. But you know what a rock isn't going to smash?"

"Paper?" Hope says slowly. She has a devious smirk on her face and I watch, transfixed as they all laugh.

How do they do that? I feel myself smiling even though my heart is pounding in my chest and I feel like I could throw up, or cry, or scream.

"Your argument is invalid," Guy continues.

"What? Why?" Chase pushes off the wall, coming closer to our side.

"Because, if someone smashes the scissors, then how do they cut the paper?"

Chase cocks his head to the side, his blue hair hanging limply. "The paper was cut prior to the scissor smashing."

"HA!" Guy jumps up. "Then paper can't cover rock. I win. You lose."

"Wait…" Chase narrows his eyes, concentrating. "But…the paper…the rock… Fuck it. You win. That game is stupid."

They all laugh again and it's just as mesmerizing as the first time. Guy settles back down next to Hope. Chase follows him, and then Annie scoots in to his side.

We're all staring at the door again.

The squeaking of shoes makes us all turn our heads. Mason's heading down the hall toward us, carefully holding a box. When he sits it down in front of Hope, he grins, pulling out a bag of Skittles. She kisses him before taking the bag. "Thanks."

Mason winks at her. He starts handing cups out. When he gives me mine, he pauses, looking back inside the box. He pulls out a little pack of powdered donuts. "I didn't know what you liked, but Hope had mentioned donuts…?"

I look over at Hope, then back to Mason. "No. That's great. Thank you."

"No problem."

Hope leans into me, her mouth close to my ear. "You see?"

I nod. "Yeah. He's pretty great."

"Isn't it weird how what works for one person doesn't work for another? We're all so different. Looking for different things."

I nod again. I think I know what she means. I just don't know what it is exactly that I'm looking for.

I hear the wheels rolling our way from a distance. Before I realize I've made the decision to do so, I'm on my feet. I pull my hair over one shoulder, twisting it just to give my shaking hands something to do. My dad says these are the situations that make a person. How you act when things are bad.

The way my stomach is twisting makes me wonder what kind of person I am.

All I can focus on is the sound of those wheels. Getting closer.

Closer.

Park's mom comes around the corner first. I search her face for some hint. But then the large hospital bed is there and I move forward. Park's still unconscious. His puffy purple eyes closed tightly.

"They said the scans look good," Mrs. Reed says and something in the air changes. Like we all may have exhaled at once. "They're going to monitor him for a while."

I reach out and let my fingers trail over his hand—the only part that isn't covered in bruises. That strikes me as strange.

Why aren't his hands bruised?

When he hit that guy at the diner, his knuckles split.

Oh, my God. He didn't fight back.

Why didn't he fight back?

"Who's first?" Mrs. Reed asks, holding the door open.

"Only two at a time," the nurse reminds us as she passes.

Everyone looks at me and I shake my head. "I'll go later," I say. "I just… I need a minute."

Hope moves around me, not willing to wait for her turn. Mason settles back against the wall and Guy touches my elbow. "Are you sure?"

"I'm sure. Go ahead."

"You okay?" Annie asks. It takes me a second to understand she's talking to me. I look back at her and shake my head.

"What's wrong, Lu?" Chase eyes me with concern and I don't know what to say. Did they notice it too? Have they already discerned that Park let three guys beat him to the point of unconsciousness?

He could have died.

I feel sick.

"Hey," Chase says softly. "He's okay." He touches my arm and I feel my lip tremble.

"He didn't defend himself."

"What? I thought you didn't see—"

"I didn't." I shouldn't have said that. He didn't know. I shouldn't have pointed it out. What the hell's wrong with me? Do I want someone else to share this new fear building in my chest so badly that I throw out Park's personal business to his friends? That's not right.

"I didn't," I repeat. "Never mind. I'm really tired."

And confused. But I don't say that aloud. Instead, I go back and sit in my spot. I lean my head and close my eyes.

26
Park

I open my eyes when I hear movement. Mason pauses, a bag in his hand. What the fuck is he doing here? I'm in enough pain already.

"Hey. Sorry. I didn't mean to wake you up." He holds up the bag. "Clean clothes. Guy said you asked for them. Everybody crashed out, so…"

"So you thought you'd be a good guy and bring them on over?"

He shrugs. "I felt like I needed to do something."

I chuckle darkly and then grab my chest as it turns into a hacking cough. Mason takes a step toward my bed and I hold up a hand. "I'm fine," I croak. I narrow my eyes. "I don't need shit from you."

"I know. I just wanted to. I hate the way things played out and I know this doesn't make up for it—"

"Not even close," I say forcefully, cutting him off.

He nods and rubs the back of his neck. "Anyway, I'll just leave them here. Lulu packed the bag, so I'm sure everything you need is in there."

"Lucy packed my clothes?" My voice comes out shocked and hopeful at the same time and I cringe. Mason looks at me, nodding again.

"She's really nice. She cares about you."

"You don't know her," I hiss. She is nice. More than nice, but I don't want him to have anything to do with her.

"I know she's been really upset. Seemed like more than this." He throws his hand out, gesturing to the room. "No relationship is perfect. Trust me. But I think..." He shakes his head. "You two make a nice couple."

I smirk at him. "We're not a couple. If you're looking for another girl to steal, you'll have to go somewhere else." He raises his brows and I point at the door. "Seriously, man. Go somewhere else."

He huffs out a dry laugh. "Hope you feel better, Park. If you need anything—"

"I won't."

He presses his lips together and nods one more time before turning and walking out the door. I close my eyes and try to sleep.

***

Guy hovers beside me as I work my shirt over my head. It's slow going, but I'm determined to do it on my own. I'm not sure I can sink any lower, but having my friend dress me might do it.

I finally get it into place and drop heavily on the bed. Shoes are next, but that's going to be harder than the shirt since it requires bending over. I'm not in the mood to get another dizzy spell. If I puke one more time, I'm not sure the doctor will let me go home.

And I really need to go home.

"You need some help?" Guy asks. He takes a step toward the bed and I shake my head. The quick movement causes the room to spin. I have to lie back and close my eyes as I try to breathe through it.

Concussions fucking suck.

Life lesson number 11: Don't talk shit to a group of guys when you're by yourself. Especially if you got a blowjob from one of their girlfriends. Not that I really remember all the details, but those parts are pretty clear.

"Just slip your feet in and I'll tie them."

I open my eyes and he's standing over me, holding my boots. Pushing myself up, I swing my legs to the floor and wait for the room to slow down. I feel like an asshole—more so than usual.

Guy drops the boots to the floor and the sound has my brain throbbing. I shove my feet inside. "Have you talked to her?" I don't say her name. I don't need to. He knows. I've asked about her every time I've seen him in the past three days.

"I saw her this morning."

"Did she say anything?"

He squats to tie my laces, keeping his eyes focused on the minor task. "She asked how you were doing and wanted to know when you'd be home."

He stands up, but still doesn't look at me.

"Did she want to know when I'd be home so she knew when to avoid my apartment?"

"She's hurt," Guy says in explanation.

"I know." I close my eyes again because the light is bothering me. "I fucked up. Again."

"You can fix it," he says, but I can hear it in his voice. He doesn't really believe that anymore than I do.

"She hates me. And she should." I went to great lengths to ensure that.

Guy exhales loudly. "She stayed all night," he reminds me. "She sat right in this chair, by your side, even when the nurses told her she needed to leave. She doesn't hate you. She cares about you and that's why you were able to hurt her. If she hated you she wouldn't care that you slept with another girl directly after sleeping with her."

I cringe. "I didn't sleep with Erika."

"Semantics. You made it perfectly clear to everybody there that night that you and she were well acquainted. And if I remember correctly, you had *plans* for her."

Yeah. I did. But now, days later and sober, I realize how completely fucking stupid those plans were. I don't want Erika. I never did. I just wanted her to erase the fucked up shit stuck in my head, and possibly help me forget Lucy.

Because I should forget.

"It doesn't matter now," I say gruffly. "She's better off staying away. Hell, I'm better off if she stays away. That girl has me fucked up thinking shit can be different." I sigh and rub my forehead. "Where the hell is the doctor? I want out of here."

Guy settles into the chair and observes me. "I'm sure you're not his only patient. He'll get here when he can. While we wait, why don't you explain to me what you mean about thinking shit can be different."

I roll my head so he can get the full effect of my glare. "Why don't we *not* do that?"

"You know I want you to be happy, right?" he asks.

I look away and laugh sarcastically. "We can't all be gay."

"Oh, you're so punny." He crosses his arms and leans back. "Anytime you want to actually start putting those extra IQ points to work, please feel free to do so."

"Are you calling me stupid or smart?"

"I'm saying you're being stupid."

"Here's a little secret, Guy: I don't give a shit."

He chuckles and shakes his head. It makes me want to smack him. "We both know that's not true," he states. "You give a shit. In fact, I think you give a lot of shits."

"Well it's still shit regardless. And stop thinking because you're wrong." He's not and he's fully aware of it. But I'm not about to tell him he's right because then he'll want to fix it. Fix me. I'm not fixable. Old dog— new tricks and all that.

Before he can reply, the doctor finally decides to grace us with his presence. He gives me some paperwork, has me sign more, and then tells me I'm free to go. I don't hesitate. I'm out of the bed and moving toward the door as soon as the words leave his mouth. He tries to stop me with some policy about a wheel chair. Fuck that. I ignore him and keep going.

By the time I stop in front of the elevator, I have a cigarette in my mouth, and I'm flicking my lighter anxiously. I'm dizzy again, but I ignore it. I'm almost out of this place.

Guy steps up beside me and hands me a pair of sunglasses. I push them up on my head. "Thanks man."

He nods as he fishes his cell phone out of his pocket. "Chase is out by the main doors."

"Is he by himself?"

"Uh, I don't know," he replies, and I stare at him, waiting for him to tell me the truth. "Hope's been worried about you. She may have insisted on coming along."

Son of a bitch.

I drop the sunglasses down over my eyes and stride into the elevator. I'll just have to deal. It's only a ten minute drive. I can do that. It's not like she'll be around much longer. She's got a life to get back to.

Guy pushes the lobby button. My thumb flicks against the lighter. My other hand is tapping against my leg and my head is light.

"Did you want to go to the police station now, or wait until tomorrow?"

"What? Why would I go to the station?" I ask, confused.

"So you can press charges against the assholes that did this to you."

The doors open and I move quickly, heading toward my freedom. As soon as I step outside I light my cigarette and take a long hit, my lungs protesting. I cough, causing pain to shoot through my head, and my chest to ache. Fucking pricks bruised my ribs.

"I'm not pressing charges," I say.

"Why not?" Guy asks incredulously.

I cock my head to look at him. *Because I deserved it.* "Because I don't remember what happened." I spot Chase's car and start walking again. He has a stupid-ass, no smoking rule in his car, so I suck as many hits as I can before I get over there.

Hope hops out of the passenger door, holding it open for me. I move around her and fall into the seat with a grunt. Everything fucking hurts.

"Hello sunshine," Chase beams. "You're bluer than a Smurf."

I haven't looked in a mirror, but I hear it's bad. "Fuck off."

"Oh, you're just precious today."

"I want to go home. That's all I want."

***

I slept the day away yesterday. All I remember is seeing my bed. Anything after that is fuzzy. My boots were sitting on the floor next to my bed when I woke up. I don't remember taking them off.

My body must have needed the sleep because I feel pretty good today. My head still hurts, but it's not as bad as my face. That's new, so it must be improvement.

I make my way to the bathroom to take a long, hot shower. My stomach clenches when I catch sight of my reflection. *Fuck*. It's not just my face. It's my neck and throat. I take my shirt off and shift from left to right.

My torso is covered in dark bruises. I stare at them, trying to remember each hit. Each kick.

"Oh, my God."

My eyes flick up to see Bree's in the mirror. I smirk. "No, just me."

"Jesus, Park," she breathes. Her gaze roams over my back and I don't even want to know what she sees. "I was going to ask how you were feeling, but…"

"Yeah. I kind of feel like I was jumped by three big-ass guys."

She nods. "You look like it."

I turn around to face her and she winces. "How's Lucy?" I ask.

Bree stands up straighter, showing off her height. She crosses her arms over her chest and glares at me. "I'm guessing she feels like you look."

Now I wince. I knew she was upset. Hurt. But the comparison hits hard.

"You need to stay away from her," Bree hisses. "She trusted you."

I swallow hard. This is unfixable. Why did I do it? Why did I fuck it up?

Bree's still looking at me, waiting for me to give her something. Some explanation. Some reason. I don't have any. I roll my eyes and grab the door. "That was her first mistake," I say, swinging the door closed.

I wait several heartbeats to see if she's going to say anything or kick the door in. When I'm met by silence, I turn the shower on and slip my jeans off. The first touch of water on my skin stings, but the longer I stand under the spray, the better it feels.

And then I can't push the thoughts away any longer. It all settles in my chest, weighing it down until I feel like I can't breathe.

I just want it to go away.

Lucy's Rules:

1. Make the conscious decision to look at others with an open mind ~~and an open heart~~.
2. Everybody needs someone in their life they can rely on. ~~Try to be that person~~.
3. Take a chance.
4. Love whole-heartedly. (<u>Unless in the presence of Park Reed—in which case, guard your heart at all cost</u>.)
5. Make it your goal to make someone smile daily.
6. Always expect more of yourself today than you did yesterday.
7. ~~No matter how many times you're let down, continue believing in the goodness of others~~.

27

Lucy

"Whatchya watching?" Bree asks, plopping down on the couch. I look up at her from my position on the floor as I stretch.

"I'm not." I toss her the remote and lean forward to grab my toes. "I'm going for a run."

Bree crinkles her nose and pops a chip in her mouth. "You have fun with that."

I laugh lightly as I stand to finish my warm-up. "You can come with."

"Mm...that's okay. I have big plans that consist of this couch, this TV, and this bag of chips. Who am I if I abandon my life goal?"

I straighten up and rest my hands on my hips, stifling an eye roll. "And that would be what?"

"To not run unless I'm being chased."

"If you ran, you'd have a better chance of getting away if you were ever chased," I point out.

"No. See I'm resting up for it. With all the running you do, if you were ever chased you'd be too tired to get away. My way is so much better. And fun. And…"

"Lazy?"

"Exactly." She smirks around another chip. "Before you go, can you bring me my laptop?"

"Oh, my God," I sigh. "You are hopeless."

"It's not my fault. My parents made me this way. All those years of being told I'm a princess…it gets to a girl."

I shake my head as I fight the grin begging to be released. "Pathetic."

"Your mom's pathetic."

"Your mom has a lazy-ass daughter," I call over my shoulder. I grab her laptop off the desk in her room and bring it out to her just like she knew I would.

"Thank you. Your mom has a sweet daughter that likes to do things for me." She puts her palms together and bats her dark lashes. "Like getting me a can of Coke…?"

I roll my eyes and head for the door. "They're called legs, B. And they can take you anywhere you want to go."

"Can they take me to Jensen Ackles' house?" she yells. "Because that's the only place I want to go right now."

I laugh as I let the door close behind me. Pressing my ear buds into place, I set up my playlist, and skip down the stairs. I pause near Park and Jessie's door for just a second before continuing on.

I haven't seen Park since he's come home. I haven't actually seen him since his first night in the hospital. I don't know how I feel about that. Or him.

Part of me feels like I should go see him. He could have died and I haven't bothered to even so much as stop by. Damn my parents for instilling stupid values in me. Guilt twists my tummy as I head out into the muggy day.

What if he's in too much pain to take care of himself?

No. If he was that bad, Jessie would tell me.

Would he though? He doesn't want me to have anything to do with Park. Maybe he would keep it from me on purpose. In which case, he's probably taking care of Park himself. And Guy's been there a lot.

Park doesn't need me.

And I shouldn't want him to.

But I miss him. I wonder if he misses me.

He doesn't miss me. He made it perfectly obvious that I'm easily replaced. Just like Jared did.

I speed my pace. I need to fall into the run, let it absorb me so I can't think about this anymore. Prying the iPod out of my pocket, I turn the volume up loud. I don't usually do this. I typically keep it low so I can hear traffic or someone approaching me. But I need it right now.

Sweat trails down my back and in between my cleavage, beads on my forehead. It's too hot to run. This late in the afternoon is the worst time. But again, I need it right now. Sitting in the apartment, knowing he's just a floor below me drives me nuts.

How could he have sex with another girl—a girl with a boyfriend—the same day as having sex with me?

Why would he do that? If he didn't want to be with me…why not just tell me?

I thought he cared about me. I thought he was going to do his best to not hurt me. He didn't even make it twenty-four hours. As soon as Hope showed up he lost it.

What did I do wrong? What could I have done differently?

No. This is not my fault. I didn't do anything wrong. This isn't on Hope either. This is all Park's fault. He lied to me. I was honest with him and told him exactly how I felt and he used it against me.

But I thought he was going to be different with me.

That's just what he wanted me to believe. I was a challenge and he conquered me. End of story.

But then why? Why all the talk about belonging to him? He didn't need to say those things.

It doesn't matter. None of it matters now.

I slow to a stop and hold my sides. I need to catch my breath. I'm cramping and I feel nauseated.

I should just go see him. If I can see he's doing better then *I'll* feel better. I can be the bigger person.

I can't believe how close he came—

What if I lost him?

No. He was never mine to lose. He ended this the moment he left me in his apartment so he could go sleep with some other girl.

I grind out a frustrated growl as I pant, still trying to get a good breath. Park Reed is not worth all this torment.

Stop thinking about him. Forget him. Pretend he never existed.

I laugh as I start into a jog.

Yeah. Easier said than done.

***

I decided the best way to appease my guilt over my refusal to go see Park is by cooking. For him. I do it under the pretense of dinner for everybody. I have been neglecting Jess since Park's come home and Bree's always down for my cooking.

Really it's my excuse to see him. If I can just see with my own eyes that he's okay then I can move on. The only problem with this plan is getting him here. It's not like I can get Bree or Jessie to make sure he comes along. Bree hates him and Jessie's not going to force him over here.

I finally come up with the idea of taking the meal down to them. I'm busy packing each course into containers and placing them into a large box when Bree pops her head in.

"What are you doing?"

"Just finishing dinner," I say casually.

"What's up with the box?" Her dark brows scrunch as she watches me.

"I thought we could go to Jessie's." I try to pick up the box, but it's kind of heavy and it's an awkward size. I can't get a good grip on it. I push it with my foot, kicking it toward the door.

"We're taking it downstairs? Why? It'd be so much easier if Jessie just comes up here..."

I shrug and keep going. I know she's going to be pissed and I really don't feel like dealing with it, but I've already started this.

"You're taking it to *him*," she says, appalled.

The way she says, *"him,"* makes me cringe.

I stop in front of the door and sigh. "Can you help me? I can't lift it by myself."

"No. You do not need to make him dinner after what he did."

"This isn't about that. I've been avoiding him since he's come home. What happened between us doesn't matter."

Bree's eyes widen. "It does matter. He doesn't deserve your cooking or your concern."

I shake my head, my arms falling limply at my sides. "I need this, Bree. I need to do this for me. For my own peace of mind."

She puckers her lips as she scrutinizes my features. "Fine. But I hope he chokes." She pulls the door open and squats on one side. "And we're bringing any leftovers home."

"Okay," I agree.

As we approach the second floor landing, Bree sniffs the air. "What are we having anyway?"

"Chicken. And pasta. And rosemary potatoes. And salad. And homemade bread. And pepperoni rolls. And a cake."

She stops, causing me to walk into the box. "Umph…what?"

"Seriously?"

I shrug, the box moving slightly with the gesture. "I made all of Jessie's favorite things."

Bree raises her brows knowing I'm full of shit.

"It's weird. Isn't it?" I ask. "Let's take it back. We can eat it ourselves."

"We're here. I don't want to take it back up."

"I feel stupid now. I thought it was a good idea at the time, but now…it's kind of creepy, right?"

"No," Bree insists. "It's…*nice*."

"Oh, my God. No it's not. It's so stupid and I have no idea what I was thinking." I shake my head and pull on the box. "I don't want to do this now."

"Lu, it's fine. I'm not taking this box back upstairs."

"I'll do it myself," I huff. I tug on the box again. "Just give it here."

"You're going to spill it."

"Then let it go," I cry.

"Okay. Stop," she sighs loudly. "Let's just put it down for a second."

I nod and we lower it to the floor right in front of Park's door. I want to dash back up the steps and go to bed, really badly. This was such a bad idea. Worse even than the Pizza Fork...or Crocs, or those banana protectors. I can't see him. I can't do it.

"Lucy, take a breath," Bree instructs. I look at her and inhale deeply. "Okay. Good. Now we're here and you spent a lot of time, I'm sure, making all this food. I'm all for saying 'Screw Park', in fact, it's kind of my new motto, but you said you needed to do this. If you really want me to lug this damn thing back up all those stairs, I will, but I want you to be sure because I'm not doing this again."

I nod. "I want to take it back up."

"Are you sure?"

I nod again. "Positive. This was dumb."

Bree sighs again. "All right. You owe me so big for this."

"I know," I agree. "You can eat everything."

She cocks a brow and stares at me for several heartbeats. "Oh, I plan on it."

"Plan on what?" I can't bring myself to look over at him, but I know it's him. Even if I didn't know his voice so well, I would recognize his scent. The crisp cologne mixed with the ashy undertone that I love so much.

No. I don't love it. I don't love anything about him, I remind myself.

Bree clears her throat and I hear the laughter so clearly when she says, "Uh, hi Park."

28
Park

"Hey…" I say slowly, stretching out the one word. "I thought I heard voices." I look at Lucy, but she's keeping her eyes trained on the box in front of her. "What are you doing?"

Bree glances at Lucy then back at me. "Um, I'm not real sure. What are we doing, Lu?"

Closing her eyes and biting down on her lip, Lucy taps her foot several times. Finally, she spins to face me. I watch her eyes widen and then fill with tears before she starts blinking quickly. My eyes are drawn to her throat when she swallows. The memory of running my lips over her skin hits me out of nowhere and I drop my gaze.

I don't hear her move, but suddenly Lucy's arms are wrapped gently around my waist and she presses her face into my chest. "I'm glad you're okay, Park."

She steps back too quickly—I didn't even have the chance to hug her back. "I made this for you guys." She points at the box. "It's food."

"A lot of food," Bree adds curtly.

"And a cake," Lucy finishes softly.

I just stand here not knowing what to say. I can't even comprehend why she would take the time to do something so nice for me after what I did to her. I get this kick of adrenaline—this jump in my torso that has me feeling scared and hopeful at the same time.

"If you'll move your ass out of the way we can get it inside," Bree says, not hiding the coldness in her tone.

I still can't manage to say anything, but I step back into the apartment to give them room. When I see them struggle with the box, I move to help.

"We got it," Lucy says. "I don't want you to hurt yourself."

I want to argue with her, but something in the way she's looking at me gives me pause. And honestly, she's right. I can't lift that box without fucking myself up more. I watch as they shove it through the door and all the way into the kitchen as I follow right behind.

Bree starts tossing Tupperware on the counter and Lucy gasps. "Easy, Bree. You can't shake them up."

Her only reply is to roll her eyes, but she places the next container down more gently.

When everything's out, Lucy turns to me. Every time she looks at me she winces and I don't know if it's because I look like shit or if it hurts her to see me. Probably both.

"This is great. I—thank you, Lucy."

She flinches when I say her name and I hate myself even more. I want to drop to my knees at her feet and tell her how sorry I am. But that would defeat the purpose of hurting her in the first place.

"Yeah, no problem. I'll talk to you later."

She's not staying.

"Will you?" I don't know why I ask. I should just let her go. I know it's better for us both if she does, but I still want her to stay. *Fuck.* I want her to want to stay so badly. I want her to want me. I need her to want me.

I'm so fucked up.

"I don't know," she says honestly.

I nod tightly and Bree nudges her toward the door.

***

I'm dumping dishes in the sink when I hear voices. Since I came home from the hospital four days ago nobody knocks anymore.

I hear Hope laugh and decide I need to start locking the door.

When I make it into the living room, I see they've made themselves at home. Guy and Hope are sprawled across the couch, chatting like I want them here.

"Hey, man," Guy says, grinning. "You look better than yesterday."

I doubt that. My bruises are starting to turn this weird brownish-green color. It's not pretty. I just cross my arms.

"Yeah," Hope agrees. "You're less swollen."

I arch my brows.

Hope sighs. "I'm going home tomorrow."

I nod. Can't say I'm going to miss her.

"We need to talk before I leave."

I chuckle and rub my chin. I need to shave. I haven't bothered with it because my face hurts, but now I'm getting itchy and I think that might be worse.

"Please," Hope whispers. It makes me go still and I narrow my eyes, scrutinizing her.

"Why?"

"I'm going to go hang out with Lulu and Bree," Guy says before heading quickly for the door. "I'll be right upstairs if you need me."

I return my gaze to Hope and wait for her to say whatever the hell she feels like she needs to say.

"I want you to know that I forgive you," she starts, and I laugh. Loudly.

"Oh, that's fucking awesome. No, really, that is priceless." I have to hold my chest because it aches still when I laugh too hard. "You forgive me?"

She gives me a sad smile. "Yes. I thought you should know."

My amusement fades. "What the fuck do you forgive *me* for?"

"For telling Mason and Guy that I cut myself."

I don't think I've ever heard her say it like that before. So honestly.

"You told me you were sorry and I couldn't forgive you then, but I can now. It hurt me when you did that, but it ended up being one of the best things that ever happened to me."

I nod. "Let me guess, Mason is on that list too."

"Yeah, he is."

"But not me," I say. I never meant anything to her.

"No, Park. You are on that list. Just in a different way."

"If I was so special to you, then why? How could you cast me to the side so easily? I leave for an hour and when I come back you're suddenly with Mason and Guy knows about it. Encourages it. How could you do that to me?"

291

Hope drops her head, shaking it slowly. "It *didn't* happen in an hour. I should have handled it differently. I'm sorry I didn't. You were one of my best friends. I counted on you for so much, but you have to know we weren't meant to be."

"That's not the point. You should have told me."

She looks up quickly, her sharp gaze focusing on me. "You didn't tell Lucy before you moved on to another girl."

I snap my mouth closed, pressing my lips together.

"You pretty much did the same thing to her. Worse even. I kissed Mason. That's it. And I did that because I wanted to be with him. I cared about him. You dropped Lucy and fucked another girl."

"Don't," I say hoarsely. "Don't talk about her. It wasn't like that. You don't understand."

"The hell I don't. I get it, Park. You care about her and it scares the living shit out of you. Cheese and rice. I get that. You pushed her away so she couldn't push you first. You're afraid she'll hurt you. But don't you realize that you're hurting both of you?"

"Wait," I say, holding up my hand. "Just stop for a second." Something about this conversation is causing a severe case of déjà vu. I close my eyes and try to think. "Lucy and I...we were never really together. It's different." *But weren't we? I told her she was mine. Fuck. I wanted her to be mine. I still do.*

Hope laughs without humor. "Neither were you and I, technically. I told you I didn't want a relationship, but I'm pretty sure Lucy does, so I think what you did might be a little shittier."

My eyes pop open. *Shit.* My chest is tightening. Did I do to Lucy what Hope did to me? God, no. I did worse because Hope loves Mason. I could give a shit about Erika.

"I didn't fuck that girl," I say.

Hope sighs. "Good. You can fix this. She's hurt because she thinks you did. And on the same day as her."

I shake my head. "I didn't fuck her, but she..." I feel awkward talking to Hope about this of all people. "She blew me," I spit.

She inhales deeply. "Okay. That might be worse."

I don't understand woman's logic. How is that worse? It doesn't even matter. "She's better off without me fucking up her life."

"I think she'd be better off with the real Park in her life. Don't push her away because you're afraid of getting hurt. It's a shitty thing to do."

"You keep saying that. I'm not pushing her away to keep myself from getting hurt." I pause as I'm struck again by a sense of déjà vu. "Were you in my room? At the hospital? That first night?"

She cocks her head to the side, watching me. "What?"

My heart is beating way too fast. I take a step toward her. "The night I went to the hospital—were you in my room with Lucy? Did you talk to her about me?"

Hope nods slowly. "Yeah. We talked."

I sink onto the couch beside her. "You said I made Lucy leave so it wouldn't hurt as much."

"Yeah," she agrees. "Did she tell you?"

"I heard you. I thought…it was a dream." I'm trying to remember the rest of it. What did Lucy say?

Hope touches my arm and I look at her. "She loves you. You can make this work, but you have to stop purposely fucking up to keep her at a distance."

Holy shit. Yes. That's it. Lucy said she loved me. But she didn't want to. Because of what I did to her.

I don't know what to feel. My veins are alive, my blood rushing with fear. I don't know how to save this. I've become way too good at fucking up.

But Lucy…she fucking loves me.

29
Lucy

I hate that nine days can feel like months. That's how long it's been since I've seen Park. He's probably a lot better too. At least, that's what I keep telling myself.

I hate that I miss him. I don't want to be that girl—the one that gets walked on, cheated on, forgotten about, and pines away for the asshole who did it.

I hate that I am that girl. I can't stop thinking about him. I try. I tell myself to stop. I remind myself of what he did.

But then I remember we were never officially together. I hate that too.

But if we were never together, then why did he say I was his?

Stop it.

I'm done.

I push myself out of bed and go to Bree's room. I tap my nails on her half open door. "Hey."

"What's up?" she asks as she shuffles through the clothes in her closet.

"Are you going out tonight?"

She grins widely at me. "Yep. Are you actually going to come with us?" she asks, her voice full of excitement.

"Yeah, if that's okay. I don't want to be the third wheel."

"Tricycles are awesome—FYI, but just so you know, you get to be one of the training wheels tonight. Chase and Guy are coming out with us too."

"Where are you guys going?"

Bree concentrates on her clothes as she shrugs. "I can't remember the name. It's a little bar near campus." She tosses a shirt over her head, the thin, black fabric hits me in the chest and I catch it. "Wear that with your cut-offs. It'll be cute and you won't get too hot while you're dancing."

"Okay Princess Bree. Anything else?" I say sarcastically.

"Leave your hair down," she says, ignoring my tone. "And at least gloss your lips."

I growl at her, but go to do what she says. I need to get out and have some Park-free fun tonight. And if that means I have to wear her clothes and slap on some gloss, I'm cool with that.

***

The bar is packed for a Thursday. That should have been my first clue. No. Scratch that. That should have been my second clue. Bree telling me all Park's friends were coming out here tonight except Park should have been the first tip off.

My eyes keep sliding to the table in the back where Park sits nursing a beer with a girl fighting to keep his attention. If she leans over any farther, her boobs are going to fall out of her push-up bra and spill all over the tabletop.

I roll my eyes and look around, trying to focus on anything other than him. I don't think he's noticed me yet and I contemplate sneaking out before he does. I don't need that awkwardness.

Bree hands me a drink and I scowl at her. "What?" she asks, innocently. I point at her in warning. I don't want to hear it. *Back-stabber.* I toss my head back, gulping down the shot and hand her the glass back.

"More," I say. I'm going to need it. She hands me hers and I repeat the process. "More," I say again.

"Damn. All right. Let me find Jessie. Take this for now." She hands me her rum and Coke and I suck on the straw. Her eyes settle on my empty glass that I drained almost immediately. I meet her gaze, daring her to say something. I'm not usually like this. She can put up with it for one night—especially since this is her fault. She knew I wouldn't have come if she told me Park was going to be here.

Why is he here anyway? Shouldn't he be home healing or something?

My gaze slips back to his table and it's empty. Good. Maybe he left with that trampy girl. My stomach churns at the thought and I feel guilty for assuming she's a tramp.

And then I giggle because seriously…she seemed pretty damn trampy.

"How's it going?"

I look up at the guy standing beside me. I turn to get the full view. He's cute with his curly dark hair and bright blue eyes hidden under a pair of squared glasses.

"Um, good," I say.

"I'm Wyatt." He holds his hand out and I shake it.

Wyatt. I like it. "I'm Lucy," I start the usual spiel, "but my friends call me Lulu or Lu."

"You can call her Lucy."

Wyatt's eyes focus above my head, and I don't move. I can't. I'm too busy having an internal debate with myself. On one shoulder, my little devil is jumping for joy. On the other, the angel is seething over Park's nerve to pull this macho bullshit when he has no right to me.

Wyatt gives me a strained smile. "It was nice to meet you, Lucy." He turns on his heel and disappears into the crowd. I roll my eyes and suck on my straw. I probably should have eaten something before drinking.

Well, too late now.

Where the hell is Bree? I still haven't turned around and I think I need another drink before I can deal with Park.

"Lucy," he says and I try so hard not to shiver, but the way my name passes through his lips is so sexy.

No.

Stop it.

I spin around and he takes a step back when he registers my anger. "What?"

He sets his half-full beer on the table next to us and rubs his forehead. "I want to talk to you."

Arching an incredulous brow, I swipe up his beer and chug it. Eck. It's warm. I grimace as I wipe my mouth. His eyes follow my movements. I try to ignore the way his white tee shirt hugs his biceps. I don't need him to be so attractive right now. "You want to talk to me?"

"Yes." He smiles. "Please?"

The "please" makes my stomach pull tightly, but I take another drink and ignore it. "Sorry," I say smartly, "but I want to dance. I'll talk to you later."

I push past him and I hear him suck in a breath through his teeth. I turn back quickly, realizing I was too rough. "Oh, my God. I'm sorry. Did I hurt you?"

His eyes are trained on me, his hand pressed into his side. "Nothing I didn't deserve."

I stare at him and he smiles weakly. "Are you trying to manipulate me?" I ask quietly.

"What?" He takes a step closer to me. "Why would I do that?"

"I don't know. Why would you fuck me in my shower then turn around hours later and fuck another girl?"

His dark eyes widen in surprise at my outburst and then I see something else flicker there. Some kind of heat that makes my stomach plummet like the drop on a roller coaster.

"Lucy, I need to talk to you."

I shake my head because I'm so close to saying okay. If he pushes it anymore, I know I will. And then I'll definitely be that girl. "There's nothing you can say that I want to hear. Not after what you did."

"Did you ever think I did what I did for you?"

"You'll have to excuse me if I can't see how you having sex with another girl is beneficial to me."

"Because it's better if you hate me."

"Don't worry, I'm almost there." I shake my head again, begging him with my eyes. I won't give into him. That will make me a stupid, weak, naïve girl just like everyone assumes I am. I can't do this.

"What the hell are you doing?" Bree demands. She hands me a shot and I take it quickly, looking for a little liquid courage. She manages to get in between me and Park, her hand on her hip. "I told you to keep your distance."

"This may come as a shock to you, Bree, but I don't answer to you."

"Fine. I'll tell Jessie," she threatens.

Park laughs bitterly. "Go ahead. I don't give a shit anymore." He looks past her, his eyes landing on me. "Lucy?"

"I want to dance."

"Okay," he says. "Let's dance."

"Not with you," Bree hisses. She grabs my hand and pulls me away from Park. I look over my shoulder and watch him until he's swallowed by all the other bodies.

I watch Lucy shake her ass and sway her hips for nearly an hour. I watch as she dances with strangers, ready to beat the first asshole down that touches her inappropriately. She's been blowing them off after one dance, which I'm happy about. Plus she has Bree by her side. Jessie's been out there for a few songs and Guy's even danced with them a couple times.

"What is it they say about taking a picture?" Chase asks from beside me.

I glance over at him and he's smirking. I hate when he does that. It makes me want to smack the smugness off his face. "It lasts longer," I say. "But it can't kick someone's ass if they touch my girl."

Chase's head snaps in my direction. *Shit*. Did I just say that aloud? "Your what?"

"Nothing. Shut up. I like this song."

He laughs and shakes his head. "Hell no. Explain yourself, oh, Delusional One." He gestures toward Lucy, swinging her hips out on the dance floor. "Does she happen to know she is apparently yours?"

I smile tightly. "She knows. She's just trying to deny it at the moment." Because I did a really good job of making her run. At least I'm good at *something*.

"I'm not sure she's the one in denial," Chase chuckles.

"We'll see," I say, but he has a good point. Even if Lucy has feelings for me, it may very well be too late for her to forgive me. And even though I know it's better that way, I can't help the selfish part of me that wants her so badly I can taste it.

Lucy pushes her way through the crowd, making her way up to the bar and I see my chance to talk to her. "I'll see you later, man," I tell Chase.

"Good luck, dude. Don't fuck up this time."

I raise a skeptical brow. "Not sure I know how to do that."

"Just…don't trip, fall, and land dick first inside some random girl on the way over there."

"I can manage that," I reply.

"You'd think, but one never knows with you," he tosses back.

"Do you have something you want to say to me?"

Chase shakes his head and takes a drink. "Nah, man. I've said all I can."

Right. Chase should start his own life lessons. Don't fuck up and don't stick your dick in random girls. Pretty legit rules to live by.

I nod at him. "I care about her. I want… I need her to forgive me."

He takes another drink, his eyes scrutinizing every feature on my face. "Then try putting her first for once. Tell her the fucking truth and trust that she's not going to use it against you."

I nod again even though my heart is stuck in my throat. The truth. What if I don't know what the truth is? What if I'm as confused as she is? What if I'm just as hurt? And trust? I don't know the meaning anymore.

I sit back down not feeling as confident as I did a few minutes ago. My gaze falls over the bar, looking for her long hair.

"What are you doing?" Chase asks.

"I'm not ready." Maybe I'll never be ready.

"You just talked all that shit. You've been watching her all night. You said you care about her."

I sigh. "Yeah. And then you said I need to trust her." And now I realize I need to earn her trust.

Chase shoots me an irritated look. "So?"

I lean forward, resting my elbows on the table. "Just the thought makes me feel like puking," I mutter.

He shakes his head slowly. "You have to trust somebody, or this is it. You get that, right? Where you are, right now at this very moment, is the best it will ever be for you if you don't let someone into that black rock you call a heart."

I drop my eyes to the table, staring at the dark wood, ringed in water marks. "I don't know how."

"It's not something you can learn to do on your own, dumbass. It doesn't happen all at once. It takes time and patience. And it's not always easy, but most of the time it's worth it."

I look up at him and laugh quietly. "When the hell did you get so fucking wise?"

"It's a new occurrence. All those Disney movies finally paid off."

"Fucking Simba, man," I say trying to keep the lighter mood going.

"Hakuna matata."

Yeah. No worries.

***

Staring at the ceiling has become my newest pastime. It's a shitty ceiling. There's a long, thin crack and a few cobwebs. Other than that, there's nothing to see. But it's all I can look at when I'm lying on my bed trying to sort through my thoughts.

It hasn't worked yet. It's all still a jumbled mess.

I've been holding my cell phone in my hand for over an hour. The only person I can think of asking for advice is the one person my pride is refusing to dial.

It's a small miracle I haven't chucked the damn thing against the wall. I've wanted to. Several times.

Shit. He said if I needed anything…

Fuck it. I'm doing it. He owes me.

I sit up, dropping my feet to the floor and hit the send button. It rings three times before he picks up.

"Hello?" Ah, he must have me programmed into his contacts because he made that one word sound reluctant and irritated at the same time.

"Hey, Mason. It's Park."

"Yeah…is everything all right?"

Is it? I have no clue. "It's fine. I just need to ask you something."

"Okay…?"

Damn. This guy gets on my fucking nerves. "You and Hope—you went through a rough patch a couple times, right?"

He's quiet for a moment, the only sound is of our mutual breathing. "We did," he confirms, but gives me no further information.

That's fine. I don't need the details of their fights. That's not what this is about. I just need to know: "How did you get her to forgive you?"

"Are you asking me to get Hope to forgive you or someone else?"

"Lucy," I say. "I fucked up really bad and I think I want to fix it."

"You *think* you want to fix it? Or you know you do?"

"I know I do. I just don't know if I should. Or how I would even go about it." I grin down at my bare feet. "And since you've been fucking up for awhile, I thought you may have some wisdom to share on the subject."

"Well when you put it that way...go fuck yourself."

I chuckle. "All right, man. I'm sorry. Seriously. I—need your advice."

He's quiet again, long enough to make me nervous. Finally he clears his throat. "Candy."

"What?"

"Hope loves candy." That's an understatement. The girl is flat-out obsessed with sugar. "Find out what Lucy's candy is and then be relentless. I mean, don't cross over into stalker territory, but walk the line if you need to."

"What if she doesn't have a candy?"

"Everybody has a candy…" He trails off and I try to think. What do I know about Lulu? She's sweet. She always puts others before herself. She likes to cook. There are her Saturday morning breakfasts. She's good with her brothers. Terrible at video games. She loves music. She sucks at Water War, but she loves to play it. She runs. And she reads as much as, if not more, than I do.

"Donuts," Mason says, interrupting my thoughts.

"Donuts?"

"She likes donuts," he supplies.

"The jelly-filled kind," I agree.

"Start there. I brought Hope candy every single day until she forgave me. And then I kept bringing it to remind her."

"Remind her of what?"

"What she saw in me in the first place. What made her care to look."

I don't think Lucy likes donuts enough to get one every day. But that's okay because I can switch it up. I'm going to do this my way. I may not know a whole hell of a lot about her, but I like what I do know. And now I realize I want to learn more. I want to know it all.

31
Lucy

I've waited a week for Park to try to talk to me again. I haven't seen or heard from him since the bar.

It's for the best. It's what I wanted, right?

But it's really not. That's just what I tell myself to make me feel better. Because the cold hard truth is this: I want Park. I want Park to want me. I don't want to forgive Park. But I want to forgive him more than anything. I hate him for what he did. But I love him. I hate that I love him. I hate that I can't stop thinking about him. And I wonder if he's thinking of me. I want him to think of me. I want him to be sorry.

I want him to love me back.

I'm a mess. A complete, hot mess.

I crank the music loud and step into the shower. Every day, this simple thing breaks my heart. It's this constant reminder of what I had for one short moment. A constant reminder of what I lost.

I've changed the shower curtain. I've thrown his toothbrush away. I even replaced mine. I purchased new shampoo and conditioner. It doesn't take any of the memories away. How can it linger this long?

It's been a month. A month since I spent one night and one short morning with Park. That's all we had. It shouldn't mean this much. It shouldn't hurt this much.

I'm not even angry anymore.

Just sad.

And lost.

Maybe I'm hurting so much because I've lost a friend. Maybe we can go back. Maybe we can at least hold on to our friendship. Can I do that?

I turn the water off and wrap myself in a towel. Yes, I think I can do that. It has to be easier than this. And I know easy doesn't always mean it's right. But in this case, it feels right.

Friends.

We never really got to be friends.

I brush through my wet hair and actually feel like smiling for the first time in a long while. As I pad back to my room to get dressed, my heart beats quickly with a nervous excitement.

There's a box sitting on the end of my bed. My racing heart stops beating all together. I glance around the empty room quickly then back to the mysterious box. I approach it slowly. It's just a simple white box. I flip the lid open and frown. There's an arrow drawn on the bottom. I look to the right—to the window.

My curiosity is peaked, but I'm naked. I throw my clothes on quicker than I've ever dressed before and practically run to the window. Throwing it open, I lean out and look around. Three steps down, there's another box.

I crawl out and open the lid. There's a small, plastic squirt gun inside, and under it, one word written on the bottom of the box: Down.

I deflate with disappointment. For a minute, I had thought this was Park's doing. But a squirt gun? It's obviously Jess. And I'm not in the mood for Water War today. I tuck the gun into my pocket and tromp down the stairs.

In front of Jessie's window is another box. I open it with less enthusiasm and then stare inside with confusion. This time, it's a silk butterfly just like the ones I have hanging from my ceiling. I brush my fingers over the smooth wings before taking it out. Where it sat, there's another arrow.

I press the soft butterfly to my chest with one hand and open the window with the other. Peeking inside first, I let my gaze scan the room. It looks like it always does. Unmade bed, clothes strewn about, DJ equipment piled against one wall. And empty. I see another box on the dresser and go straight for it.

I hesitate, looking around once more before I flip the top up. My stomach tightens. It's the book I got Park. The second one in the series he and I were reading. My heart is pounding against my ribs. I can feel it in my head. My hands are shaking as I take it out of the box. On the bottom, one word: Out.

I pause. Out the door or the window? I came in the window, so I decide to go out the door. I can't help it—I look for him as soon as I step into the hall. He's not there, but there's another box. I nearly trip in my hurry, dropping to my knees to open it. Even though I have no idea what's going on, I like this game.

The third and final book of the series is inside. I pluck it out and hug it to my side as my gaze follows the arrow. Right into Park's bedroom. I stand and take a deep breath.

I can turn around and go back home. I don't have to go in there.

It's my decision.

Looking down at the books in my hand, the silk butterfly resting on top, I touch the squirt gun in my pocket and make a choice.

I step inside his room.

I'm alone, but there's a box on his bed. I set everything down and slowly raise the lid. And then I smile. A single jelly donut. I move it to the side and read the words beneath: Turn Around.

I read it once more before spinning on my heel. Park's in the doorway, eating an ice cream cone. A vanilla ice cream cone with hot fudge dripping onto his fingers. He licks it away slowly and I swallow with difficulty.

Everything has significance. From the stupid water gun—just like I shot him with the first time we met, to the butterfly—I have fifty more like it hanging from my ceiling, to the books we were reading together, to the ice cream in his hand—just like when he told me I was vanilla and he wanted to lick the hot fudge off my body.

"Hi," he says softly.

"Hi," I whisper.

He moves toward me and I take an involuntary step back. I don't make it far, my calves hit the bed and I freeze.

"We need to talk."

"About what?" I rasp.

His eyes lock onto mine. The determination there makes my breaths come faster. "You and me."

"There is no you and me," I reply, my voice barely coming out.

"There's a you and me, Lucy. There has to be," he says firmly. "Just answer something for me?"

I nod.

"Is there a chance—any chance at all—that you can forgive me?"

"I don't know. I want to." His eyes spark with some emotion I can't identify. He takes another step. I have nowhere to go.

"Can I ask another question?"

I nod because I've lost my voice.

"Do you miss me even a little? Because I miss you. You're all I can think about."

My pulse is throbbing furiously. I nod, and then I shake my head.

He cocks his head to the side, studying me. "I'm sorry, Lucy. I'm so sorry. I know that's not good enough, but if you give me another chance, I swear I'll prove myself to you."

I don't respond and he takes another step, putting him just inches away from me. I lift my chin in order to keep my eyes on his.

"Last question," he murmurs. His breath caresses my cheek and I shudder. "I know I have no right to ask this, but...are you still mine?"

I eye the ice cream in his hand just so I can look away. Can I tell him? Can I put myself out there again? I close my eyes and choose. "I never stopped," I breathe. "But you were never mine."

"I was always yours," he states adamantly. "I didn't have sex with that girl."

My head snaps up quickly. "You didn't?"

He shakes his head. "We fucked around. A lot. And I was going to sleep with her because I was trying to forget you, push you away, make you hate me...something. But I didn't do it."

I feel the tears build in the back of my throat. "But you were going to."

"I freaked out and fucked everything up. But I know something now that I didn't know then."

"What?" I ask. What could he possibly know to make him so sure right now?

"I don't want to go another second without you." He moves in a way that brings our bodies as close as they can be without touching.

"How do I know you aren't still scared?"

"I'll probably always be scared," he says, shrugging.

I feel my brows draw together as I shake my head. "We can't do this if you're scared."

"I have every right to be scared." His eyes rake over my face, searching.

"Because of Hope? You're still not over her. How can we ever be together if you're still hung up on her?"

He grinds his teeth and steps back slightly. "I am over Hope. I'm just not over what she fucking did to me. Do you have any idea what it feels like to think you have something and then out of the blue one day you realize it was never truly yours? Not ever? Not even for a second?"

I feel my mouth drop open. "Yes, Park. I know *exactly* what that feels like."

"Maybe you do know."

"You treat me like I'm her. You treat me like she treated you."

"I…we're…" He shakes his head. "I'm so sorry." He closes that little bit of distance. "Tell me you'll give me another chance and I swear it will never happen again."

"We're different, but I'm not sure you'll ever see it."

"I see it. I see you. You are worth it to me. Please, Lucy."

"I don't…I don't know what to say." I can't stop shaking. My eyes are burning. I want to give in. I want to run away.

"Say you'll give me another chance. Tell me you want me. Tell me you care about me. Tell me *I'm* worth it."

"I do want you. I do care. And you are worth it—"

His fingers cover my lips. "Stop there," he says hoarsely. "Please." He moves his hand and skims his mouth over mine. "Just say yes. One chance." His tongue teases my lips and I close my eyes, shivering. "Say yes," he demands.

"Yes," I sigh.

Park stills and my eyes fly open. He drops the melting ice cream cone and before I register what's happening, I'm on my back on top of his bed. He pushes everything to the side and lowers himself over me.

"You and me, Lucy, we're like a fire: Hot and unpredictable, scary and mesmerizing all at once. We started with a spark and before I knew it, I was consumed. I love the way you burn me up from the inside out."

I don't know what to say to that. All I know is I couldn't have said it better myself. I dig my fingers into his hair and pull his mouth down to meet mine. We merge like two flames, fast and out of control. Because sometimes that's just how love works. We may smolder, we may blaze, we may rage without reason. But it's always beautiful.

32

Park

I've missed the way Lucy tastes. I've missed the way her skin feels under my hands, her smell, and the little noises she makes. I've missed the way she kisses, wholly uninhibited. As if each kiss could be the last.

I've missed everything about her.

She pulls back suddenly and I reach for her, not wanting this feeling to end.

"Wait," she breathes. "Hold on." Her palms are pressing into my chest, pushing me away.

"What's wrong?" My voice is low, calm, but inside I'm panicking. I can't—I won't lose her again. I don't care what I have to do—I'll do it. But I'm not going to live without her in my life.

"I need to slow down." She adds more pressure, her breathing growing heavy. I roll to the side and she sits up quickly. "I can't fall back into this."

I watch her run trembling fingers through her damp hair and I force myself to stay where I am. I want to grab her and hold her against me until I'm sure she won't leave. I want to tell her to fucking go—old habits die hard. I want to beg her to stay.

"Lucy," I croak. "Don't do this."

Her hair brushes the bed as she shakes her head. "You have no idea the power you have over me," she says.

I don't respond. Too many things are running through my head and I don't know which thought to put a voice to.

"I know I'm a pushover. I know I put up with a lot because I always try to give people the benefit of the doubt. Sometimes too much. Sometimes I see something that isn't there. But with you, if I let myself think… How do I know it's real this time?"

I stand up and look at her. I take in the true fear in her eyes, her fingers bunching into hair, the way she bites at her lip. And then I kneel in front of her, resting my hands on her shaking knees.

"It's real, Lucy. It's always been real. That's why I freaked out. What you make me feel, I've never felt that before. Ever."

Her gray eyes dart over my face. "What about Hope?"

I shake my head. "No. Not like this. It was nothing like this."

She tips her head, concentrating on my hands, still over her knees. "The day I asked you about *A Fool's Paradise*, and you got out of my car, I knew then. I sat in my car for twenty minutes, waiting for you to come back. And when you didn't, I called Guy. I wanted to make sure you didn't have to walk all the way home. He told me Chase was taking care of it, but I still sat there waiting on you. I wanted you to come back." She looks up and meets my eyes. "I knew then that you were going to hurt me. I asked you not to and you were honest. You warned me that you would. And then you did. And I realized that I never stopped waiting on you. I can't give up on you. I don't know how and that gives you all the power over me. The power to keep me waiting. The power to hurt me again and again." She looks back down and shakes her head. My throat is closed off, blocked by my heart. I tighten my grip on her.

"You left me sitting in your kitchen when Hope showed up. That's all it took. One minute, you're claiming I'm yours. You're pledging to do your best by me. Then the next you're leaving me to go mess around with another girl. You didn't just hurt me by accident. You did it purposely. And still I waited for you. I stayed in your apartment all day, waiting for you to come back. Waiting to make sure you were okay." Lucy shoves my hands off her and stands up. She paces in front of me.

I slide down until I'm sitting on the floor, unable to do anything else. I knew some of this already, but to hear it come from her mouth, to hear the pain in her voice, to see the anguish in her eyes, it strikes me so much harder.

How could I have been such a cold-hearted bastard to her? To Lucy of all people.

I'm sorry sits on my tongue, leaving a bad taste in my mouth. It's not big enough. It can't be. I've said it too many times now. I have to show her. I have to prove it.

"I don't know if I can spend my life waiting on you, Park. No matter how much I want to. Just because I want you doesn't mean you're good for me."

I shove myself to my feet and barrel into her. I back her up into the wall. I have to make her see. If I can just get her to find something redeemable in me…

"I can't take any of it back. Fuck, Lucy. I would if I could. All I can do is try to make it up to you. Prove to you that I won't pull that shit again. I don't want to lose you. The past month has been hell and I can never make you understand how sorry I am for putting you through this. I'll make it my goal each day to make you happy."

Her eyes are bright with that storm that makes me weak. Our chests are rising and falling in sync. I can't take my eyes off her. I can't stop touching her. I can't lose this again.

"You call me Lucy."

I feel my brows draw together as I shake my head in confusion. "That's your name," I say slowly.

"Nobody calls me that. Nobody that really knows me. *My friends.* If you can't even do that, how can I believe you?"

I chuckle lightly without humor. "Because, Lucy, you and I are not friends. We never have been and we never will be." I press my body into hers and lift her chin so she's looking at me. "We have something bigger than that and I don't want to call you what everybody else does. When I label you with a nickname, it's going to be mine, and only mine, to call you by."

Her mouth opens then closes, her eyes a whirlwind of emotions, and her body quivers against mine. "Oh," is all she says.

"We'll take this slow," I whisper against her hair. "We'll do this right. Dates, meeting the family, all of it. I know I can never be good enough for you, but let me at least try. Give me the opportunity to show you how great we can be together."

Lucy closes her eyes. "Please don't hurt me again."

I drop my head, leaning it into hers. "Never again. Not on purpose. I swear on my testicles."

She laughs and opens her eyes. We stare at one another for several seconds. I want to kiss her. I need to. She must see it in my gaze because she tilts her head just enough to bring our lips together. I nearly sigh at the pleasure this brings.

I think I love this girl, and as much as it scares the shit out of me, I'm even more frightened of not loving her.

She breaks the kiss and I almost groan. "What does this mean?" she asks.

"What does what mean?"

"For you and me. What are we?"

I smile. We've been here before, but I was a chicken-shit then. She wants it clear this time and so do I. No more bullshit. I hold her face in between my palms and touch the tip of her nose with a kiss. "You're mine. I'm yours. I want everyone to know it."

"But Jessie—"

"Jessie can deal with it. If he can't, then I'll move. But he doesn't get a say in this. And neither does Bree. This is between you and me. The only person's opinion that matters to me is yours. I'll be yours until you tell me differently. Only yours."

"You can't take that back," she murmurs. "You can't flip out and take off on me again."

All I want is her trust. I know I don't deserve it, but *I will* earn it. I want her to have no doubts. I want to be the person she knows she can always count on. "I may flip out from time to time, but I will never take off again. You'll see. You'll get tired of me being around so much."

"I'm not so sure about that. You're too fun to look at."

"I'm even better to touch," I say, smiling at her deviously.

"And to taste."

Fuck. I go completely still because I just promised to take this slow, but I'm already thinking about ripping her clothes off and tossing her onto my bed. She laughs at my reaction.

"You're going to be in trouble if you keep talking like that," I warn her.

Lucy arches a brow in challenge and I growl.

"You decide when we stop because I don't think I'll have that ability," I tell her. I wait for her to acknowledge me. As she nods, I slam my mouth against hers and start showing her how much she means to me.

33
Lucy

I had a hard time finding the stop button. When he starts touching me, everything else fades away. It's just me and him. His hands, his mouth, his chest pressed into mine. His legs tangled with mine, his scent engulfing me, his words whispering in my ears. I get caught up in his taste. I get lost in his caress. And I never want to find my way back. I could live in the moment forever.

I know it's not like this with everybody. I know what Park does to me is special. Everything feels so much better because it's him. Because I love him.

It also means things can hurt so much worse, too.

How do you love someone and still protect yourself? How can you give your heart away and trust it will be safe in another's hands?

I don't know.

But I guess I'm going to find out.

He's going to be here soon. We decided last night, while we were twisted in the sheets, our hair tousled and our fingers intertwined, that today we were telling Jessie and Bree. I'm not looking forward to the aftermath. Bree can be seriously scary when she's angry.

She thinks I deserve better, and I love her for it. But what she'll need to understand is I want Park. He's not perfect and neither am I. We aren't going to have an easy relationship, but that's okay. Nothing of worth is simple.

My phone beeps an alert and I know it's time. I look at myself in the mirror. Even though my tummy is a little queasy, I look calm. And happy.

"Okay, Lucy. You can do this," I tell my reflection. I've pissed Bree off plenty of times. She always gets over it. And Jessie…he'll eventually see that Park is different. He's not Jared.

God I hope that's true.

I catch movement over my shoulder and turn just as Park pushes my window open. I watch him, the way his bicep flexes with his movement. How his hands curl around the windowsill. The grin that lifts his cheeks.

"Hey, gorgeous."

"Hi," I return.

He glides inside with ease and makes his way directly to me. As his long fingers knot into my hair, I breathe out in relief. I hadn't realized how worried I was, but now that he's here, touching me, I notice the way my whole body relaxes.

I still feel sick to my stomach and I'm still shivering with nerves, but I'm good now.

Like all over, from the tips of my toes to the roots of my hair, I feel joy. The kind that makes you feel light. Makes you feel invincible.

"You ready for this?" Park asks, his lips brushing my hair.

"Yep. Are you?"

"I'm actually kind of excited." He pulls back, his fingers moving to hold each side of my jaw. "Everybody will know how I feel about you."

I frown, my brows pulling together.

"What?" he asks, his features matching mine.

I shake my head slowly and he drops his hands. "Everybody will know but me. How do you feel about me, Park?"

"You're everything I want."

It's the simplest sentence. Just four words. How does he do that? How does he make something so plain mean so much?

People have no idea how so few words can affect a person.

He has no idea.

I tug his shirt, pulling him against me until I can reach his lips. I need them against mine because I feel like a crybaby at the moment. I want to burst into tears because I believe him.

When I've kissed him thoroughly, I pull back slowly, making sure to soak up every last bit of his lips. "Let's do this."

He smirks. "Do you think Bree will go for my nuts or just throw shit at me?"

I bite my lip and shrug. "It could go either way. Or, more likely, both."

He winces. "Just promise you'll kiss any injuries I incur."

I laugh quietly. "Promise."

I start for the door and he grasps my hand, tugging me back. "Just one more thing," he says slowly. "I need to borrow something." I raise a brow and he steps into me. "I'll return it, I swear."

"Okay…"

Park wraps his arms around me, embracing me tightly and touches his mouth to mine softly. My lips curve up and then I feel his do the same as it occurs to me this is what he wanted. A hug and a kiss.

"All right," he murmurs. "I'm ready now."

I think I like sweet Park.

***

Bree's eyes narrow as soon as Park and I enter the living room, our fingers clasped together tightly.

Her lips twist and she sits forward, perching on the edge of the couch. Jessie's gaze barely touches on us before he reaches for Bree.

"Nu-huh," she hisses.

"B, just listen," I say, my tone composed. I want her to be okay with this—need it, actually. But I'm keeping this relationship. Whatever it is. Wherever it takes me. I'm keeping it.

"Are you really this stupid?"

"Whoa," Park says. His voice is full of warning, but Bree ignores him. She crosses her arms in front of her and shakes her head harshly.

"He cheated on you," she spits. "Don't be a doormat."

"Baby, calm down," Jessie whispers.

"No. She's being stupid."

Park's hand squeezes mine almost painfully. "Hey. That's enough. You don't agree, fine. But don't call Lucy stupid."

"Oh, my God. Are you for real?" She stands up and places her hands on her hips. I've seen the gesture more times than I can count. She's gearing up for a fight.

"I know you think this is a bad idea," I begin.

She barks out a dry laugh. "Bad idea? No, Lu, the bangs you sported in ninth grade were a *bad idea*. This is insanity. He treated you so wrong."

"I did," Park agrees before I can respond. "And I'm going to regret it forever. But Lucy and I talked and she's giving me another chance." His eyes dart over to Jessie before sliding back to Bree. "And I'm going to prove to her, to you, to everyone, that she can trust me. I care about her and I won't hurt her again."

"Pretty words Park. You should be a performer. Oh, wait. That's your job." She rolls her eyes. "I told you to stay away from her."

Park smirks. "I tried. Couldn't. And again, Bree, I do not answer to you."

Jessie rests his hand on Bree's hip as she opens her mouth to reply. "Stop," he says firmly. He looks at me, his eyes studying my face. "This is what you want?"

I nod. "Yeah, it is."

He nods back and glances at my best friend. "It's their choice. Their business."

Her mouth drops open. I think mine may have as well. "It'll be our business when he fucks her over. Again."

"If that happens we'll deal with it then."

Both of her brows shoot up and she makes a disgusted sound. "You know what?" She throws her hands up, the movement jerky. Angry. "I don't care. You do whatever you want and when he hurts you again, I don't want to hear about it." She stalks past us and out the door. I flinch when it slams loudly.

Why is someone always walking away from me?

"You knew?" Park says and I flinch again, pulling away from my thoughts.

Jessie leans back, resting his head against the back of the couch. He props his feet on the table. "Not at first, but I added until it equaled this." He flicks his index finger back and forth between me and Park.

"And you're cool?" Park questions.

Chuckling, Jessie sits forward again. He props his elbows on his knees and looks at Park. "Bree will come around. And as long as Lulu's happy, I'm cool. You fuck this up—that's a whole different story."

<u>34</u>
<u>Park</u>

This is my first show since the infamous beat down. It's also my first show with a girlfriend. I keep a tight grip on Lucy's hand as we move through the crowd. It's a good turn out since we've been M.I.A. for more than a month.

I've never had to side-step a fan before, but things are still unstable with Lucy and I'm not about to fuck this up because some drunk chick is getting handsy. Before Lucy, I would have been trying to remember the girl's face so she could take me home after I played my set. But now I'm holding the hand of the only person I want to go home with.

I purposely maneuver us around the frisky female earning me a few slurred curses.

Lucy's eyes widen and I pull her tighter to my side. I press my lips against her hair. "Stay close. I may need protection."

Breathing out a surprised laugh, Lucy shakes her head. "You're on your own, buddy. That girl is scary."

I glance over my shoulder and shudder. "Hell yeah she is."

"I'm pretty sure you can handle it," she says, her mouth turning up into a smirk.

"This may come as a shock to you, but I have no idea how to handle women." Both of her brows rise and her head tilts slightly to the side. "That I'm not having sex with," I amend.

She pauses, frowning at me. "So what you're saying is you don't know how to treat a woman if you aren't seducing her?"

I squint at her, not sure how to answer that question. But yeah. That's exactly it. Lucy's eyes narrow and I decide it'd be better if I kept that information to myself. I'll just have to figure it out. "Come on. I need a drink before I'm on."

Tugging my keys from my pocket, I hand them over to Lucy. "Keep a hold of these for me?"

"Why?"

"So you can drive. I don't drink and drive."

She sucks her bottom lip into her mouth and my gaze is instantly drawn there. "I've wanted to ask you about that." She accepts the keys, tucking them into her pocket and I lean into the bar.

"What about it?"

The bartender stops in front of me, smiling invitingly. "Haven't seen you in awhile," she says. Resting her elbows on top of the bar, she inclines forward giving me a perfect view down her shirt.

Is this what it's always like? Have I never paid attention before? My brows draw together as I try to remember if I ever got with her. She obviously knows me, but I don't recall her at all.

"Missed you around here," she continues and her eyes drop, scaling my chest.

I almost laugh because I have absolutely no desire to draw this out any longer.

And I almost want to hug her because this is the moment that I'm absolutely certain, without a shadow of a doubt, that I am mind-blowingly, 100% in love with Lucy Braden.

I tug Lucy up onto the stool. "Did you want something?" I ask, my voice low. She shakes her head and I reluctantly turn back to order a beer. The bartender sets it down in front of me slowly, eyeing Lucy before she moves on to take the next order.

I take a long drink, watching Lucy the whole time. She's struggling with something and it makes me nervous. Especially with my new insight.

"What did you want to ask me?" I prompt again now that there are no more distractions. I'd rather just get it out and over with.

She sits up, bringing herself closer to me. Instinctually, I reach for her, clasping her fingers within mine. "Is there something there? A reason other than the obvious that you're so big on not drinking and driving?"

I stare into her overly perceptive eyes and once again feel stripped bare in her presence. I'm not sure how she does this. How she sees everything. That itch to run and put some kind of distance between us presents itself with a frightening force. I release her hand and take a step back as I rake my fingers through my hair.

Clearing my throat and taking another drink, I brace myself to cut my chest open in front of this girl that I self-admittedly love. She's seen a hell of a lot of my demons surface from the shadows, but this one—this is my darkest.

"In high school," I say, but my voice catches and I have to start over. "In high school, I went to a party and got drunk." I shake my head and begin peeling the label off my bottle so I don't have to look at her as I pour my guts out.

"That's not true. I was already drunk when I got there. I got drunker. It got out of control, a fight broke out, and cops got called. I took off and Guy followed. That's common knowledge." I rub my forehead and swallow down the bile trying to rise. What I'm about to tell her nobody else knows but Guy.

Inhaling deeply, I close my eyes for a moment before chugging down the rest of my beer. And then I laugh harshly at myself. What kind of person drinks while telling the story of the time they almost killed their best friend in a drunk driving accident?

Me. I'm the kind of person.

I stretch over the bar and motion for another.

The bartender holds up a finger, telling me to hold on and I turn back to Lucy. Her warm, gray eyes watch me closely and I feel my stomach tighten. I've never cared much about what people thought of me. I'm not a good person. I know that. I've come to terms with it. And I've never tried to hide it. But I care what Lucy thinks.

"I don't want to tell you this story, but you deserve to know who I am."

She nods and I open my mouth just as another beer appears. I pick it up and take Lucy's hand, pulling her toward the back corner. I don't want to do this in front of an audience.

We sit and I lay my palms flat on the table, staring at them as I recount the events of that night.

"Guy tried to stop me from driving. He asked me—he begged me not to. He tried to take my keys and it pissed me off. I fucking shoved him. I was so mad at him for so many things and that was just the final straw." I shiver as the memory swarms up around me bringing with it all the emotion I've fought so hard to keep at bay these past two years.

"I got in my car and he stood there, this shocked look on his face. And then..." I drop my head into my hands. My eyes sting and I honestly cannot remember the last time I cried, but I feel like it could actually happen right now. I stand up, my legs pushing the chair back so quickly it topples over. I glance down at it before I kick it out of the way and walk out the side door.

As soon as the door closes behind me I light up a cigarette and take a deep hit. I need something to calm me or I'm going to lose it.

The sounds from the bar grow louder, and then small, warm hands wrap around my stomach. I place my own hands over Lucy's.

"Park," she whispers.

I pivot quickly so I'm facing her and I grip her tightly, tugging her into a hug. I breathe in the scent of her hair. If I can stay like this...

"You don't have to tell me."

"Yes I do." I pull away and pace in front of her. This is better. Just me and her. I can do this. And now that I've started, I think I need to do this.

"I don't know why I told him, Lucy," I say. "But I did. I told him..."

She doesn't rush me. She waits, her eyes wide, her hands shaking. I want to comfort her, but if I touch her I'm not sure I'll be able to get the words out.

"I told him I wanted to die."

Lucy takes in a sharp breath, but doesn't say anything. I'm glad. I'm so fucking glad she doesn't say anything because I don't think I can handle it at the moment.

"I don't know why the hell he got in the car, but he did, and I floored it. I was so drunk. I had no right to be behind a steering wheel. But I swear, if I hadn't been drinking, I never would have driven the way I did. I never would have let him get in when I was like that. I didn't... I just didn't care at the time. I wanted to be away from the party as fast as I could and I couldn't see past my own pain. I kept going faster and the next thing I knew, my face was slamming into an airbag.

"Guy almost died. He had to have emergency surgery and physical therapy. I almost killed my best friend because I didn't care if I lived or died."

I can't look at her. But I can't stand her silence either. I lean against the brick wall and finish off my cigarette.

"Say something," I rasp. I just want it over with.

I look up and meet her eyes. "Did you do it on purpose?"

"No. I don't think so. I don't know. It all happened so fast."

"Was it because of Hope?" she asks.

I pop another smoke between my lips and light it quickly. I hate this conversation. My legs are begging me to walk away, but I promised I wouldn't do that again. I started this—I'm going to see it through.

"No. Yes. It was a lot of things. It was Hope, it was my dad, it was my life. I just didn't want to keep struggling. Everything fucking hurt and I was so sick of it."

"Do you still… Do you still not care if you live or die?"

I move in front of her with determination. "I've been searching for a reason to care. I didn't even know I was fucking looking, but then you shot me in the face with that squirt gun and everything that happened before slowly stopped mattering."

I dig my fingers into her mass of hair and pull her into me. "I care," I whisper against her ear.

"You still drink. After that, you still get drunk night after night."

It's not a question. It's not an accusation. She says it so calmly, so matter-of-factly. And that's exactly what it is. It's a plain and simple fact. But I feel the tension in her body and I know it scares her. It scares me too. I'd like to reassure her, but she needs to know who I am.

"Yes, I still drink. Because that's the kind of person I am. I'm a careless, selfish bastard and I will always put my needs before anybody else's. But I don't want to be this way."

"You don't *have* to be this way," she murmurs. "You're better than that."

I don't know what it is about this girl, but when she says shit like that, I fucking believe her.

35

Lucy

The door opens quickly, slamming against the brick wall. "Hey, man. We're on." I look up at the drummer from Park's band and he lifts his chin, acknowledging me.

"Give me a few more minutes, Lewis. Okay?" Park doesn't look away from me, so he doesn't see Lewis nod his agreement before heading back inside.

As Park leans in to kiss me, I catch the remaining faded bruise near his eye, and a shocking realization hits me. I press on his chest, holding him back. "If you care, why didn't you fight back?"

His dark brows draw together in confusion. "What?"

I feel my eyes beginning to water. My stomach twists and I feel sick. I reach out, resting my hand on the building for support. "You didn't fight back when those guys jumped you, Park. I know you didn't. And if you care now, like you say you do, then why would you do that?"

I study his face, waiting for some kind of explanation. For him to give me something. Some kind of hope. Anything to take this feeling away. He shakes his head, his face paling more and more with each passing second.

"Tell me," I plead. Was that what he was trying to do? Was he trying to die that night? I think I'm going to throw up. "Tell me," I say louder.

"I don't know what to say."

"The truth." My voice quivers over the two small words. "Did you care the night you let those guys hurt you?"

"Yes." He twists his fingers into his hair, his eyes flicking over my face. "I cared, but I couldn't take all the shit that was running through my head. There was just too much. I wanted to feel less...or different. I don't know. Once they started on me, everything else faded, and... I honestly don't know. It was stupid, but I learned my lesson. I've paid for it, believe me."

The door opens again and Park closes his eyes, his jaw tight. "Dude, they're getting impatient," Lewis calls. "You need to get in here."

I reach out and take Park's hand. His eyes open, peering down at our interlocked fingers and I tug lightly. "Come on. Your fans are getting rowdy." I offer him a smile and he finally moves toward the door with me.

Just before I'm about to step inside, he twists us away, pressing me into the wall, and kisses me. His lips on mine, his taste on my tongue, it eases the anxiety of the past few minutes. I melt into him, holding on to this moment.

He pulls back and draws his thumb across my lip. "I don't love you," I breathe.

His head tips to the side. One side of his mouth twitches up into a smirk and he cocks a brow. His thumb trails down until he's caressing my neck. "I don't love you either," he says softly. "Not at all."

"Dude, *seriously*," Lewis announces, the frustration evident in his voice. "Crazy, horny females getting out of control in here. Let's go, dickhead."

"You better go." I give him a little shove and he grabs my hand.

"Are you going to be with Jessie?"

I nod. "And Bree. If I can find them."

"They should be up front." He pauses and grins. "I'll see you after the show."

"Okay," I agree. "Good luck, break a leg, and all that."

His smile widens. He leans into me, his breath warm on my skin. "Just so you know—I lied," he states. And then he saunters off, leaving me to watch as he hops up on the stage and grabs the mic from the stand.

What did he lie about? The same thing I lied about? I bite down on my lip and turn to find Bree. I take two steps and slam into a hard chest. I bounce back, nearly falling. Large hands reach out gripping my arms.

"I'm so sorry," I say, embarrassed. "Thanks for the save." I tip my head back to see who I nearly trampled and my heart jumps into my throat.

"Hi Lulu. You look good."

"Jared." I yank my arms from his grasp, crossing them over my chest.

"How've you been?" he asks. He moves closer as if to hear me better over the crowd, but I don't want him that close. I step back.

"Great. You?"

"I've missed you."

He missed me. *Right.*

I narrow my eyes, taking in his long, sandy colored hair that I used to think was so sexy, and his hazel eyes that used to captivate me. And I feel nothing. Absolutely nothing for this man. He's just a stranger now. And I wonder how I ever cried over him.

I smile at him sweetly like he's one of my difficult customers. "I can't say the same. Enjoy the show. I'll tell Jessie you said hi."

He rubs his lips together, his fingers working through his mane of hair. "Jessie's here?"

I nod as I glance around. "Mm-hm. Somewhere."

"He still pissed at me?"

"I couldn't say." I'm done with this conversation. I just want to find my friends and watch my boyfriend sing. I look over my shoulder, wondering why they haven't started yet and meet Park's eyes. His brows lift in question and I shake my head.

"You know that guy?" Jared asks, drawing my attention back to him.

"He's my boyfriend." I sidestep him and he turns with me, cutting me off.

"You're joking, right?"

I finally spot the top of Bree's head, bouncing up and down. I can picture her springing back and forth from her toes to her heels like she does when she gets impatient. "What?" I say, distracted.

"You're not really with Park Reed, are you?"

I put my hands out at my sides, palms up. "Why?"

"You had a stick up your ass over me, but you'll get with him? Doesn't make sense." He chuckles, his eyes roaming over me.

I feel my nose crinkle in disgust. "Don't compare yourself to Park. You don't even come close to measuring up."

I look back up to the stage. Park's placing the mic back on the stand and I know he's getting ready to come down here. Jared needs to back up now.

"I have to go," I add as I push past him. The instant I make contact with him, the night of the party rushes in with a series of bad memories.

"Hey, you should take my number," Jared calls reaching for my arm. "You can hit me up when he's done with you." I jerk away. I don't want his hands on me.

Asshole. Asshole. Asshole. I glare up at him. He puts his hands up and shrugs.

"Just being honest."

"No, you're being a jerk." I glance back and I can't see Park on stage anymore. "Look," I say, "you need to walk away. I don't want your number. I don't want anything to do with you. I haven't since the night you showed your true colors."

"Yeah. All right," he replies. "It was nice seeing you, Lulu." His eyes cling to me as they travel my body. "Good luck with your *boyfriend*." The way he says boyfriend makes me want to punch him, but I just turn around and start making my way through the crowd, searching for Park.

Like he has some special radar I'm attuned with, I find him quickly. I wiggle past a few girls circled together talking loudly in their drunken states. And then he's in front of me.

"Hey."

"Who was that?" He looks over my head as if he's trying to locate him.

I wave my hand through the air, brushing away his question. "Jared. He's just this guy I used to know."

"Jared?" Park's eyes narrow. "Jessie's last roommate?"

I frown at him. "Yeah. You know him?"

"Just what Jessie's told me. What'd he fucking say to you? Did that motherfucker touch you?"

"I took care of it," I say. "Shouldn't you be working?" I remind him.

He shakes his head sharply, taking my hand. "Not until I get you over to Jessie. I know he'll kick that dude's ass if he fucks with you again."

He takes his cell out of his pocket and clicks out a quick text before returning his attention to me. "What'd he say to you? You looked upset."

"It doesn't matter," I say.

"It matters to me," Park counters, his voice turning almost scary.

"He was just being a jerk. I handled it. You'd have been proud of me." I wink, trying to reassure him.

"I'm always proud of you." He squeezes my hand. "But if he comes near you again I'm going to beat his fucking ass."

I huff out a laugh. "Calm down, caveman."

"I'm serious, Lucy. I didn't like the look on your face when he was talking to you. It makes me want to kill him. I'm actually using a hell of a lot of self-control not going after him right now."

My peace loving parents would be appalled over his speech, but I'm overwhelmed with the desire to pounce on him and kiss him silly. Because not only is it his first instinct to protect me from someone who upsets me, but also for the simple fact that he's holding that instinct back to stay and make sure I'm okay.

I'm pretty sure I'm falling helplessly in love with him.

**

As soon as the last song ends, Park hops off the stage and makes his way straight to me. Taking my hand, he tugs me out of my seat, and wordlessly pulls me out the door.

"What's wrong?" I ask as we near his car.

He swings me around quickly, his hands sliding around my hips as he backs me up against the door. His body invades my personal space, making my heart beat erratically how only Park can. "The only thing wrong is that we're here, talking about what's wrong, instead of at home. In bed."

"Oh, you're tired?" I tease breathlessly.

"Hell no. Sleep is the last thing on my mind. But I do want you in my bed. Naked. For the rest of the night." His fingers tighten, pressing into my skin in this way that makes my whole body come alive for him. Only him.

"What are you waiting for then?"

"This…" Leaning in, he licks his lips just before touching them to mine. And that's all it takes. My hand goes to his stomach. I twist his shirt, pulling him closer in order to deepen the kiss.

He draws back, focusing his attention under my ear. "I'm so close to ripping your clothes off right here, right now, in this parking lot." His mouth drags across my neck as the words leave his lips and I shiver. I know Park undoubtedly has full control over me because I'd let him. I'd let him tear the clothes from my body if he really wanted to. I'd let him do whatever he wanted to me.

His hand slides into the space between my skin and my jeans. My hips automatically move into his touch. He slips in further until the tips of his fingers dip inside my panties and I'm so desperate for him to make contact, a small whimper sounds from my throat.

"Fuck, Lucy," Park groans. "I don't know what the hell you do to me, but I have never in my life wanted someone like I want you."

"Oh, my God," I moan. "Touch me, Park. Please."

He retracts his hand and I nearly cry out at the loss. Reaching past me, he grips the door handle. He shifts me to the side and then he's pushing me into the car. I'm all for a hot and heavy backseat viewing, but he takes the keys from my pocket and starts the engine instead.

"Pout those gorgeous lips all you want, Lucy. I'll be turning that frown upside down as soon as we get home." His long fingers settle over my thigh and he squeezes. "And I'll have you smiling, too."

I laugh at his devil's smirk, but it doesn't come out right. It's raspy and breathy from the way my insides are twisting with anticipation.

<u>36</u>

<u>Park</u>

"Mine or yours?" I ask, my hands cupping Lucy's face.

"Yours. It's closer."

God I was hoping she'd say that. I practically shove her through the door, kicking it closed behind us. I'm so torn because I want to take my time with her. I want to draw this out, make it last as long as possible, but at the same time, I want to ravage her. I want to eat this girl up and drink her down.

I stop guiding her and she comes to a standstill in front of my bed.

I take a second to appreciate the miracle that she's here. I love the way she looks, standing there in her tight jeans, her shirt hanging off her shoulder, and her long hair loose and wild. There can't be anything more perfect.

Her eyes fall over my movements as I stalk toward her. I remove her shirt first, letting it fall to the floor. "I've had dreams that begin right here," I say, my voice low, husky. "Dreams so fucking vivid that when I wake up and you aren't in my bed it physically hurts. I want you here all night. I want to see the sunlight on your bare skin in the morning. And I want to taste everywhere it touches."

She nods, the motion fluid, hypnotic.

I flick the button on her jeans and drag the zipper down slowly. Her eyes haven't left me for a second. I meet her gaze and the sight of that stormy gray makes me suck in a harsh breath. "You're beautiful."

Without a word, she takes a step, landing us chest to chest. She works her hands under my shirt, her fingers gliding up my stomach. "You make me feel beautiful when you look at me like that."

"I'll never look at you any differently." I lower myself in front of her and work her pants down her legs. The moment they're past her feet, she drops to her knees, and her lips meet my neck. Her wet tongue leaves a trail of heat followed by a chill of cold as the air cools it. It feels so good I shiver as instinct has me grasping her neck.

Lucy directs me back, her chest pressing into me until I'm lying down. She pushes my shirt up, baring my stomach and most of my chest. Her nails caress the skin there, following an invisible path to my pants. She has them open quickly, releasing me from the restricted space. I thrust my hips off the floor as her hand takes hold of me.

"Get on," I moan.

She stares at me, sucking her bottom lip into her mouth in a way that makes me jerk in her hand. "Condom?"

"Fuck. In the drawer." I push myself up and tug my shirt over my head as I hurry to the dresser. I pluck two out of the box and let my jeans fall as I make my way back to her. I watch her unhook her bra and even though I've already seen every inch of Lucy, my breath still hitches in my throat.

She wiggles as she maneuvers her panties over her thighs and I can't stop staring at her. Every single movement—every single twitch of her muscles has me spellbound. I sink to my hands and knees and crawl over top of her. My mouth slams into hers and I follow her as she lays back, our lips never separating.

I feel her take the condoms from my hand and as I move from her mouth to her breast, I feel her place the condom on me. I shift to give her better access as I continue to massage her flesh with my tongue.

She guides me inside and I moan, sinking my teeth into her nipple. She gasps, digging her fingertips into the back of my head and holding me in place. I begin to move, gradually at first, and she feels amazing. I sweep her leg up, positioning myself deeper. The sweetest sound emanates from between those flawless lips and I know this is my heaven. This is my permanent bliss.

"Lucy," I murmur. "Tell me." I shift quickly to her other breast, pulling her nipple between my teeth. "Say it."

She doesn't ask me what I mean. She doesn't even hesitate and I realize how important this is.

"I'm yours," she utters. She places her hands on each side of my face, drawing my head up. Our eyes meet and she brushes her thumb across my cheek. "And you're mine."

I go still as I gaze down at her. Something's just ripped open inside of me with those words. Or maybe it's been mended. I honestly don't know what the hell just happened, but Jesus, I want to feel this every second for the rest of my life.

I press my forehead to hers and just breathe.

"You've just surpassed all my best dreams," I tell her weakly.

***

Lucy and I have fallen into an easy pattern over the past week, which basically consists of spending every available moment with each other. It's actually not been a lot of time with us both back in classes and Lucy working full time. We've had two dates. Nothing big— we went out to lunch once and to a movie last night. It's weird because I've never done this whole dating thing before. Not even with Hope. But I like it. I like the small things, like holding her hand, or the way she ordered me a milk when I was out smoking, or how she raised the armrest at the theater and snuggled against me.

The best part is at night when she curls into my side, resting her head on my chest. No matter how busy our days are, we have all night with each other. Sometimes we stay up talking. Sometimes we make love. Yeah—I said make love. I'm not even sorry.

If this is what it's like, I'm cool with it.

Life lesson number 12: As your life changes, change your rules accordingly. Nothing is set in stone when it comes to living.

I lean back on her bed, waiting for her to finish in the shower. I wanted to join her, but she hasn't been feeling well. Part of me wonders if it has anything to do with Jared. If that fucker upset her enough to make her sick to her stomach, I swear I'll kill him. She still hasn't told me what he said even though I've asked a few times. She just brushes it off, but since that night, she's been tired and queasy. I know anxiety can do crazy things to a person's body.

Maybe she's doing too much, wearing herself down.

I hope I didn't cause this. That was the same night I confessed some pretty big shit. My jaw clenches with the thought.

I watch her when she finally glides into the room. She falls onto the bed, her hair wet and smelling of honey suckle. Inhaling deeply, soaking up her scent, I roll to my side and rest my hand on her hip.

"I love finding you in my bed," she says quietly. "It might be the best part of my day."

I lean in and kiss her softy. She grasps my hair and pulls me closer, deepening the kiss. Her lips move with need as her tongue searches mine out and I growl deep in my throat.

Her body stiffens and she pulls back.

"You okay?"

"Hm-mm," she groans.

"Lucy? What's wrong?"

Shaking her head, she sits up and takes a deep breath. "I'm really dizzy. I just need a minute."

Her skin is pale. I push myself up so I can reach her face. She doesn't feel feverish. Pushing my hand away, she darts out of the room and I try to follow. But I get the bathroom door shut in my face.

So that's what that feels like.

"Lucy, baby, you okay?"

"What's going on?" Jessie steps out into the hall shirtless and looking like he just woke up. He rubs his face and yawns.

"She's not feeling well."

"Again?"

I nod.

"Damn," he sighs. As he runs his hand through his hair, I catch sight of something on his inner bicep.

"What the hell's that?" I tip my head, indicating what I think is a tattoo on his arm.

Jessie's mouth twitches as if he's holding back a smile. He crosses his arms over his chest and shrugs. "It's a bee."

"A bee." I deadpan.

Clearing his throat and scratching his chin, he shrugs again. "Yeah. Ya know, a bee, as in B—for

Bree." He touches his inner arm. "This is where her head goes when we sleep. It's her spot."

I raise a brow. "Well isn't that sweet?" I say flatly. "I cannot believe you actually did that. There is no way in hell I'd ever permanently ink my skin with a girl's name." He's been acting like a dumbass ever since he and Bree became exclusive.

Jessie smirks, shaking his head. "First, it's not her name. Second, I'm not you."

"Clearly," I retort.

He opens his mouth to respond, but stops short at the sound of Lucy losing her last meal.

"Shit," I murmur. "Lucy, you all right?" I hate being on this side. Shouldn't I be in there with her? Like holding her hair back or some shit? I want to at least let her know I'm here. I reach for the doorknob and Bree pushes me out of the way.

"Idiot," she hisses as she flings the door open.

Lucy sits back, pressing her back into the side of the bathtub and draws her knees to her chest. Bree wets a washcloth and kneels beside her. I'm not sure what I'm supposed to do and I don't like it. I don't like feeling helpless. I need to do something to make her feel better.

Bree leans into her and whispers something. Lucy's eyes snap up to meet mine and she nods her head slowly.

"You need to go to the store," Bree tells me, her voice firm and icy cold.

"Yeah, whatever she needs," I say, relieved to have something to do. Someway to help.

"Ginger Ale," Jessie says. "That's supposed to help with stomach issues."

Lucy drops her head and hugs her legs.

"Morons." Bree huffs out a frustrated breath. "She needs a pregnancy test."

Wait.

What?

No.

Just wait.

"What the fuck?" Jessie spits. "I'm going to fucking kill you."

"Wait," I say aloud this time. I hold my hands up, palms out. I need to think. I can't think right now. My gaze falls on Lucy and her eyes are shining with unshed tears. She's still pale and she looks confused. Scared.

That halts my panic immediately.

I step into the bathroom and rest my hand on the door. "Get out, Bree."

"Oh hell no. You—"

"OUT. Now."

Lucy closes her eyes and trails her fingers over her bare knees. "Give us a minute, B. Please."

Narrowing her eyes on me, Bree pushes herself up. She pokes her finger into my chest. "You better not say one God damned thing to upset her or I'll rip your nuts right off."

"I don't doubt it."

As soon as she passes me, I close the door and turn to face Lucy. "You're pregnant?"

Her shoulders jerk and she sighs. "I think I might be."

"But we've always used—"

"The shower," she whispers.

Ah, the shower. I almost laugh. The one and *only* time I don't use a condom… I shove both hands into my hair and tug. Why did I do that? *How* could I do that? I wanted her so badly that I didn't think. I didn't *care*. I just needed her and nothing else mattered.

I drop in front of her, resting on one knee. "It'll be okay," I say. "We'll do whatever you want. Hell, we don't even know yet."

She smiles weakly at me. "I'm pretty sure, Park. I keep getting sick and my period's late. I just..." She shakes her head and bites down on her lip. "I'm pretty sure," she repeats.

"I'll go get the test. We'll go from there." I stand up and offer her my hand. I refuse to believe anything until I have a definitive answer in front of me.

***

The door opens and my eyes automatically go to the thin plastic tube sitting on the counter.

"Three minutes," Lucy says. Her voice is shaky. I want to comfort her, but I can't. I'm pissed off at myself and it's holding me back. And I don't know what she's thinking. She probably hates me. I hate me.

If this test comes back positive it ruins everything. I'll have ruined three lives because I couldn't fucking bag it.

I don't know how to be a dad. I'll fuck it up.

I fuck everything up.

I need a cigarette so badly, but I won't leave Lucy alone. Damn it. My chest hurts. My stomach is knotted. I can't lose her. The past couple weeks have been the best of my life. It can't end now.

I look at my phone. One more minute.

One more minute and everything could change.

I'm nineteen. Lucy's only twenty. We're too young to be parents. What about school? How do we finish school? We have to finish. Can't get a good job without school. Can't raise a kid without a good job.

Maybe she doesn't want to keep it. She's adopted, maybe she'll want to put it up for adoption. Maybe she'll want an abortion.

I bite my thumb nail as I watch her. She's perched on the side of the bathtub, her eyes refusing to move anywhere near the counter where our future sits.

A kid.

There could be a kid—my kid—growing inside her right now. It could have her eyes and her lips. Her voice and her sweet personality.

Would that really be so bad?

But it'd have a part of me in it too. That can't be good. Even if it were to be like her, I'd probably do something to screw it up.

I look down at my phone again, tapping my foot. I stare at the numbers. "It's time," I choke out.

Lucy's chest rises as she takes a deep breath, but she doesn't move in any other way. "What's it say?"

Fuck. She wants me to look?

I step in front of the counter and pick up the box. I want to read the directions one more time. Okay...two lines means positive. One line is negative.

I set the box down and pick up the test.

And I just stare at it, trying to grasp one of the emotions rushing through me.

"What's it say?" she asks, her voice low.

I blink. Check the box one more time and shake my head slowly. With a trembling hand, I hold it out to her.

I'm going to be a fucking dad.

37
Lucy

I'm going to be a mom. I knew it, but I couldn't believe it. My hand automatically goes to my stomach. There's a person inside of me. A teeny, tiny, little person.

I hope he looks like Park. I hope he has his eyes and his hair.

Oh, my God. I'm pregnant.

I stare at the test as if it will change if I keep looking.

"Okay," I stammer. "Okay. This is probably the last thing you expected—or wanted to happen." I take a deep breath, my eyes still focused on the small, plastic stick in my hand. "I'm not going to ask anything of you. You don't have to be involved."

"What?" Park croaks. "What are you saying?"

"It takes a lot of commitment to be a parent…" I flick my wrist, shaking the test. Maybe I should take another one. This could be faulty.

"So you want to keep it?"

Park's words hit me and I lift my head to read the expression on his face, but it's indecipherable. "I want to keep the baby," I confirm.

"And you don't want me involved?"

His dark eyes hold me in place as I try to express one of the many thoughts in my head. "I can't make you be someone you're not."

He takes a step backward and crosses his arms, his head dropping until his eyes are hidden from my view.

"You don't want me involved. Just say it, Lucy."

"That's not it. That's not it at all. I want you to be there every step of the way, but how can I trust that you'll do that? I can't have you take off on me again. Not with a baby in the picture. You can't…you can't do that to a child. You can't just decide one day that you don't want him."

I blink several times, trying to will the moisture away. I don't know why I always tear up. I've heard pregnant women are even more emotional because their hormones get all out of whack. Great. Something to look forward to.

"Jeremy's mom was young when she had him. I don't know all the details because my parents wouldn't tell me everything, but from what I was told, she couldn't handle the responsibility. She bounced him around from home to home, whoever would take him in for awhile. Eventually she ran out of people willing to help her out and when it came down to partying or Jeremy, she chose the party."

I take another deep breath and sigh. "He was five, Park. He remembers some of it. He remembers that his mom chose to give him up rather than give up her lifestyle. It took a long time…" I shake my head quickly and push my hair off my shoulder. "He still has a hard time with it. My mom has to constantly remind him that we want him. That we chose him."

"And you think that'll be me?" His eyes are like weights bearing down on me.

"It could be. You can't blame me for thinking it."

"No, I can't. I've given you every reason to think that about me." He moves cautiously toward me before lowering himself to sit on the floor. "But I'm going to give you a reason to be certain that I'll never do that to my kid."

My stomach tightens as he claims his child and I nearly launch myself at him. Instead, I slide off the tub's edge and get comfortable beside him.

"Guy, Hope, Chase, they're the only ones that know about my family. I don't really share personal shit about myself."

I laugh dryly—I can't help it. His brows raise and I touch his hand. "Sorry. Go on."

"My dad's come and gone in and out of my life so many times... It's different, but I know how Jeremy feels. The whole: Why wasn't I enough? What did I do wrong? What could I have done better? What could I have done to make him stay?

"I know all that well." He scoops my hand up, engulfing it in both of his. He stares down at my palm as his thumbs rub over my skin.

"Dad's been married...three times? I can't remember for sure. And after every marriage, every girlfriend that doesn't work out, he comes home." He shakes his head and pulls his gaze up to meet mine. "Mom always takes him back because he's my dad. Because she loves him. Because deep down he's a good person. She has more excuses, I just can't think of them all right now.

"So he comes home, he's my dad for a few months, and then he takes off again. I found out—that night I told you about, the night of the car accident—I found out he had another kid. A daughter. She's older. I've never met her and until two years ago, I never knew she existed.

"It wasn't just us he was always leaving. He'd been doing it to her even longer."

"Park," I whisper. I open my mouth again, to say something—anything to take away his pain, but I have no words. I crawl into his lap and wrap my arms around his neck. He pulls me in tight, burying his face into my hair.

"I may not be good for a baby—hell, Lucy, I know I'm no good for *you*—but I'm going to try. I won't abandon my kid."

"You're good for me," I say firmly. And he is. He isn't a perfect man, but he's perfect for me. "I swear I don't love you one bit," I say softly.

He nods. "Not one single bit."

***

"Can I come in?" Bree asks as she hovers in the doorway.

I nod and she settles beside me on the side of my bed. I'm still holding the test. I can't stop looking at it. Her fingers wrap around my wrist. She pulls my arm toward her and reads the results.

"I get to throw your baby shower. Your mom can help, but the planning is all mine."

I laugh, a quick burst of air from my chest that echoes off the walls. This is precisely why she's my best friend. Without a shadow of a doubt, she knows I'll keep this baby.

"So...where'd Park go?"

I shake my head and shrug at the same time. "He just said he had something he had to do."

"Is he freaking out?"

I lie back, my feet hanging off the side of the bed. "Actually, I think he's taking it really well. Possibly better than I am."

"Bullshit." She leans back on her elbows so she can see me better. "Seriously?"

"Seriously. He's obviously freaked out—I mean we're talking about a human life and Park being responsible for said human life. He's scared the same as I am. But he…" I turn my head and smile at her. "He wants to be there."

"And you trust him?" She cringes. "I'm sorry. As your best friend and godmother to your unborn baby, I have to ask."

"I trust him. I don't know why, but I do. I believe him. I believe *in* him."

"You know, if someone had told me three months ago that you'd be having Park Reed's love child, I would have punched them in the face, and then I would have rolled on the floor laughing."

I chuckle as I shift, staring up at the butterflies hanging from my ceiling. "I know, right? If anybody would've told me that I'd be having a baby—period. My mom is either going to be ecstatic or disown me."

"Mary's cool. She'll roll with the baby blow. Now your dad...he may hurt Park in ways that make it impossible for him to ever father another child."

Pressing my lips together, I nod at the ceiling. "That's the honest to God truth."

"Mm-hm." The silence stretches as the image of my dad chasing Park through the apartment fills my mind. Bree sits up and turns to face me. "Can I come with you when you tell them? And can I bring my camera?"

38
Park

"Hello?"

"Hey, Hope," I say into the phone. "It's me."

"What's up?" She says it lightly, but even after all this time, I recognize the slight tremor in her tone.

"I wanted…" I take a deep breath and release it slowly as I try to focus my thoughts. "I needed to tell you that I understand. I didn't get it before, but I get it now."

"I need you to be a little more specific," she replies quietly.

"You can love someone, hell, you can love a lot of someones, but when you find the right person—the one that you're meant to be with—it's like…"

"You can breathe for the first time," she finishes for me.

"Yes." I can't help but smile. "I needed to find that to understand."

"And you have," she says softly. "Lucy."

"Lucy," I agree. "You forgave me for hurting you. I just wanted to do the same."

She's quiet for a moment and I wonder if she heard me. "Thank you, Park. That means a lot. And I'm happy for you."

"Shit, Hope. Me too. I'm happy as hell." I shake my head, still surprised that I can feel this way. "Do me a favor?"

"Sure."

"Tell Mason I said it worked. And...tell him thanks."

"Okay," she agrees. "I'll talk to you later." It comes out almost like she's asking.

"Yeah. Talk to you later."

***

I roll onto the bed and shake my head. "I can't do it."

"Why?" Lucy's delicate brows crinkle in confusion and I run my finger over them. She grabs my wrist, pulling my hand away from her face. "Why?" she repeats.

I let my head fall back onto the pillow and sigh heavily. "What if I do something wrong?" I can't look at her as I say it aloud, so I stare up at the swaying butterflies floating above our heads. "What if I poke it and hurt it."

Her burst of laughter causes me to narrow my eyes as I turn back to her.

She pouts out her lips and I feel desire stir for her, but I ignore it. I'm not doing it. Ever since the doctor confirmed what we already knew, all I can think about is my dick jabbing my kid in the forehead over and over. How the hell do guys have sex with pregnant women? How is that shit not running through their heads every second?

"You're giving yourself an awful lot of credit, don't you think?" One eyebrow arches as she regards me. "I mean, not once in the history of the world has a single unborn child been poked and hurt during sex, yet you think you're capable of doing just that."

"Yes," I hiss.

"You know that the baby is surrounded by amniotic fluid, inside my uterus, right? And my uterus is completely protected by my closed cervix?"

"I paid attention in health class, trust me," I say. "So I also know that the cervix can dilate early and your water can break."

"Not this early."

"You can't be sure," I reply.

She opens her mouth as she searches for an argument, her head shaking slowly from side to side. "The chances are so slim that both of those things would happen and I wouldn't be aware of it."

That's actually a valid point. She'd probably notice her water breaking at least.

"And even if that did happen, I still don't think you'd *reach* far enough to cause any damage."

I scoff at her. "Oh, I'd reach."

She eyes me with an unbelieving expression and shrugs her shoulders. "Okay, you'd reach."

"I would," I insist.

"What? I said you would."

"You said it, but you didn't mean it. Don't humor me."

"I think I was actually patronizing you," she quips, her mouth twitching as she fights a smile.

Damn it. She's right. I tip my head, watching her for a moment. "Have you decided what you want to major in yet?"

I catch her by surprise with the change in subject. The crease between her brows appears once again and I smooth it with my finger.

"No."

"I think you should be an English major."

Lucy turns onto her side to face me, resting her cheek against her hand. "I've actually thought about that. It doesn't really matter now though. I'll probably just finish this semester and then go back whenever I can."

Whoa. Wait.

"What? You can't quit. I agree you'll have to take a semester or two off, but you have to finish school."

She twists her hair and flings it over her shoulder. "Babies cost money, Park. I'm going to have to work. I was thinking I could be home with the baby during the day while you're in classes and then I could work at night. I can try to work around your shows, and any shifts I can't get around, I'll have Bree babysit."

I rub my hands over my face roughly. "You have it all worked out."

"I'm working it out as I go."

"What if I stayed with it while you went to school? And if I picked up extra gigs you could just work on weekends or something."

"When would you go to school?"

I shrug. "I wouldn't."

Lucy sits up and glares at me. "You have to go to school."

I push myself up, mirroring her. "Why? Why do I have to go, but it's okay for you to drop out? You're farther in than I am. You're throwing away more."

"That's bullshit and you know it. It makes more sense for me to take the time off. I'm not on academic scholarship."

That pauses my retort. I close my mouth audibly.

"Hope told me," Lucy says quietly. "I can't believe you think throwing away a scholarship is better than me taking time off when I'm going to need the time off anyway." She puckers her lips and looks away. "You weren't even going to tell me you have a free ride."

"It isn't free. I worked my ass off for it."

She huffs out a dry laugh. "You're just proving my point. I'm not letting you give it up."

I sigh. "I fucked up your life enough. I don't want to take school away from you too."

"Hey," she says harshly. "First of all, I was there too. I hold just as much responsibility for this pregnancy as you do. Secondly, you aren't taking anything away from me. College will still be there when the time is right for me to go back. And third—it's seriously messed up to say you fucked up my life. This baby isn't fucking up my life. Yes, I was shocked and scared—I'm still scared, but I'm also happy. We're having a baby. It's not ideal. We didn't do this anywhere close to how I always pictured it happening, but that doesn't mean this is a bad thing. And when you say things like that, it makes me feel like you think you're life is fucked up now because of me and the baby."

She inhales deeply and exhales with a large puff of air. I don't think I've ever heard Lucy say "fuck" so many times in one rant. She's really upset.

"Okay," I say calmly. "I don't think you fucked up my life. Not at all. You make my life better. It's just a lot of change and I've only had a week to adjust. I'll get this right, Lucy. I'm going to make a lot of mistakes. I always will, but I'm trying."

"I know you are," she agrees softly. "I know you are."

***

"You're going to have to say that again, much slower this time," Guy states as he sits heavily on the couch.

"Lucy. Is. Pregnant," I say clearly. "She's almost eight weeks. She's keeping it."

"Yours, right?" Chase asks as he leans back in the chair, resting his hands behind his head.

I point at him, my eyes narrowing as I contemplate punching him in the throat. "Fuck you. You know it is." He chuckles, dropping his hands to his knees.

"Why do you keep calling the baby an 'It'?" Guy asks.

"What?"

"'It'. You keep referring to your baby as 'It'. He. She. The baby. Any of those will work. 'It' is what people call animals and inanimate objects."

Shit. Have I been doing that?

Son of a… I have.

That's kind of fucked up.

"Shut up," I reply. I pace in front of the coffee table, my hands on my hips. "I don't know what the hell I'm doing. Okay? I need—I need someone to tell me what to do."

I watch Guy cross his arms in front of his chest and his cheeks lift as he smiles. "Dude, you're going to choke. *Daddy.*"

"Right?" Chase laughs in agreement. "You can't even keep a girlfriend. If you can't handle an adult, how in the hell do you think you're going to handle a baby?" He sits forward and smacks the table. "Oh shit. You're going to have to change diapers. Shit and piss. Baby puke."

"You guys are the shittiest friends, ever. I don't know why I tried to have a serious conversation with either of you."

Guy stands up, holding his hands out in front of him. "Man, we're just messing with you." He rubs his forehead and sighs. "This is big."

"Huge," Chase concurs.

"Enormous," I add.

"So what are you going to do?" Guy asks.

I shrug. "I'm having a baby."

Chase grins. "We're having a baby."

Guy hands me a controller and settles back onto the couch. "We better get in as much gaming as we can now before your progeny gets here."

"We'll teach the next generation of Reed to play too, right?" Chase verifies.

"We're talking about my kid," I say. "He'll come out holding a controller."

Chase shakes his head and smiles deviously. "Hopefully that's all he's holding. If your kid comes out with a liquor bottle and a pack of cigarettes, I'm going to be a little scared of him."

I press the back of my head into the cushion as the image fills my mind.

"This is Lucy's baby too," Guy reminds Chase.

"Oh, yeah. Okay, maybe not cigarettes. Maybe a fat sack of pot and flowers."

"Lucy doesn't smoke pot," I tell him.

He scrunches his nose. "What kind of hippie doesn't smoke pot?"

"Lucy," I say. "She doesn't smoke, she barely drinks. She's good."

"Then why in the hell is she with you?"

"I honestly can't tell you the answer to that." I smirk at him. "You'll have to ask her. I'm just really fucking glad she is."

<u>39</u>

<u>Lucy</u>

Park and I are on our way to my parent's house. Today is the day I'm telling them about the baby. I'm nervous. And I'm not sure if the nauseous feeling in my stomach is morning sickness or my shattered nerves.

"You doing okay?" Park asks. He picks up my hand, his fingers intertwining with mine. This small gesture quiets some of the worry and I smile.

"Yeah, I'm good. How are you doing?"

"I've been better," he mutters. "This isn't the way I wanted to meet your parents. What am I supposed to say? 'Hi, I'm the asshole that knocked up your lovely daughter. Nice to meet you?'"

I tip my head like I'm thinking about it. "You may want to start off with a better opening."

He grunts. "I'm serious. I've never done this meet the family bit. I've never cared if parents liked me." He squeezes my hand firmly and his gaze meets mine quickly. "I care now. I don't want your mom and dad to hate me. This..." He sighs. "This is important to me."

I have to look away because my stupid eyes are tearing up once again. I wonder if he realizes the impact his words have on me.

"Maybe that should be your opening line."

"'Please don't hate me because your daughter means everything to me.' It could work." He grins. "If that doesn't work, I could always hook your dad up with my supplier."

"Mm. A mellow dad is a happy dad." I pull my sunglasses out of my hair and cover my eyes as I lay my head back.

"You tired?"

"A little." I'm always tired now. I don't know how someone so tiny can wear me down so much. The doctor assured me it's normal. I've been taking my prenatal vitamins and Park has been on top of making sure I'm eating. Bree treats me as if I'm made of glass, not letting me do much around the house. And even with all that, I can't keep my eyes open past 10 PM.

That's not even close to being the worst of it. My breasts hurt. And I have cramps. The doctor said that's my uterus stretching. This is only nine weeks in. I still have thirty-one more weeks of this and I don't know what to expect next.

It has to get better, though, right?

***

I haven't brought a guy home since I started college. In my twenty years, I've only ever had two serious boyfriends outside of Park. So it shouldn't have surprised me when my parents fawned all over him to the point of embarrassment.

We sit down for lunch and before Park can take the seat next to me, Ozzy hurries to fill it, forcing Park to sit across from me instead.

"Are you in school with Lulu?" Dad asks.

Park nods. "I'm a sophomore."

"He's attending on an academic scholarship," I add. I figure it's better to point out Park's attributes before I tell them I'm having his baby. Maybe I should wait. Maybe I shouldn't tell them today. I mean, it's the first time they're meeting. I shouldn't ruin this by igniting a nuclear bomb.

Yeah. I should probably wait. I have plenty of time to tell them later. Today can just be about them getting to know Park.

Yeah. That sounds like a good idea.

"How are classes going, Lu?" Mom inquires.

"Uh…good. They're good."

"And your professors? You like them this semester?"

"Um, yeah, I guess."

"You guess?" Mom sets her fork down and focuses her full attention on me as she studies my face.

"No. I mean, they're good. Everything is good."

Mom locks her fingers together as she continues to watch me. Her eyes narrow slightly and she clears her throat. "So everything's good. That's good."

"Park," Dad begins and I hear the silent laughter in his voice. "Has Lucy told you about her complete disdain for clothing during her preschool years?"

I roll my eyes, shaking my head. And here we go...

"Couldn't keep clothes on her for anything," Mom continues.

"She was kicked out of preschool," Dad goes on.

Mom nods as her eyes light up. "Poor Sister Marie was nearly hospitalized from the sight of little Lucy running through the halls in her birthday suit."

Park releases a bark of laughter and I sigh audibly. Every single time. They live for my humiliation.

"We aren't Catholic," I remind Mom. "And I never went to preschool. That was Jeremy."

"Not the naked thing," Jeremy corrects. "Just preschool."

"No," Dad muses. "I'm pretty sure it was Lucy."

"I haven't heard that story," Park announces. "But I understand she had an unusual addiction to toilet water...?"

I cup my hand over my mouth to keep from spitting food. Mom and Dad exchange a look before erupting in hysterics.

"Oh, I like you," Mom tells Park. She turns to me and grins. "He's a keeper."

Dad leans over and slaps Park on the shoulder. "Quickest game of bullshit I've ever played."

"Lucy really did go through a phase where she hated clothing," Mom says. "She was two and every time I turned around she was peeling off her clothes."

Park nods. "I'd say it was more than a phase. No matter how hard I try, I can't keep her from stripping naked every chance she gets."

My mouth pops open in shock and the entire table quiets.

"Did…" Dad looks at Mom and shakes his head slowly. "Did he just flip our game on us?"

I close my mouth as Park's lips twist up in a superior smirk and he winks at me before taking a bite of his pasta.

"Kudos, Mr. Reed." Mom salutes him with her glass of wine. "Like I said, keep this one."

***

"Coffee's ready," Mom says as I load the last glass into the dishwasher.

"Oh, no thanks." I press the button, starting the cycle and straighten up to Mom peering at me over her cup.

"You always have coffee."

I press my lips together as I try to come up with an excuse. The only thing that keeps running through my mind is caffeine is bad for the baby. "I just don't want any."

She sips from her mug as she keeps her eyes glued to my face. I watch her scrutinize me for a moment before turning to the sink. I grab the dishrag and start wiping the counters down just to give myself something to do. Some reason to not have to look at her.

"Are you sure everything's all right?"

"I'm positive. Everything's—"

"Good?"

"Exactly," I whisper.

"Fine." She pivots on her heel, her long, dark hair swinging behind her as she leaves me in the kitchen. I blow out a breath and lean over the countertop. I drop my head, letting the marble cool my face.

"Hey, kid," Dad calls, peeking around the doorway. "Ride with me on an ice cream run?"

I could use the break away from Mom for a little bit. I hesitate as I contemplate it.

"Come on," he insists. "I'm getting old. There are only so many trips to the freezer section left in me."

He pouts his lips and blinks at me. I laugh, giving in. "Okay, let's go."

40
Park

As soon as Lucy left with her dad, I had a feeling something was up. The moment Mary sent Jeremy and Ozzy upstairs to their rooms, I confirmed it. So now I'm just waiting.

"How do you like school?"

"It's all right," I reply. I bite down on my thumb nail, my knee bouncing.

"What did you say were taking?"

"I didn't. Computer science." I glance around, wondering how long Lucy's been gone. And how much longer she's going to be. Mary pulls her hair to the side and starts braiding it deftly. Even though she isn't her biological mom, I can see Lucy so plainly in her movements. I've watched this same routine more times than I can count.

"And you and Lu, how'd you meet?"

"Jessie," I explain. "I moved in with him at the beginning of summer and she shot me with a water gun."

Mary smiles at that and tucks her finished braid over her shoulder. "You care about her."

She doesn't state it as a question, but I nod. "Very much."

"Then tell me what's going on with her. Something is off, I know it. But she keeps saying everything's good."

I scratch my head, feeling tremendously uncomfortable. It's not my place to tell her, but I don't want to lie to her either. "You need to ask her," I say apologetically. "But just so you know, she plans on telling you."

Her jaw twitches and I realize belatedly that I shouldn't have said anything. She's upset and I feel like shit.

"Is it bad? Is she okay?"

Fuck.

I don't know how to answer. I shake my head. "She's... She just... I'm not sure—" The door opens, cutting me off and I deflate in relief.

Thank God.

"We got cookies and cream," Ryan announces. He pauses, his gaze moving over his wife, sliding over to me, and then back to Mary. "What's wrong? Where are the boys?"

"Upstairs," Mary says. She turns to Lucy and gestures her over. "I think we need to talk."

Lucy's eyes widen and she looks at me quickly. I shake my head once, letting her know I didn't say anything. Barely. But I didn't tell her mom she's pregnant.

Ryan follows closely behind Lucy. "What's going on?"

My discomfort level has just skyrocketed and I want to take off so badly. I touch the cigarette pack in my pocket, wishing I could hit one real quick before whatever's about to happen happens.

"Is there something you wanted to tell us?" Mary asks. Lucy's gaze darts over to me again and I realize I need to man up. What's done is done. We're both adults. It's definitely not the best situation, but it is what it is.

I stand up, going to my girlfriend's side. She takes my hand, pulling me closer.

"I'm pregnant."

Okay, I thought there'd be something leading up to the big reveal, but no. Lucy just put it out there on the table all at once.

"What?" Mary asks. It's clear from the tone of her voice that she heard exactly what was said. She just wants verification that she heard correctly.

"I'm having a baby."

"But—what…" Mary sputters before choosing the question she wants to ask first. "How far along are you?"

"Nine weeks."

Everyone is silent as the news sinks in.

"If you're happy then we're happy," Ryan says roughly.

"I am," Lucy assures him. "I'm a little scared, but I'm happy."

Ryan's eyes shine and he shakes his head. "Where the hell have I been? I've just been living my life and time's been passing me by. When did you grow up?"

"I'm still working on it," Lucy says.

***

"We should move in together," I announce.

Lucy lifts her head from my chest and stares at me with big eyes. "What?"

"We should do it. I mean, we pretty much do already. And don't you think it's stupid to live in two separate apartments when we're having a baby. He—or she—should have one stable home. Don't you think?"

"It's too early for this," she groans. "I just woke up and you make this declaration out of nowhere."

"I've been thinking about it for awhile." I shift to my side so I can look at her better. I rest my head on my fist and brush the hair off her face and shoulder. My fingers graze smoothly across her collar bone and I want to kiss her there.

"Moving in together is a really big step."

I quirk a brow. "Not bigger than having a baby."

She bites her lip and I hope she's considering it. "What about Bree and Jess?"

"They can stay where they are. Or, hell, they can move in with each other. They spend most of their time together anyway."

"You're serious?"

"Completely," I agree. "Move in with me."

"Let me talk to Bree. I need to make sure she'll be okay."

I grin at her. "Okay." I bend forward and trail my lips over her neck. "Today. Talk to her today."

Lucy pulls me closer, shifting her leg to the side. "Do something for me first."

"Whatever you want," I say against her throat.

"Make love to me."

While Lucy worked last night, I spent her shift reading. Everything I found says sex is safe during a healthy pregnancy. I needed the reassurance and it couldn't have come at a better time because sharing a bed with her every night and not being inside of her was beginning to be too much.

I sit back and tug her panties off. "You know what...? I'll be right back."

"What?"

I hold up my index finger as I slip out the door. I open the cupboard and pull out the bottle of chocolate syrup I bought the other day. It's not hot fudge, but it's close enough.

I rip the plastic off as I saunter back into the room and crawl over Lucy's legs. I drop the bottle on the bed and she arches a brow, a slow smile lifting wickedly on her lips.

"I think I like where this is heading."

"You're going to love where this is heading," I promise.

I slip her tank top off of her. She settles back, looking up at me expectantly. I pop the cap and start drizzling a thin line up her leg, over her knee, across her thigh, her hip bone, and finally make a circle around her belly button.

I touch the ring there. "Are you going to be able to keep this?"

She shrugs slowly. "I'll keep it as long as I can."

"That's good. I like it," I say as I lower my mouth to her leg. I work my tongue over the smooth skin there, lapping up every bit of chocolate. As I make my way up her thigh, Lucy whimpers breathlessly and I make a detour because as good as the chocolate tastes, I know for a fact that she tastes better.

Her hips rise in a reaction I'm not sure she's even aware of. I slide my hand up, my fingers resting in the thick, dark syrup. I pull back, letting it drip from my fingers to coat her and I savor this experience. It doesn't take long for Lucy to float off the edge.

She forgets about the rest of the sticky mess on her stomach as she pulls me up. She wipes away a smear of chocolate from beside my lip and I suck her finger into my mouth before easing into her gently. She makes the best damn sound as I find my pace.

"I've missed you," she murmurs.

***

"Where do you want this one?" I ask, holding up the next silk butterfly. Bree and Jessie jumped on the idea of moving in with each other. We all decided it would be easier for Lucy to move in with me. Two stories are easier than three with a baby.

So now I'm hanging her butterfly collection from my ceiling.

"Right here," she says, pointing at an open spot. I move the crate I'm using as a makeshift ladder and press the tack into place.

"So I was thinking," I state as I hop down. "Since you can't drink because you're pregnant, I'm not going to either."

She doesn't respond, so I turn around to make sure she heard me. She jumps into me and I barely catch her before I fall backwards onto the bed.

Lucy kisses me deeply and I wish I had made this announcement sooner.

She pulls back, straddling my lap. Her hand smoothes over my chin. "You know, I can't smoke either."

I cock an eyebrow and regard her seriously. "You didn't smoke before you were pregnant. You didn't have to give it up."

"That's true, I guess."

I tuck her hair behind her ear, letting my fingers linger. "Do you want me to quit smoking?"

"I don't want you to do anything you don't want to do. Our lives are changing enough."

"That's not what I asked," I say.

"I wish you didn't smoke because I know it shortens your life and I want you with me as long as possible."

My heart starts beating out of control against my ribcage. She's talking about the rest of our lives. She's talking about forever.

"But," she continues, "I know all you've given up for me, Park. I won't ask you to lose anymore."

"Lucy," I rasp. "I haven't lost anything. Hell, I don't even remember anything before you. You've erased it all. All that shit from before, none of it matters. None of it means anything now. I tried to avoid this. Us. I tried to ignore the way I felt about you. But it just wouldn't go away. Before now I just didn't care. Before now I was just surviving. But now—now I have you and I know…I know I've gained everything. Because I want more than right now. I want the rest of my life with you."

I slip my hand behind her neck, drawing her closer. "I am so fucking in love with you, Lucy."

Her eyes grow glossy and she blinks quickly, sending tears off her lashes. They hit my neck and my heart lurches in my chest. I slide my thumbs under her eyes, willing her not to cry as I dry her tears. Good or bad, I can't stand to see her cry.

"I've loved you for so long," she says.

I close my eyes as her words replay in my mind. This. Right here, is pure happiness. Her lips touch mine, just verification that this moment is absolutely perfect.

Lucy's Rules:

1. Make the conscious decision to look at others with an open mind ~~and an open heart~~.
2. Everybody needs someone in their life they can rely on. ~~Try to be that person.~~ Be that person.
3. Take a chance. Take a lot of chances.
4. Love whole-heartedly. ~~(Unless in the presence of Park Reed—in which case, guard your heart at all cost.)~~
5. Make it your goal to make someone smile daily.
6. Always expect more of yourself today than you did yesterday.
7. ~~No matter how many times you're let down, continue believing in the goodness of others.~~ Learn to forgive.
8. Make memories.

41

Lucy

Park makes a face at me when the nurse focuses her attention on my arm. As she pokes at my inner elbow, searching for a good vein to drain, I try not to laugh.

We heard the baby's heartbeat today. Yes—I cried. I think Park may have even gotten teary for a second, but he fought it well.

Now I'm getting blood work done. Which kind of sucks, but I'm still floating high from knowing our baby is healthy.

"I'm having a hard time finding a good vein," the nurse says, straightening up. "You might be a little dehydrated. I'll get you some water and we'll try again."

Park pushes off the wall and moves to my side. "Why are you dehydrated? Are you still getting sick?"

The nurse ducks out the door and I shrug. "No, I haven't had morning sickness in over a week. It's just early. I'm not drinking anything while I'm sleeping and I just had that bagel before we left."

"You didn't drink anything? I didn't even notice."

My brows pucker as I look at him. "Why *would* you notice?" I brush my hand through the air. "She's getting me some water. It'll be fine."

Before he can respond, the nurse comes back in, handing me a small bottle and I start working on it immediately. I want to get this over with so I can go home and enjoy the next few hours with my boyfriend.

"How much water should she be drinking?" Park asks.

"A lot," the nurse says. "Aim for at least eight glasses a day."

Park nods and I can nearly see the wheels turning in his head. I almost groan, but I refrain, sipping from my bottle instead. I'm certain Park's going to turn into a water peddling tyrant for the remainder of this pregnancy.

As soon as we're finished at the doctor's office, Park drives straight to the grocery store, proving me right.

I watch him lift a package of bottled water into the cart, his biceps flexing with the movement, and his shirt pulling tightly over his back. And I realize this isn't so bad. My stomach clenches with desire, the power overwhelming.

"Maybe you should get another one," I suggest.

Without question, Park bends down for more and I get to enjoy the show.

"Keep looking at me like that, Lucy," he says, placing my water in the cart, and looking at me over his shoulder. "See what happens."

I press my lips together, as he grins wickedly at me. "I can't help it," I cry. I fling my hand out, gesturing at him. "You've got all that going on and I've heard stories about pregnant women, but I didn't realize it would be like this." I take a deep breath and sigh.

"Wait. Back up." He takes my hand, twining his fingers through mine. "You didn't realize it would be like *what*?"

"I'm hormonal," I say quietly, glancing around to make sure nobody can hear me.

"Hormonal?"

"…yes…"

His eyes flick over my reddening face and his smile turns so lecherous I have to press my thighs together because that look makes me want to jump him in the middle of aisle five.

"You mean horny."

I yank my hand away. "Yes. Now shut up. People will hear."

Park chuckles, totally loving this. "So pregnancy makes you hot," he muses.

"So I've heard," I say tightly. "Can we go?"

"Right here?" He arches a brow, smiling deviously. "I'm down, but I didn't know you were an exhibitionist. I think I'm going to really enjoy this pregnancy."

"I hate you right now," I mutter.

"No you don't," he says confidently. "You love me. You know how I know?"

I cross my arms. "How?"

422

He steps into me, resting his hands on my hips. "Because," he murmurs against my hair, "you can't keep your eyes off me."

"That doesn't mean I love you. It means you have a sexy body and my hormones love you."

"Close enough," he decides. "Why don't we stop talking about it so I can get you home? I want to make your hormones happy."

Sounds like a damn good plan to me.

***

"Your mom is so mean," Bree says in way of greeting. She flops down on the bed, shaking me with the harsh movement.

I yawn and glance at the clock. I can't believe I napped so long. My shift starts in a little over an hour. I slept the whole day away.

"Lu, did you hear me?" Bree taps my arm, regaining my attention.

"Mean Mom," I confirm hoarsely.

"Yes. She said I can help with your baby shower."

I rub my eyes and try to catch up. "Okay…"

"She's not letting me throw it. I want to be in charge of your first shower." She flings her arm over her forehead and exhales loudly. "I'm your best friend. You're like my sister—my pasty white, soul sister."

I scoff. "I'm not pasty. I'm creamy."

"You're mom's creamy. NO. She's mean. This is my right and she's stealing it from me."

"B, as my mother, don't you think it would be her right to give me and her grandchild a baby shower?"

"No…" She looks away, her lips puckering.

"Stop making duck lips," I say. "She said you could help, right? So help."

"It's not the same," she whines. "I want to pick the decorations and the location. I want to choose the invitations and cake. And I want to play really crazy games that have awesome prizes. She'll just have candles or bottles of body wash. Everybody does that. I want to make your party special."

Awe. That's sweet. "Well can't you still do that stuff by helping her?"

"No," she sighs. "She told me I can be in charge of *party favors.*"

"I bet they'll be the best party favors to ever grace a baby shower," I sing.

"Oh, they will be. You can count on that. I'm going to show your mean-ass mom."

"That's the spirit—the psychotic, over-the-top spirit."

She sits up, nodding excitedly. "Mm-hm. That's right. Oh, ho-ho…you just wait. The best thing to happen to you will be my contribution to this shower."

Hopping up quickly, she heads for the door, fueled by her proclamation. "Where you going?" I call after her.

"I have research to do."

I let my head fall back and laugh quietly. The bedroom door opens again and I turn to see Park coming in, a plate in one hand, a bottle of water in the other. Of course.

"Hey you. Hungry?"

"Not really."

He sets everything down on the nightstand and pulls the blanket back gradually. His eyes follow the length of my body, starting with my toes, before resting on my face.

"You are so sexy when you first wake up." He shakes his head, licking his lips. "You're sexy all the time." He climbs onto the bed, hovering over me. "But when your hair's messy and your cheeks have that deep sleep pink to them, I just want to consume you, inch by beautiful inch."

Park's mouth comes down on mine, kissing me greedily. He pulls his hands over my chest, dragging them down to my hips. His hand glides over my small belly pouch, pausing there for a moment, before continuing on. He slips inside my sleep shorts and I break apart.

His finger slides inside me, moving in a circular motion, and I begin to breathe heavy. I love the way he touches me. The way he knows exactly how to make my body respond to him.

I open my legs farther and move into his hand. Park makes a low murmur of approval before he severs the kiss. He works his way down my neck, continuing over my chest, and places a kiss on my stomach.

I lift my hips as he begins slipping my shorts off. Before I have time to register his next move, his tongue is delving into the same spot his finger just vacated. I grab a handful of his hair, gripping it tightly.

Park growls, pulling back slightly. "You taste sweeter after sleep, too."

Holy hell. I bite into my lip as he draws his tongue over me intimately, stroking flawlessly. His hands hold me in place as I begin to wiggle, searching for relief from the intense pleasure.

I think I say his name. I can't be sure because I'm shattering into a million pieces. I'm dust. Falling. Floating. I'm fire. Pulling. Clinging. I'm ash. Soaring. Sinking.

"Jesus, Lucy," Park chokes. My eyes fly open and meet his. "I have never been so fucking turned on before. That was, hands down, the best thing I've ever witnessed."

I'm panting, trying to regain control of my breathing, and all I can think about is how I want more. I unhook his pants, guiding him exactly where I want him. He gives me what I need, thrusting his hips forward.

"I need to see that again," he breathes. "Daily."

I think I should be embarrassed, but I just can't find that emotion right now. Right now, all I can think about is him.

42
Park

While Lucy's at work, I decide to go see Guy. There's been so much on my mind lately. I've changed a lot in the past few months and with everything happening so fast, I can't help thinking about what's really important to me.

Guy is high on that list.

He opens the door and I can see the surprise on his face before he steps aside, inviting me in.

"What's up Daddy?"

"You need to quit calling me that. It's fucking creepy."

He chuckles. "Just trying to get you acquainted with the term." I follow after him to the kitchen. The makings of a sandwich are set out on the counter. He pulls out a second plate, handing it to me, and I work on fixing a snack.

"So what's up? You haven't sought me out since the night you took off. How'd you even know where I live now?"

"Chase," I say, answering his last question first. I scratch my chin with the tip of my thumb, my eyes on the counter. "I wanted…" I drop the bread in my hand and face him. "I'm sorry."

He stares hard at me for several seconds and then puts the back of his hand to my forehead. "You dying?"

I duck out under his hand and push his arm away. "I'm serious. I'm trying to apologize for—well, for every shitty thing I've ever done to you. You're my best friend and I've been fucking worthless in this relationship. You've stuck it out and I have no clue why, but I…I'm glad you did. I just…"

He nods, clearing his throat. "We're good, man." He throws a slice of cheese, hitting me in the face. "Now quit being a little girl."

I laugh, tossing the cheese onto the bread. "This coming from the dude that rents chick-flicks twice a week."

"This coming from the dude that used to watch those chick-flicks with me twice a week."

Damn. Good point.

"Maybe I'm a little bit better of a friend than I thought because I hated those movies. I only did that so you wouldn't have to watch them alone."

Guy cocks his head to the side and raises his brows. "Don't make me check your movie collection. I can guarantee I'll find Titanic."

I drop my sandwich. "Hey," I say defensively, "that is a classic. And Kate Winslet is hot."

He smirks at me. "I knew it."

"Shut up."

He takes his plate to the table and I join him. "So," he says, "how's Lulu doing?"

"She's good. Getting a little baby bump." I smile, thinking of the way her belly is showing the first signs of rounding, growing with life. "I fucking love it." I sit back, tapping my fingers on the table. "I'm in love with her."

He has no reaction and it throws me off. I expected him to jump out of his chair and check my head for fever again.

"I know. I'm happy for you, man."

I lift my chin, acknowledging him. "It's weird," I confess. "I thought I was in love with Hope. All those years, I really thought she was who I wanted." I pick at the bread and shake my head. "But that was… Hope just wasn't the one. Lucy is—everything. She's everything I want and everything I need. I didn't think I'd ever find this."

"And now you have a baby on the way."

I nod. "A baby. Can you believe that? I'm scared shitless. I've picked up extra shows, trying to save money. I know we need shit, but I don't even know what yet. I bought books. Read everything I can, but I still don't know how to prepare. But, Guy, when I heard the beating of his little heart…" I rub the sting from my eyes. "Best damn sound, ever. And it made it finally sink in. I'm going to be responsible for a person. A person who I'm going to care about every single aspect of their life."

"I think you'll be all right. The fact that you can sit still and talk about this with me speaks volumes. You, my friend, have grown up."

Is that what I've been doing? Growing up? Hell. Lucy's dad had it right. Where have I been while this was happening?

***

Jessie and Bree come over for our pre-Thanksgiving dinner before we head home for the real thing later this week. Lucy likes to cook and thought it'd be fun to have our own thing. And it was, but the second we're alone, I pull her to the bedroom. I take a deep breath, inhaling her scent to compose myself.

"I decided what I want to call you," I say and my voice is thick with nerves.

"Oh yeah?" she replies. "What?"

"I was thinking it'd be really nice to call you Mrs. Reed." I watch her carefully, trying to figure out what she's thinking.

The muscles in her throat work as she swallows and my chest is throbbing as I wait for her reaction.

"I thought you wanted a name only you could call me. Mrs. Reed is something everyone will say." Her voice quivers over the last sentence and I don't know how to take that.

"Yeah," I agree, forcing my tone to sound light. "But no matter how many people call you that, it will still be all mine."

"I don't need to be married just because we're having a baby."

I step back, my heart racing. "That's not why I asked."

"Did you ask?" she says breathlessly.

"Yes. That was my way of asking." This isn't going well. I knew I'd fuck this up.

"Okay, if I weren't pregnant, would you still have asked? And before you answer that, just think about it. At nineteen and twenty, without a baby, while we're still in college—would you have asked me to marry you?"

When she lays it all out like that, no. I wouldn't have. But that's not how things are. "I probably would have waited, but I love you, Lucy. And the fact is we *are* having a baby. I plan on being in both of your lives forever. So why not? Why not get married? We live together. We're starting a family. It's the next natural step."

She perches on the end of the bed and I settle beside her.

"I love you too, Park. You know that. But I don't want to get married because it's the next step we should naturally take. I want to get married for us. And no other reason."

"It is about us. About us loving each other."

"That's not what you said. Loving each other was presented as a perk. Not the purpose."

"That's not how I meant it."

"I know," she sighs. "And I'm not saying no. I'm just saying not yet. Let's have this baby first. Maybe finish school."

"So you're not saying no?"

She shakes her head. "Is that the only part you heard?"

"It's the only part that matters. I can wait as long as you want. I just want to know it'll eventually happen."

"Oh," Lucy squeaks. She presses her hand against her stomach and panic fills my throat.

"What? What's wrong?" My hand hovers over hers, afraid to make contact.

Her eyes are wide as they meet mine. *"I felt the baby."*

What does that mean? "You felt the baby do what?"

She's grinning, making my racing heart slow. "Moving. The baby's moving."

I inch my hand closer. "Can I..?"

"I don't know if you'll be able to feel it, but here…" She pushes my fingers into her stomach and I hold completely still, focusing all my attention there. I try to hide my disappointment when I can't feel anything.

"Maybe this is his way of telling you we should get married," I say. She arches a brow and I shrug. "I'm just saying. You never know."

"What I do know is we need to start thinking about names." She lies back and I follow, keeping my hand in place just in case.

"Isn't that exactly what we were doing?" I smirk. "Discussing your name?"

"Baby names," she sighs.

"All right. Fine. What did you have in mind?"

She shrugs one shoulder. "I don't know. I need to get a book of names. I want something unique. My birth mom named me so plainly."

"I like Lucy. It's unique to the time." I brush her long hair back, trailing my fingers through the soft locks. "You've never told me about your mom. Your real mom, I mean."

"She died. I don't remember her. I was only two."

"How'd she die?"

"She got sick." Lucy rolls onto her side, throwing one leg over mine. "She went into renal failure."

"Renal failure," I repeat. "Have you been tested? Are your kidneys healthy?" Why haven't I asked her about her mom before now? I should have known this.

"She was diabetic. I've been tested for that. And they just ran all those blood tests. I'm healthy."

I pull her into me, wrapping my body around hers protectively. "What else don't I know about you?"

"I'm allergic to cats," she says.

"What? That sucks. I love cats. I guess we'll have to get a dog."

"What about you? What don't I know about you?"

I think about it for a moment. She knows all the bad. She even knows my darkest secret. What's left? "I looked my sister up. I have her number and address programmed in my phone."

Lucy lays her palm against my cheek. "Do you think you'll ever call her?"

"I saved her information for security. Just to know I have it if I ever decide I want to use it. But I don't know if I'll actually do it. Maybe one day. I'm not sure she knows about me, but if my dad told me about her, then I'm sure he told her about me. And she hasn't contacted me either."

"Maybe she thinks the same things you do."

"She could," I agree. "I'm not ready to find out yet, though."

"What's her name?"

"Emari Jessup."

"Emari," Lucy echoes. "I like that."

"In general, or for the baby?"

"Both," she says.

"All right, but I get to pick the boy's name." I squeeze her hip, my fingers lingering against her smooth skin.

"Okay," she murmurs. "Because I've been having this feeling lately that we're having a girl."

"What? You can't know that."

"I have a feeling."

"I guess we'll find out next month," I say, referring to her scheduled ultrasound.

"Unless you want to wait. We can be surprised when she's born." My heart beats faster with her statement. *When she's born.*

I kiss the top of her head and tuck her in closer to me. *When she's born*. A little girl. God, I hope she looks like Lucy. I hope she's like her in every way.

43

Lucy

I hang up the phone and head upstairs to Bree's apartment. It's still so weird to think of it as her apartment without me. It's even weirder to take the stairs instead of the fire escape, but it's not as easy to scramble out the window now.

"Hey, baby," Park calls when I open the door. "You coming to play?" He holds out a controller and I laugh.

"No. I just got a call from the diner. The new girl no-call-no-showed. I told them I wanted any extra shifts they could throw my way, so I'm going in."

"All right," he says. "Let me get my keys."

"No, I'll drive myself. I just wanted to let you know." I kiss his cheek and he takes my hand, pulling me onto his lap.

"I want to go with you. I hate you working the midnight shift with all those drunks."

"You're not going," I insist. "You have an early class in the morning." He growls, but I ignore him, going on. "I worked there for months before you came along. I'm a big girl and I can handle myself."

"I know you can. I just feel better being there." He trails his lips down my neck and I shudder. He's going to make me want to stay home.

Love: a feeling of deep affection, or romantic attachment.

I have the deepest affection for this man. And my attachment...is definitely romantic.

I stand up and swipe his hands away as he reaches for me. "Stop that," I laugh. "I have to go change. I'll be fine. Get some sleep and I'll wake you up in an extra special way when I get home."

"Gross," Bree yells from the kitchen.

"I'll bring home muffins, too," I add loudly.

"Oh, yum," she calls. "Blueberry."

I grin at Park. "I'll see you in the morning."

"'Kay. Love you."

"I love you, Lucy," Jessie mocks, enjoying the fact that he can finally mess with Park after all the times

Park messed with him. He puckers his lips, making kissing sounds in Park's face.

"Love you too. Both of you."

"She doesn't really love you," I hear Park say as I open the front door. "She's just being nice because you're right here."

"Nah. We have a secret love affair going on behind your back," Jessie retorts. I shake my head. "She told me she loves me more, but since she's having your baby—"

I pull the door closed and skip down the steps to change into my uniform.

***

We've been dead for the last forty minutes, and I've been craving a muffin since I told Bree I'd bring her some. So I get a glass of milk—something Park's gotten me addicted to—and grab a strawberry muffin before sliding into a back booth.

Kimmie drops across from me, propping her feet on either side of my thighs. "I'm dragging tonight."

"I know," I empathize. "Me too." I pull my phone out of my apron, checking the time. "Only two more hours and we're free."

"Blah. Two whole hours? I wanna be done *now*." She lays her cheek on the table and closes her eyes. "Wake me up if I get a table or if Hugh wanders out of the office."

I chuckle at that. This late, it's a guarantee Hugh's fast asleep at his desk. "Will do."

The bell above the door chimes and Kimmie groans. "I'll babysit free for life if you get this one."

"I'll take it," I say, swallowing my last bite of muffin. I eye the two guys that just came in and click my tongue. "And you're off the hook for the free babysitting."

She raises her head. "Why?"

I nod my head toward the door and she follows my gaze. "Oh, man. They're hot." She lets her head fall back to the table. "Get me a number if you can."

"For your list?"

"Mm-hm. I'm always on the lookout for the list."

I laugh quietly as I head over to the new customers. "Hi guys," I greet. "Just the two of you?"

"Yep," the taller one confirms, smiling.

I grin back at him as I grab menus. "Okay. Right this way," I say, leading them to a table in my section.

"You guys are slow tonight," the shorter one says.

"The bar rush has come and gone. It's nice to slow down." I wink at him. "And that just means you get extra attention."

He laughs. "Any attention from you will make my night."

I smile bigger as I pull out my notepad. I'm pregnant—not dead. Flirting is part of the job. The more I flirt, the better my tips. And these guys are nice. I get their orders in and go back to the kitchen to make sure Rob, the cook on shift tonight, got the order. He likes to sit outside and smoke when we're slow like this.

"Got it Lu," he calls before I make it all the way back. I reverse and fill the guys' drinks instead. And then

I take a minute to refill the straws and put on a new pot of coffee.

The bell chimes again and I round the corner, glasses in hand. "I'll be right there," I say. The man steps in front of me, opening his jacket. Everything slows down as my eyes focus on his hand, dipping into his inside pocket. I know before I see it. I know what he's getting and my hands start to shake. The condensation on the outside of the glasses makes them slippery and they slide out of my trembling fingers, falling to the floor. Shattered glass flies in every direction and my legs are covered in icy cold fountain drinks.

"Open the register," he shouts as the gun appears in front of my face. "NOW."

But I can't move. It's like one of those dreams I used to have where I try to run away from the monster, but my legs won't work, so I try to scream, but nothing comes out.

But I hear Kimmie scream. My gaze is stuck to the gun, inches from my nose.

"Hey, man," someone says. "Be cool."

"Put your hands on the table," he bellows. "Open the register," he says again and I can hear desperation in his voice. That kicks me into action. I raise my hands in front of me, palms up, as I back toward the counter. If I just hurry up and give him what he wants, he'll leave. And if I can get behind the register, I can protect my stomach.

Protect my baby.

A strangled cry erupts from my throat with the thought.

I swipe my card and tap in the code, opening the drawer. I start plucking the cash out, laying it on the counter between us. When I get all the bills, I eye the coin rolls. I don't know if he wants them too, but I'm not about to ask. I scoop them up and lay them on top.

"That's it," I say, my voice shaking over the words. "That's everything."

"Empty your apron," he demands. His head turns from me to the guys at the table. Back and forth quickly. The guys are watching him, their hands flat on the table. Kimmie is standing perfectly still just outside the booth she was napping in.

I reach into my apron pocket and the first thing I feel is my phone. My mind flashes to Park. To the last image of him, sitting on the couch, video game controller in his hand, smiling at me as he told me he loved me.

I'm so glad he didn't come with me tonight. I close my eyes and exhale, moving past my phone—I need that so I can call him when this is over—to the wad of tip money. That's all this guy wants. Just give him what he wants and he'll leave.

I slap it down and slide sideways, trying to put more space between us. He starts shoving everything into a carry-out bag, the gun waving around with his every move. I put my hands over my belly, over the small bump.

Please just leave now. Please just go.

"You, get over here," the man barks. "NOW."

My head swings to Kimmie as she stumbles her way between the tables, her legs quivering so badly she can barely take a step without falling. She stops several feet away, her hands out in front of her.

"Empty your apron," he instructs. He holds the bag open, but she has to come closer in order to put her money inside. She shakes her head, refusing to go near him. "Now, bitch," he spits. I hear the gun click and I jump at the ominous sound.

"Kimmie," I plead. The man swings my way, the gun shifting back to me and I flinch. "Do what he says."

He turns back to her and I start trying to memorize what he looks like. Black jacket, blue jeans, gray baseball cap, brown hair. What color were his eyes? It doesn't matter.

Black jacket, blue jeans, gray baseball cap, brown hair.

Kimmie finally drops the cash into the bag and ducks quickly behind the counter. She clings to me, sobbing into my neck.

Black jacket, blue jeans, gray baseball cap, brown hair.

"Come around the counter," the man yells.

I'm shaking so badly I feel like I'm going to throw up. I have to push Kimmie to get her to move and we scuttle away from the little protection we had.

Black jacket, blue jeans, gray baseball cap, brown hair.

"Get down on the floor," he screams.

I slide down immediately, pulling Kimmie with me. She's crying louder now.

Black jacket, blue jeans, gray baseball cap, brown hair. I look up and note that his eyes are green.

Black jacket, blue jeans, gray baseball cap, brown hair, green eyes.

I'm still looking into his eyes when the gunshot rings out.

<u>44</u>

<u>Park</u>

I woke up for the fourth time and couldn't fall back to sleep. The bed feels so empty without Lucy. Deciding I'll stop in and surprise her, I take a quick shower, and make her a bagel with the fruit spread she likes.

There's only a little over an hour left in her shift, but I'll at least get that hour before she goes home to sleep and I have to go to school. I'll take what I can get. I laugh at myself, getting up before the sun just to spend a few minutes with my girl. I never thought I'd see this day.

I turn the corner and the flashing lights catch my attention right away, but it takes me a moment to realize they're coming from the diner. My foot hits the brake, jerking me to a stop in the middle of the street.

Terror seizes me with an unrelinquishing grip. I squeeze the steering wheel to keep my hands steady as I step back on the gas pedal. A small group of onlookers are gathered on the corner, and I can't go any further, so I pull next to them. It takes two attempts to get my door open once I've thrown the gear into park.

"Someone was shot," I hear someone say. I trip over the curb, catching myself at the last second.

"What'd you just say?" I choke.

"Someone was shot," the woman says excitedly. "Some guy shot up the place. Robbery I think."

No.

No. She's wrong. She has to be wrong.

I propel myself forward and an officer stops me as I approach the building. He places his palm on my chest as I try to move around him. "You can't go in there right now."

"My girlfriend works here," I practically shout. "What happened?" I grip his wrist, ready to toss him off me.

"Armed robbery," he informs me. "Was your girlfriend working tonight?"

"Yes," I say urgently. "Lucy Braden. She's a waitress." I look past his shoulder in an attempt to see through the glass doors as I use my whole body to push him back. "Is she okay? Can I go see her? Please?"

"Sir, I need you to calm down and listen to me." I shake my head and shove him back. I just want to see Lucy. I just need to see her.

The officer grabs my arm and I jerk away. I make it two quick steps before he wraps his arm over my shoulder, crossing it over my chest. And now another cop's joined in, taking my neck into a choke hold. Between the two of them, I can't move.

"Sir," the first cop pants. "If you calm down I can try to get you some information, but you *have* to cooperate with us."

What the fuck is wrong with me? I'm struggling with the police and I have no idea where Lucy is. I stop fighting as realization hits, piercing through my panicked brain. "I'm calm," I rasp. "I'm calm. Just tell me she's okay." My voice drops as I plead with him to reassure me the images swirling through my head aren't true.

They release me slowly and I rub my hand over my chin. My fingers are shaking so fucking bad as the first officer says something into his radio.

"What's your name?" the second one asks me.

"Par—Park Reed. I'm looking for Lucy Braden."

The first one turns back to me and I can tell it's bad. I can see it on his face. I take a step back as if that will make the news change.

God no.

Please no.

"Both females were taken to Roddenberry about ten minutes ago."

Ten minutes ago. While I was driving over here, Lucy was in the back of an ambulance.

Oh, my God.

"That's all the more I know right now," he continues. "I suggest you go up to the hospital." He pauses, placing his hand on my arm. "They only let family in," he adds.

It takes a second for that to register through my fear-filled thoughts as I run toward my car. Just a few feet away, I'm stopped by my cell phone chirping in my pocket.

I fish it out quickly, nearly dropping it. Lucy's name on the screen blurs my vision as moisture fills my eyes. "Hello?" I croak.

"Park?" Lucy breathes and my legs give out. I hit the ground, knees first, and catch myself with my free hand as the tears spill over.

"Lucy, baby," I murmur. "Lucy. Lucy." I can't stop saying her name. I try to get a handle on it, but the relief is so overwhelming, I just keep weeping like a child. "Are you all right? Tell me you're all right."

She sniffles and my stomach twists. I squeeze the phone as my head spins. "I'm okay," she says, her voice small.

"The baby…"

"The baby's okay too. They're going to do an ultrasound to be sure, but the heartbeat…the heartbeat was go-good." She's silent for a moment and I'm thanking God over and over as I kneel in the road. "Kimmie," Lucy cries as she releases a sob. "He killed Kimmie, Park. She's dead. She's—" Her words catch and she begins to cry audibly.

"I'm on my way, Lucy. I'm coming right now. Just keep talking to me."

I shove myself up and rip the door open.

"I can't believe she's gone." She begins to cry harder and my heart is breaking for her.

"Baby, I'm so sorry. I'm so sorry. I'm almost there."

"Please…hurry. I need you."

Fuck. Fuck. "I'm hurrying. I love you, Lucy. I love you so much."

"I love you too." She grows quiet, crying quietly into the phone. I don't say anything else, just letting her get it out.

"I'm pulling into the ER right now. Where are you?"

"I'm in the waiting area. I'll meet you at the doors." The line goes dead and I hate the way it makes me feel. I need to see her. I need to touch her.

I tuck my phone into my pants and run. The doors slide open and she slams into me. My hands glide over her back as I hug her to me. I swear I search nearly every inch of her, checking for any injuries beneath her blood stained clothes. She presses her face against my neck and I hold her tightly.

My skin grows wet from her tears and I'm at a loss for words. Nothing I can say will make this better. And as horrible as I feel, I can't stop being grateful it wasn't her.

***

Lucy hasn't let go of the sonogram since the doctor placed it in her hand. She even holds it now while she sleeps, wrapped securely in Bree's arms. It seems to be the only thing keeping her together.

I close the door lightly after checking on her for the tenth time since I got her home.

"How is she?" Guy whispers.

"Sleeping," I say as I lower myself into the armchair. I rub my face, the exhaustion finally starting to hit me. We spent several hours at the hospital, then a couple more at the police station before we were able to come home. Lucy showered and passed out almost immediately.

"What the hell happened?" Chase asks.

I've heard the story several times now through Lucy's recounts to the cops, but I still can't believe it.

"The guy came in to rob the place," I say, my eyes flicking to the bedroom door to verify I shut it. "He had a loaded gun." I have to stop again, this time to take a breath because even though I know she wasn't hurt, what could have been fills my head.

"He got all the money he could and made the girls get on the ground. He was getting ready to leave, I guess, but the cook came out to see what all the yelling was about. Lucy said it startled the guy and the gun just went off." I shudder as I say the words. It could have been her. A few inches to the left and it would have been Lucy's head struck by a bullet.

I shove myself out of the chair and grab my keys. "Stay here until I get back," I tell Guy. "I don't want her waking up and wondering where I am. Not after... Not after what she saw."

"Where're you going?" he asks.

"I need a cigarette. But don't tell her that. I quit."
I squeeze the keys in my palm. "Or I did. I will. I just
need a smoke or a drink right now and I think a cigarette
is the lesser of the evils."

"I'll get them," Chase offers. "You need to be
here when she wakes up."

I nod. He's right.

I hand him my wallet and sink back into the
chair. I can't stop thinking about it. Wondering what I'd
do if something had happened to Lucy. To Lucy and the
baby. There's no way I would make it. Now that she's
become part of my life, I don't want to live it without
her.

"How are *you* doing?" Guy says, snapping me
out of my dark thoughts. "Looked like I was losing you."

I shake my head. "I have fifty different notions
running a marathon through my head, and none of them
are good."

His eyes rake over my face as he silently regards
me. As I look back at him, it occurs to me that I more
than likely wouldn't have ever met Lucy had it not been
for our fight the night I tried to call Hope.

The more I think about it, the more I start to realize. "If I had never met Lucy, she wouldn't be pregnant right now," I say. "She probably wouldn't have been working tonight because she wouldn't have felt the need to pick up an extra shift."

I drop my head into my hands. I can keep going back, farther and farther, all the people that would be better off if I had never walked into their lives.

"So you think she'd be better off to lose her friend and you and the baby?" He sits forward now, mirroring me. "You can't know what could have happened if something was different. Stop having a pity party for one." He points his slender finger at me and leans back. "She loves you and the baby. And you're both better people because of it."

I don't respond. I quietly consider his words, trying to decide if there's any truth to them. In the end, I recognize the fact that it doesn't matter. Maybe he's right. Maybe I am. But it just doesn't matter because the simple truth is this: Lucy and I could have walked different paths, but we didn't. And nobody can be sure that had we taken different roads our paths wouldn't have crossed again at some point.

Life lesson number 13: Focus on what is—not what could have been.

45

Lucy

"Would you like to know the sex of your baby?"

I glance at Park. His gaze is intent on the small screen. They hadn't been able to tell during my first ultrasound. I think it was better that way because I couldn't have appreciated it at the time.

"Yes," I say. "I want to know."

Park's hand finds mine as the technician turns back to the monitor. "I'm obligated to tell you there's a chance I'm wrong," she says, "but I'm 99% sure you're having a girl."

My eyes instantly fill. Park's hand tightens around mine.

"We're having a girl," he says, his tone so soft I barely make out his words. His eyes drop to mine and he grins. "You were right." He leans in, placing a quick kiss on my lips before he returns all his attention to the screen. "A girl," he says again.

"You have a name picked out?"

"Emari Kimberly Reed," I tell her. I try to fight off the memories from a month ago, but I fail miserably as images of the funeral flood my thoughts. I still have nightmares. I'm not sure they'll ever go away. My next breath is more difficult and the tears that trail down my cheeks are for a different reason.

"That's beautiful," she says.

"Thank you," Park says for me because I can't speak right now. He slides his thumb under my eye, trying to dry away the salty trail. I catch his hand and hug it to my chest.

***

Jess pops the lid on the paint can, his brows crinkling as he leans back to read the label. "It's blue."

"It's sky blue," I say.

"Lucy doesn't want the baby to be surrounded by gender stereotyping," Park explains.

"But…it's blue," Jessie repeats.

463

I sigh. "Sky blue. And her bedding's pink. Just because she's a girl doesn't mean she needs everything *pink.*"

Park grins at me. "Damn straight. I want a tomboy. That way I don't have to worry about kicking some kid's ass that steps out of line. She'll be able to do that on her own."

"We should do a rainbow on one wall," Bree says eagerly. "That way she can have a lot of color." She folds her hands under her chin, bouncing on her toes. "Please? Can we? I'll do all the work. Pretty please?"

I laugh, my palm resting against my belly. I look to Park and he shrugs. "Fine," I agree. "But you're in charge of it. I'm going to go read a book."

"If you find Guy out there, tell him to get his ass in here and help," Park says.

I open the door and look up, meeting Guy's eyes. He raises his finger to his lips, shaking his head. "Yeah," I call. "I'll tell him."

Holding up a box, Guy gestures me to follow him. "Donuts. I need some sugar before I'm put to work." He hands me one as we settle onto the couch. "How'd Chase get out of this, anyway?"

I shrug. "He didn't. He's just not here yet."

"Lucy, baby, can you come check this color?" Park yells.

I groan. *I just sat down.* Guy jumps up, offering me his hand, and I take it appreciatively. I don't know why I need to check the color. It looked fine in the can.

I push the door open to the nursery and step inside, my gaze shifting from wall to wall, not seeing any fresh paint. "Where?" I ask. I turn around and Park's on one knee, a small velvet box in his hand.

"Right here." He opens the box and I gasp. "What do you think? Is this white gold or silver? I can never tell the difference."

"That's…beautiful," I murmur behind my fingertips.

He grins. "I'm glad you think so." I watch him, paralyzed as he removes the ring from the box and stretches out his hand. "I know you want to wait, and I can wait. As long as this is on your finger." His dark eyes meet mine, crinkling at the corners as he smiles widely. "Lucy, I love you. Will you let me call you Mrs. Reed?"

I nod my head. "Yes."

Park stands up, positioning the ring onto my finger and envelops me in a hug. "One more time, just so I'm perfectly clear."

"Yes," I say. "Absolutely yes."

"I'm throwing the damn bridal shower," Bree announces. "I don't care what Mary says this time."

Epilogue

Park

One year later

"I can't get over how cute she is," Annie says as she gazes at my baby girl sitting happily on my lap. "I never thought you could make something this precious."

"I don't take credit for this." I wiggle Emari's chin, causing her to smile up at me. "She looks just like her mommy."

Annie nods in agreement. "Everything but the hair."

"She needs to eat," Lucy says as Chase spins her on the dance floor. "Vegetables," she adds breathlessly.

"Yes, ma'am, Mrs. Reed." Damn I like calling her that. "Mommy's no fun," I say pressing a kiss to Emari's cheek. "We like Tutti Frutti Dessert, don't we?" Grabbing my lip with her tiny fingers, she squeals and I take that as her agreement. "Tutti Frutti it is," I say. "When Mommy's not looking."

"I heard that," Lucy calls over her shoulder.

I chuckle as I lean over, digging through the diaper bag. I grab the jar and position Emari on the table in front of me. Today is a special occasion. My little girl should get to enjoy it too. I offer her the first bite, which she takes enthusiastically. This is why she's a daddy's girl. I peek over at Lucy to make sure she's not paying attention before slipping the second bite into my own mouth. They should seriously make this shit for adults. I'd buy it in bulk.

"Everyone's gone," Bree says as she drops into the chair beside me. "My maid of honor duties are officially over." Jessie takes a seat beside her and she places her feet onto his lap with a sigh.

"I can't believe the entire day went off without a hitch," he says.

"Except for Park having to hold Emari while they exchanged their vows," Bree points out.

What can I say? The girl has me wrapped tightly around her little finger. I couldn't just stand by, listening to her fuss when I knew all she wanted was for her daddy to hold her. So I vowed to love Lucy until the day

I die with our daughter in my arms. I can't imagine doing it any other way.

Bree takes the jar from my hand, checking the label. Her eyes flick over to Lucy before she sticks her finger in, claiming some for herself.

Jessie makes a face and she shrugs, unabashed. I look past them, watching as Chase and Mason exchange dance partners. For just a second, my chest tightens when Lucy moves happily into Mason's arms, but her ring catches the light, and I let out the breath I was holding.

"At least Lulu's little brother didn't bite anybody," Guy chimes in as he sits across from me.

Ozzy. That little zombie wannabe. I shake my head, chuckling lightly. "And nobody got kicked out this time."

Everybody laughs and Annie's eyebrows lift in question.

"Hey," Hope trills. "You better not be blaming me again."

"Wait." Annie laughs. "What the hell did I miss?"

"Hope got us thrown out of the hospital when Lulu had the baby," Guy says, filling her in.

Annie throws her hands up. "I didn't hear anything about this. You got kicked out of a hospital?"

"We were all hungry," Hope says defensively. She sinks into a seat, gearing up to defend herself.

I roll my eyes. "You ordered pizza and had it delivered to the maternity ward," I say flatly. "Did it ever occur to you that women in labor may not appreciate that?"

"I. Was. Hungry," she says again. "We had been there all day."

"In her defense," Mason says as he joins the table, "that pizza was delicious."

"It really was," Hope agrees. "And the nurses wouldn't have been half as angry if Ozzy hadn't bitten the doctor."

"I can't believe you didn't hear this story," Jessie tells Annie. "Epic."

"Chase didn't give me details," she huffs. "All he said was Lucy had the baby, it was a girl, and they were both okay. That's it. *He didn't tell me any of this.*"

"So he didn't tell you the part where he wept uncontrollably at the first sight of Park's offspring?" Guy asks, chuckling.

"Dude," Chase breathes as he falls into a chair. "Park cried too."

I grin. "My kid, dude. That's all I'm saying."

"Screw you guys," he says, ripping the tie from his collar. "I'm not ashamed. She was so sweet, all wrapped up in her little blanket... Nobody could look at that face and not be moved to tears."

Hope holds her hand up. "I didn't cry."

"I didn't either," Jessie adds with a smirk. "But that's just because I actually own a set of balls."

"Whatever," Chase grunts. He takes Emari's hand, shaking it gently. "She's an angel and I regret nothing."

"Hell yeah she is," I state in full agreement.

Lucy makes her way over, her dress bunched in her hands, and I know she can't wait to take it off. And then I smirk at her because I can't wait for her to take it off either. She catches my devious smile and winks as she takes the last open spot at the table. Emari stretches, reaching for Lucy immediately, and I hand her over. Watching my wife bounce our daughter in her lap, I kind of feel like crying now. That's my whole life right there. I didn't think I could ever love someone more than I love Lucy, but the all-encompassing love a parent feels for a child is like nothing I even knew existed until the day Emari was born. No matter how deep my devotion runs for Lucy, there is this unexplainable and undeniable attachment to my daughter.

Even though she's only been in the world for seven months, it feels like Emari has always been a part of my life. And I can't fathom anything different now.

"So did you go natural or did you get an epidural?" Annie asks and every single one of us loses it. Emari looks around with wide eyes and an unsure half smile, startled by the outburst.

"Yes, Lulu," Bree sings, batting her eyelashes. "How long did you last Miss I'm-Having-A-Natural-Childbirth?"

"I blame Park for that," she says, jetting her chin out stubbornly.

I lean toward Annie, gaining her full attention. "Okay, this is how it went down. Lucy made me promise that no matter what she said—no matter how much she begged—I wouldn't let her get an epidural."

Annie nods, resting her chin on her interlocked fingers.

"Her water broke around five in the morning. By noon, there's still no baby, but Lucy's been in labor for seven hours. I've watched her, laying there in pain, listened to her cuss and cry for hours—"

"I was cussing because it was only the second time I had met your mom. The first time you were unconscious in the hospital and the second I was in the hospital having your child," Lucy mutters. "That was awkward to say the least."

"So," I continue, ignoring that because I honestly have no defense, "I didn't stop her from getting the damn epidural." I shrug as I pick up my glass of water and take a drink. "But she was so sweet after the drugs kicked in."

"The first time I said I wanted it, he caved," Lucy adds. "He didn't even try to stop me. And I wasn't sweet. I was high."

"He caved because he likes his vital organs attached to his body," Bree says.

"You threaten to rip off one appendage in the heat of the moment and nobody ever forgets," Lucy sighs.

Hope nods, flinging her hands in the air. "I know, right?"

Guy chuckles. "Lucy Lu, you were pretty damn scary."

She narrows her eyes. "There was a *person* coming out of my *vagina*. Until you can say the same, no judgment."

I have nothing to say to that because seriously, she has a valid point, but Guy cringes and Bree makes a strangled sound deep in her throat.

"So," Annie says, looking for a subject change. "I heard a rumor about you, Park."

"Yeah, I want to see it," Jessie says, leaning into my view.

"What?"

"The tattoo. I have to see it with my own eyes."

Oh, that. I smirk at Jessie and start unbuttoning my shirt.

"I have to get a picture to document this. Park Reed permanently inked his body with not one, but *two* girls' names."

"Me too," Annie seconds.

I slip out of the dress shirt and lift my tee, exposing my chest. "Document away," I say as they each snap a photo of Lucy and Emari's names displayed proudly over my heart.

Lucy stands with Emari held snugly to her chest. Before she can move away, I drop my shirt and pull her into my lap, lacing my fingers through hers.

She looks over at Chase, inclining toward Annie. All of his attention is focused on her every word. "I can't figure out if they're together or not."

"Chase and Annie?" I laugh dryly. "They're like brother and sister. They usually hate one another."

Lucy shoots me a doubtful look. "They don't look at each other like siblings."

"Boys are so clueless," Bree sighs.

"Completely blind," Hope adds.

I glance back and forth, from Annie to Chase. They haven't heard a word we've said about them. I chuckle, squeezing Lucy's hand, and drawing her attention back to me. "I see you."

She grins, bringing her lips to my ear. "I love you," she whispers.

I kiss her neck, letting my lips linger. And then I nod as I inhale her scent. "I love you, Lucy. You don't even know how much. You make happy. I was miserable before you. Since we've been together, before now, everything has been incredible. But *now*—now that you're my wife, I'm pretty damn blissful."

"Blissful is good."

"Hell yeah. It's perfect."

The End

Playlist for Before Now

Kiss Me by Ed Sheeran

Lucy In the Sky With Diamonds by The Beetles

Locked Out of Heaven by Bruno Mars

Arms by Christina Perri

I Will Wait by Mumford and Sons

I Walk the Line by Johnny Cash

Stay by Rihanna (featuring Mikkay Ekko)

Hurts So Good by John Mellencamp

Little Lion Man by Mumford and Sons

One and Only by Adele

About the author

Cheryl McIntyre is a mother, author, and insomniac, as well as a reader, movie critic, and incredibly bad singer. She's lived in the same area of Ohio her whole life, though she secretly has dreams of moving somewhere a little warmer—preferably near a beach.

Her life revolves around four things: family, music, books, and really bad scary movies. If she doesn't have a kid on her hip, an iPod in her hand or a laptop in front of her face, it's one of those rare moments when she's actually sleeping.

You can follow her author page on Facebook where she lives part time. On Goodreads—which is like crack for avid readers. Or on Twitter, though it's rumored she has yet to master the art of tweeting.

Find Cheryl at:
www.CherylMcIntyrebooks.com

Acknowledgements

I want to say thank you to my family. Mom, you've been so helpful taking Mini-Me off my hands so I could actually get my thoughts out of my head and into print. To my big sis, Tammy, for losing sleep to create my website. You've done a wonderful job and I appreciate it so much. To my step-dad, Daryl, for designing my swag, and not making one, not two, not even three covers, but seventy-two on my last count. Your patience with me matches that of a saint. To my oldest sister, Dawn, thank you, thank you, thank you for not only all the encouragement, but for your diligent editing. For creating all my swag, which has turned out awesome, and for everything else you've done and continue to do for me on a daily basis. And to Sean, thank you for believing in me even when I didn't believe in myself, and for the countless dinners you made while I was off writing. You have all been so supportive. I love you.

I want to acknowledge my Wonder Woman of an agent, Rebecca Friedman. Thank you for holding my hand through this process. You've lead the way and I couldn't have done any of this without your enthusiasm and priceless advice.

I've made some great author friends along the way, but two have gone above and beyond when it comes to support and encouragement. To Beth Michele, thank you for our many conversations. I smile every time I see a new message from you because I know you'll have a funny story about hot-boy pictures or incredibly nice words of wisdom. And to my good friend, Tex. Sometimes people just click and I clicked loudly (as you would say) with you. Thank you for your ever-present ear and advice, and for random conversations about books, movies, music, and Anime. I appreciate it more than you will ever know.

And last, but not least, THANK YOU to my readers, and to all the awesome bloggers out there. I love each and every single one of you. I wouldn't have anyone to tell my stories to if it weren't for you. You guys rock!

481